forever and all the afters

K.I. LYNN

Forever and All the Afters

Copyright © K.I. Lynn

This book is a work of fiction. Names, characters, places, and incidents either are products of the author's imagination or are used fictitiously. Any resemblance to actual events or locales or persons, living or dead, is entirely coincidental.

This work is copyrighted. All rights are reserved. Apart from any use as permitted under the Copyright Act 1968, no part may be reproduced, copied, scanned, stored in a retrieval system, recorded or transmitted, in any form or by any means, without prior written permission of the author.

Cover design by T.E. Black Designs
Photo credit: Lindee Robinson Photography

Editor:
Evident Ink
Marti Lynch
Danielle Leigh

Publication Date: September 23, 2019
Genre: FICTION/Romance/Contemporary
ISBN: - 978-1-948284-18-9

forever
and all
the afters

intro

G RIEF. IT'S AN EMOTION THAT DEFINES US ALL. WE'VE all lost, we've grieved, but we as humans don't always move on. Why is that? Is it because it's such a strong, visceral reaction that no matter how much time has passed or how we say we've moved on, a part of us never does?

It's a nagging little twinge in our hearts that sows doubt and fear. The reason we guard ourselves. There's nothing more painful than tearing open a still-festering wound. Pain is to be avoided, and at times that means avoiding things that once made you happy.

I grieved deeply for the loss of Pike. He didn't leave this world, but one minute he was my world and in the next, he was gone. I've never recovered from the pain of his absence—the loss of the man I believe was my soul mate.

Now, every time I see him, I'm blindsided by so much sorrow that it steals my breath. My only recourse is to avoid him, at all costs, to avoid the utter devastation that I feel when we part ways. Pike was my first love, and his leaving devastated me. He was mine, but we were teenagers.

We grew up.

We moved apart.

I've moved on. Shouldn't that mean I've made peace with him and our past? Shouldn't that make him nothing more than a familiar stranger?

After everything, I know why. I promised forever, and my heart meant it.

I never, not for one second, stopped loving him.

chapter 1

THE AIR BURNS MY LUNGS, MY MORNING RUN underway. For months, I've been running, building up endurance and trying to slim down my thighs. I've never been one to exercise, but I've managed to make it up to about three miles, which is good, considering when I started I could barely do one.

While my shape has improved, I still have a lot of work to do. The wedding is fast approaching, and I want to look perfect for my fiancé, Caleb. On Monday, I'm going to push myself and do four miles.

My mind whirls through my schedule, plotting out my packed morning, designing rooms in my mind, and trying to forget about the fact that I've still got two miles to go. A half an hour later, I'm finally jogging into the house to change and get ready for the day.

As soon as I walk in, my phone goes off with a text from Caleb.

Hey, babe, when are you bringing my coffee? Xxx - Caleb

Shit. My morning is already a mess, and it's only eight.

Where are you? - Aubrey

Before I even get to shower, I'm in my car and off again.

Starbucks is so close that I'm still sweating when I step in. While the run helps get me going, I need coffee. At least the delay in getting home will give it enough time to cool down.

I can drop Caleb's off before heading home.

Warmth spreads through me as I smile down at the screen and the little kisses. In just over six months, I will be Aubrey Manning. Someone different, and hopefully better than my former self. I want to be better—for him.

There is still so much to do. We've barely scratched the surface, and I'm grateful my mom and my best friend, Nora, are around to help. Thankfully, we were able to secure the location. It isn't my dream venue, but Caleb was able to book it on our shorter timetable. Considering we got engaged at New Year's, we are doing pretty well.

"What can I get started for you?" the barista asks.

I manage to remember my order and pay before stepping to the side to wait with the others.

While I wait, my phone goes off with a slew of notifications. I wake the screen up and find nearly a dozen messages from my best friend, Nora.

What do you think of this dress?

What are the colors again?

OMG I am dying!

This is the one and if you disagree I'm disowning you as a friend.

There's a bunch of photos attached. I like the first dress and try to hold in my laughter at the one that follows. It's atrocious with layers of multi-colored tulle.

This is for Halloween, right? - Aubrey

You totally need a themed wedding - Nora

Oh, it has a theme, but gaudy trash is not it - Aubrey

As I type, a tingle spreads across my back. Almost like a wave of heat from a fire. I've felt it before. Years ago.

The energy radiating from behind me flickers in the back of my brain, igniting memories from long ago. Forgotten times buried under heartache. I can never forget it—forget him—but I refuse to turn around to believe it.

Pike isn't here.

He lives in New York. Why would he come back to Indianapolis after all these years?

Not only that, but how in the world would the two of us end up at the same place at the same time?

I draw in a ragged breath as heat surges through my body.

One man in my entire life has made me feel this way. Only one.

My knees grow weak. I want to blame it on my run, but I know the truth. The mere thought of Pike being close has sent every part of me into chaos. Ten years of silence is suddenly as loud as a rock concert surging through me.

I don't even have the courage to turn around, to see if it's him. I'm too scared that I'll have to face him after years apart. That I'll have to admit that it's him doing this complete system hijack.

I take a deep breath that is shaky as hell, and peek over my shoulder. The hair of my ponytail over my shoulder hides my face some, but with one small glance, every fear is confirmed— Pike Warren is home. Not only is Pike back in Indiana, but he's at the same Starbucks as me at the same time, just a few miles from where we grew up.

His lips are parted, blue eyes dark as he stares at me, catching me in my casual attempt to spy. It almost looks as if he is just as shocked as I am.

"Aubrey?"

Suddenly he seems to be growing taller, and it isn't until I feel the shock of his hands on my waist that I realize it's my knees giving up the ghost. Warmth crawls through me from his touch, taking over.

"Whoa, are you okay?" he asks as he pulls me up and toward him.

Okay? Okay?

No, I am not okay. I was perfectly fine before he got in line behind me minutes ago. But after, my life is suddenly in an upheaval of epic proportions.

Fuck you, Pike.

"Yeah, fine," I say as I struggle to get my legs under me again. But my hands are on his chest and he's holding me close, and everything is wrong but so very right. Stronger, larger, angular, and still every bit the boy I loved. "Um…Hi."

"Hi."

"Grande skinny vanilla latte and a venti red eye mélange for Aubrey," a barista calls out.

"That's me," I say, waiting for him to release me while also making no effort to move. I'm locked in some time warp that has more comfort than it should. I shouldn't feel like this in another man's arms.

"Americano for Pike."

Neither of us move.

"If you don't get your drinks, I'm going to take them," a man says from behind Pike.

That seems to break the circle of energy that ties us together, and I step forward as Pike apologizes.

I swallow hard, looking forward as I pick up the two cups and then swiftly head toward the door. My escape plan is thwarted by the magical man and his long legs beating me there.

"Two coffees?" Pike asks as he holds the door open for me.

I give him a soft, "Thanks," as I step outside. "One is for Caleb."

"Who is Caleb?"

I stop to look at him, my gaze bouncing between his eyes. "My fiancé."

While his expression is neutral, I can see something stirring beneath the surface in his eyes. His eyes were always so expressive.

"What are you doing here?" I ask.

"I moved back a few months ago."

"You did?" *And you didn't call me?*

The news catches me off guard. It's almost gutting. After all these years, he finally came home and I had no idea. A part of me acknowledges that it's almost worse that he didn't try to contact me.

Months? Months he's been here, so close, and he never came.

Stop it, Aubrey. He's the past. Caleb is your future.

He nods. "I got a great job offer. Too good to refuse."

"That's great." I start making a path to my car. "I'm sorry. I have to get going."

"Aubrey, wait," he calls.

I stop and turn back to him. There's so much that hangs in the space between us. It's electric, pushing and pulling. A veritable war between past and present emotions. All the things never said, never done. The door that never fully closed when he left.

It's terrifying. So powerful I know it could easily tear me apart if I let it.

"Can I see you sometime? To catch up. Coffee?"

I shake my head. "That's not a good idea." I have to stay away.

"Why?"

Because you're toxic to me.

"I just can't," I say as I unlock my car with the fob. "Bye, Pike."

I'm still shaking as I step away from Pike and slide into my seat. The disorientation and surprise throw me off. After nearly a decade of not seeing him, of not talking to him, the effect he still has on me seems somehow stronger than when he left.

Being near him is a risk my heart can't take.

There is nothing wrong with my life, with my relationship with Caleb. He's a good man, and I love him, but there's just something about a first love that never seems to leave, which is why I can't see Pike again.

He's still standing in the middle of the parking lot as I pull out, and I can't stop myself from glancing at him. Our eyes meet, if only for a fraction of a second, and then I'm gone. They say you shouldn't look back, but that doesn't stop me from watching him in the rearview mirror standing there much like I did the last time I saw him, when he walked away.

For years I've tried to forget him, but I admit it—I couldn't stay away. I Facebook stalked him. And Twitter. Instagram.

Over the years, I've watched him go through relationships. Some lasted a year, some lasted a month, and every one of them was a knife to the heart. Prettier than me, maybe a bigger rack, wilder, or even tamer, but they all seemed more special than I was.

And they were, because they had Pike's attention. They were with him, being touched by him, even loved by him.

Months may have passed since I last snuck a peak at his social media, but I've come to terms with the fact that he is someone I will never be able to forget.

Instead of heading home, I race to Caleb's job site. I need affirmation, for him to shake these feelings from me. Because he is the man I love, and he loves me. My future is Caleb. Pike is only a memory.

I pull in a deep breath, then grab his coffee and head inside. In the middle of the family room stands a fit man with sandy blond hair and a chiseled jaw. He's so handsome. His light brown eyes give a sparkle when he spots me, making my heart jump.

My new happily ever after—Caleb Manning.

"Hey, babe," Caleb says as I step through the door. "Watch out."

I look down, noticing the huge hole in the floor from at least two squares of missing plywood. The three-foot edge around the perimeter of the room calls upon all of my balancing skills as I carefully make my way around.

"Coffee?" I ask, holding out his cup.

He smiles and leans forward, giving me a peck on the lips. "Thanks." He takes a sip, letting out a low moan. "Where have you been all my life?"

"Hey!"

His lip twitches up. "I meant you, babe."

"Riiight."

His brow furrows as he looks at me. "I thought you were changing after your run?"

I look down and realize I completely forgot the whole shower step in my race to get away from Pike. There is a heat wave and so I broke my shorts out from their winter hideaway and paired them with just a sports bra. "I…yes, I just got distracted."

His lips form a thin line. "Not very professional. The crew keeps staring at your ass."

I swallow hard. Why is it that sometimes I feel like I'm being scolded? "Sorry, I wanted to get your coffee to you before it got cold."

"And I appreciate it, but next time dress appropriately."

I nod, then look around at the progress made since I'd last seen the place. The large wall that separated the kitchen and the family room is mostly gone—only the studs still stand.

"I thought the wall was going?"

"It is. As you can tell by the hole in the floor, we're having some structural issues."

"Great, another house with problems."

"Yeah, I didn't plan for this severe of an issue."

"Do you want to talk about the layout later, then? I can go get some samples. I have this fabulous marble in mind that I saw last week."

He nods. "That would be great. I've got an engineer coming by at three, so anytime after that."

"Is he going to look at the Carmel property as well?"

"On Friday. Today's pressing matter is this mess," he says as he guides me back around, his hand on my lower back the whole way down to my car. "Now, go change."

Walking me to my car is something Caleb has always done. More than just an excuse to kiss me like crazy before I left, but also for my security.

"Yes, sir."

He grins and pulls me to him, chest to chest, his arms around my waist. It's the same as with Pike, but there is a difference.

He presses his lips to mine, drawing me closer. "I am going to fuck you so hard for that."

I bite down on my lower lip as I smile up at him. "Looking forward to it."

I cry out as his hand slaps against my right ass cheek, his fingers digging in. "Tonight, I want you in that red teddy and those black fuck-me pumps."

"Maybe I'll wear those pumps when I see you this afternoon," I say with a wink as I pull away from his arms and slide into my car.

While I drive away, I glance in the mirror, but Caleb is already back inside.

I really can't wait to see him, to spend time with him tonight, but something still bothers me. The entire time he touched me, all I could think of was the reaction I had to Pike, and how much Caleb's touch paled in comparison.

chapter 2

THREE HOURS LATER, THE VEIN ON MY FOREHEAD IS throbbing. Listening to Matt and Dana Walker fight over cabinet styles for the last hour hasn't helped my situation, and I'm tempted to smack them with the samples I brought—the samples I didn't even get to show them before they started bickering.

"Can I interject?" I ask for the tenth time. Finally, they stop talking and turn toward me. "Matt, I know you are a traditional man, and Dana, you love modern, clean lines." I pull the cabinet sample from my bag, now that I have their attention. "I think this Shaker style is a perfect mix. We can use the quartz counter Dana wants and a slick subway tile backsplash."

They both stare at the samples I've placed out, then at each other.

"I suppose it could work," Matt says.

"Compromise, right?" Dana's lips slide up into a smile as she steps to press her body against his.

"Right." He grins back to her. "Compromise."

I want to roll my eyes, but instead I plaster on a smile. *Newlyweds.*

Who am I to talk? I, myself, am about to become a newlywed.

In a few short months, I will walk down the aisle to my fiancé, and we will start our lives together.

"It looks great, Aubrey," Dana says.

"So, we're set with this?" I ask to be certain. They both nod, excitement rolling off them. "Excellent. I know you want a light, bright kitchen, so I have some paint chips and tiles as well."

I pull out the colors I'd picked out for the cabinets as well as the tile, explaining both and why I chose the colors and textures. It takes another few minutes of hammering it out, but they make their decision in record time—compared to how long I waited to get a word in edge wise.

"I'll get all this ordered and get Briar out to start the demo ASAP."

"Who?"

"Sorry, Briar Prescot from Done Right Construction."

"We're not using your soon-to-be husband?" Matt asks.

It's a question I know I'm going to have to get used to, especially with us merging our businesses. Simply put, Caleb's crew is working too many projects, so the work has to be subbed out. The list of contractors he works with is small, and they are all highly skilled and vetted by him.

"Caleb has his crew, but he also hires out contractors, and Briar is one of the best. You're in good hands."

"If he recommends them, that's great."

I force a smile at Matt, trying not to think about how my word seems to mean nothing. It was me who introduced Caleb to Briar in the first place. Done Right Construction is a company I've worked with almost since I started, which was years before I met Caleb.

"How's the wedding planning going?" Dana asks as I pack my bag up with the samples.

"Good," I say with a genuine smile this time, eyeing the two-carat ring on my finger. "Invitations are due in any day."

"That's cutting it a little close, isn't it?"

It is, and I'm beginning to get concerned about whether I'll be able to put them together, address them, and get them ready to go on Monday all in one weekend while Caleb watches sports. "Well, we wanted to get married in the fall, but Caleb didn't want to wait a full year more."

"Ah, that's true."

"It's March, so there's time."

"Trust me, it goes super fast. You'll be up to your eyeballs in planning in no time. But then you'll have your happily ever after."

Dana is beaming up at Matt, and I know I'm smiling as well, but something about her words strikes a chord in me.

We part ways, and I climb into my car. As I drive, Dana's words continue to resonate inside me.

Happily ever after.

I have to admit, as a teenager there was only one man I ever imagined marrying and having my happily ever after with— Pike. But we said goodbye ten years ago when he hopped on a plane bound for New York. We reluctantly separated when he passed through security.

It was the end of a great love story, and I never forgot that last look. The way his brow crinkled, his blue eyes searching for one last glimpse as I hopelessly stared after him, is burned into my memories.

It crushed me to say goodbye to my first love, but NYU was a thousand miles away, and I still had one more year in high school. It never would have worked, as much as my devastatingly in love teenage heart wanted.

Foolishly, I hoped it would, that we could stay together despite the distance, but by Christmas that was squashed when I saw a photo of him with a new girl on Facebook. I was crushed, despite my mother's soothing. For weeks I typed out text messages, only to delete them. It was the only way to get my feelings out, to tell him how devastated I was without starting some big row of drama that I couldn't handle.

My destiny was not far from home—Purdue University. They had a great interior design program. It was there I met my first college boyfriend, Jack. He helped me forget the fissure in my heart that had created a chasm since the day Pike left.

I scrunch my brow as I look around, wondering how I got to my neighborhood. I spaced out for a minute.

"Wow, Aubrey, way to get lost," I say with a sigh, doing a hard U-turn. In my trip down memory lane, I'd gone on autopilot and was almost home versus on my way to another appointment.

I shake my head to rid myself of memories of the man I've put on a pedestal for far too long. After all this time, he almost seems like a fantasy—an inhuman being and a relationship that couldn't have been real.

What is real is Caleb. The one who is waiting for me, who asked me to marry him, who isn't going to leave me after promising me forever.

I pull into the older suburban neighborhood, taking in the tall trees and tired homes. The houses were all built in the sixties and seventies, and some are in desperate need of rejuvenation. One house in particular is a two-story home with the smallest kitchen I've ever seen in a house over two thousand square feet.

There were a few work trucks with Home Works Flipping scrawled across them, along with a few other cars sitting in the driveway and on the street in front of the house in question. I park my car in front of the driveway, blocking it, but I'm only stopping for a minute. From the backseat, I pull out another large bag and head in.

The front door is wide open, the sound of hammers and saws buzzing filling the air. I peek in, noting the centrally located staircase a few feet in front of me, and try to decide on whether to head left or right when I see him.

"Hey, babe!" Caleb says with a huge grin. "You're late. I was getting worried."

I wave my hand in front of me. "They spent almost an hour arguing over style before I even got to show them my idea. We hadn't even started talking about it when they were off."

"What do you give them? A year?"

"Maybe."

He pulls me in for a quick kiss, then steps back. "They've ripped the kitchen out."

"Yeah?"

He jerks his head to the left before walking through the doorway leading between the family and dining rooms. The whole house is compartmentalized into designated rooms and I know he wants to open it up for a more contemporary floor plan. One obstacle to that is the staircase that is situated in the center of the space, surrounded by all the rooms.

The dining room has a bump-out addition, doubling the space of what was once a small room, and when I look to the right I'm amazed at how open the once small galley kitchen looks now that it's empty.

"Wow."

"I've been trying to figure it out for two days."

"The layout?"

He nods. "The central staircase is killing me."

I step back to get a visualization of the space if the walls were gone. "If you take out the wall between the family room and these two rooms…" I trail off and shake my head, realizing my idea isn't going to work.

"Hey, Jim, can you have the guys bust a couple of holes through the drywall real quick?" Caleb asks his construction manager, knowing where I'm going.

We exit into the backyard while two guys get to work on the wall. It only takes them a few minutes, and we give it another few minutes for the dust to settle.

"What if you bump it out to where the dining room ends?" I ask, looking at all the concrete that surrounds a large, L-shaped pool.

"I've been thinking about that. My worry is the cost."

I nod in understanding. An extension would be a huge financial investment along with time. We step back inside to take a look. Light now streams in from the front windows through the still standing two-by-fours, but the only thing blocking the view is the central staircase.

There's a fireplace in the living room, and an eat-in-like space on the other side of the house, but both rooms are small. Probably best to keep as is. There is one other option.

"I'm going to say it."

He shakes his head. "Don't say it." After over a year and a half working together he knows where I'm going.

"Move the stairs."

He lets out a groan. "It's not that it can't be done, but the amount of restructuring…It would require a reconfiguration of a bedroom that still needs a closet."

"But if you move it, you can steal one of the closets from

the big bedroom. It has two." There were once five bedrooms, but the wall was knocked out between the two smallest ones to create a larger space.

"Then beams and headers. In the end it would be easier to do the bump out. It would take less time, too."

I shrug. "Get an engineer in and see what they think. If that's moved, we can replace the sliding door with French doors and put in a huge kitchen storage system against the wall."

"I'll get an engineer out here later this week. If the stairs stay, I would bump out the section of the casual dining room as well."

I nod. "That would help with the kitchen size and doesn't decrease the usable concrete area around the pool."

"Nothing in that bag is of any use right now, correct?"

I shake my head. "Not until you have all this figured out."

He leans down and places a kiss on my lips. "I better get back to work. I've got a couple of showings of potential investments and I need to check the progress on the house in Zionsville."

"Well, I have the afternoon off. Want company?"

His hand rests on my lower back as he walks me out. I notice him glance at the workers while he shields me from their view. Caleb has jealousy issues, but I don't mind, because that jealousy is a reminder of how much he wants me.

"Why don't you go home. Relax, and I'll come over for dinner," he says as we walk down the driveway.

"Okay," I say, trying not to let the disappointment show. Then again, I was looking forward to the downtime to catch up on *Lucifer* since I can't watch it with him around. "Anything in particular you want?"

A flash of a smirk enters my mind from long buried memories. *"You. The only thing I ever want is you."*

I shake the image from my mind and notice the way Caleb's lips purse as he thinks.

"Some tender beef with gravy sounds good. Do some mashed potatoes and salad. Red wine, and a homemade dessert. An apple pie sounds good. And some brie and fig for a starter."

The list is big, but not an unusual request. However, it does take the wind out of my sails.

"Tender beef will take a while," I point out.

"You've got that pressure cooker I got you for Valentine's Day."

"Right." The pressure cooker that is still in the box and stuffed in a corner of my condo.

"Why don't you make it at my place? We can relax after dinner. I'll be tired."

"Okay." Once again, not an unusual request, especially not since I'll be moving in soon and it will be *our* place.

One last kiss and I climb into my car, making a mental list of all the things I need to pick up at the grocery store. I glance at the clock and groan. It's nearly two and I still have to go home and pack a bag and grab the pressure cooker, go to the grocery store, and cook a four-course meal from scratch by the time he gets home.

At least we'll get some cuddle time later. I need it.

Three hours later, I'm elbow deep in ingredients and the kitchen is an absolute mess, but at least the pressure cooker recipe I found online is working its magic. The potatoes are boiling, and I'm covered in flour as I make some yeast rolls. I still have pie and salad to make, but the dough needs to rise.

Of course, in the middle of this kitchen nightmare, my

phone rings across the six-foot island and my hands are covered in crap. With dusty, sticky fingers I poke at the screen and manage to answer and hit the speaker button.

"Hey, Nora," I say. Come hell or high water, I was answering my bestie's call.

"Oh my God, Aubrey, he asked me out! It's happening!" Nora's voice screams out, echoing off the walls.

"Who did?"

"The guy I've been talking to. He finally asked me out and so I have a question for you."

"Shoot."

"What's your Friday look like?" she asks.

I wrack my brain, going through my mental calendar. "Caleb and I—"

"Ugh! Don't even finish."

I dig a bowl out from the cabinet and spray it before placing the dough inside and covering it. "Why?"

She sighs. "Our date is Saturday, and I need serious help figuring out what to wear."

Crap. Our dinner will probably run late. Knowing Caleb, there will be wining and dining until late into the night. "What time Saturday?"

"It's a lunch date."

I pull on the refrigerator door, my brow scrunched. "A lunch date?"

"Yeah. He lives in Ohio. I met him on a dating site."

The fridge holds the pie crust that I hadn't pulled out yet. I let out a small curse as I grab it and the lemon juice. "I have no appointments Friday afternoon."

"That's nice. I'll be at work." I can almost see her infamous eye roll.

My shoulders sag as I try and figure some way to help my friend out. "Saturday morning?"

"I'm freaking out!" Nora has a tendency to overreact to almost everything. But first dates were hard on her, since she and her boyfriend of three years broke up a year ago.

"Breathe, Nora. Just breathe."

"I really like this guy."

Those words are a shot to my chest because it's the first time she's said them since the breakup. I know she's been talking to this guy for a while, but I didn't realize how much she'd connected with him. In the last two weeks, we've barely had a moment to talk due to our work schedules and the wedding planning I'm doing at lightning speed.

Normally I would just ask Caleb to switch dinner to Saturday, but it is a work related-dinner with one of his investors. They have a huge project in the works, and Caleb is going to endorse me to do the design.

"I can't skip this dinner, but I have an idea. Send me pics of the outfits you're thinking, all different combinations, and we can narrow it down. I'll come over early Saturday with breakfast and coffee, and you can fashion show the narrowed-down outfits."

She blows out a hard breath, and I can tell she's settling down. My idea is enough to calm her.

"Okay. I'm going to need some carbs to help calm me down. Think biscuits or pancakes or something."

"Got it."

"Thanks, Aubrey."

I smile at the phone, not that she can see. "Anytime. Start taking pics."

"Aye, Aye, Capitano."

A chuckle leaves me. "Later, Number One."

The click of the call ending pulls me back to the bag of apples in front of me. With each apple I peel, I mentally go through her closet and think of outfits I've liked on her, reminding myself to text her when I am free again.

Taking in the state of the kitchen, it's going to be a while.

chapter 3

T HE SUN SPARKLED, HIGHLIGHTING THE STRAY BLOND strands in his brown hair, giving him an almost magical aura.

His hips pressed against mine, rocking in a slow, sensual pace. My breath stuttered as his fingers left my clit and brushed against my nipple on their way up to my hand. His fingers linked with mine. With my other arm I pulled him closer, wrapped my legs around his waist. I needed him closer.

In the distance, birds sang and the cicadas hummed—the sounds of summer surrounded us in our secluded camping spot deep in the woods by a small lake. The sun began to pass the tree line, and his clear blue eyes bore into my hazel ones with each deep thrust. Everything was there, every emotion.

Love and desire and hope—all the happiness we shared. There was no other love like ours, I just knew it. It was like my chest was completely open to his, our hearts tied together as one.

His breath mingled with mine as my back arched up to him. Sweat glistened on his skin, pooling before rolling down the curves and dips of his body. He was my heaven on earth, the one I knew was meant for me. In my bones, I knew Pike was my soul mate.

"No matter what happens, no matter how much time passes, I will always love you," he said as his movements picked up.

"Really?" I asked with a gasp.

"Forever." His lips crashed to mine, our tongues mingling as he continued to drive me to the edge. "I'm yours. Now and forever. No matter what."

My breath hitched, tears of happiness filling my eyes. "I'll never stop loving you," I said against his lips before tumbling into ecstasy.

He groaned as he stilled above me, but his eyes never left mine. "Never stop."

My eyes snap open, and I draw in a quick breath. I sit up and look around in confusion, searching for him but not finding him. Sweat dampens my cool skin.

It takes a moment for clarity to come, and I scan the bedroom. A lone tear trickles down my cheek, and I brush it away with the palm of my hand.

What the hell was that? I know what it was—one of the last days I had with Pike—but why? Was it because I saw him?

That has to be it, because I haven't even had a dream about him in a year or more. Not since before I got engaged, and of course the dream had to be *that* day. A reminder of all the things I never told him.

It probably happened because I'm in a good place right now, planning my wedding to the new man in my life—the new love I've found.

I lie back down, but after dreaming of Pike, I barely manage to fall back to sleep. I keep going over our meeting, my skin burning in memory of where he touched me.

When I wake a little while later to my alarm, I'm greeted by a headache that's threatening to become a migraine. The headache started coming on last night when Caleb got a call about an emergency at one of his houses, and he had me go on home because he didn't know how long it would take. Based off my dreams, it was probably a good thing.

I try and push past the throbbing, hoping a run will relieve it, but the tension only rises.

With each block, my head thumps louder. It beats almost in time with my footfalls.

The dream still floats around my mind, and I'm unable to shake it or the emotions it evokes. It's the most gut-wrenching memory, taunting me with one of our last days together. That day was perfect in so many ways.

As I run, the tension in my shoulders grows. Each time I think about Pike's body on mine, his kisses, his voice when he said he loved me, my muscles cramp even more. By the time I'm done with my run, I'm desperate for the tension to drain from my muscles.

The headache has exploded into a full-on migraine. I should have taken my medication before I left. I'm migraine prone, so I should know better by now.

Instead I'm in agony, popping pills and pulling ice packs out of the freezer. There's too much light in the family room, so I move to my bedroom and its blackout curtains, and shut the door.

I lie down, one ice pack on my forehead, the other on the back of my neck, and in the dark. Through the pain, one thing is still perfectly clear and bright—Pike's eyes locked with mine as he rocked into me.

I close my eyes in an attempt to blot the vision out, but when I open them again nearly an hour has passed. The pain wracking my brain has lessened. I feel marginally better, and slide out of bed and into the shower.

The hot water helps release the last of the tension in my

neck and shoulders. Still, my mind wanders. I hate myself for each minute I think about Pike, which is more than I care to admit.

Luckily, I don't have any appointments and can work from my home office, which is just my second bedroom. A few hours later, I'm deep into a design when my phone goes off beside me.

Babe, I need a coffee. At the Tuxedo house - Caleb

I stare down at my phone, my head thumping. Agitation crawls in. Let me stop what I am doing. Again. When did I become a secretary?

I blow out a breath to calm myself. It's just my headache talking. Caleb doesn't know, and he loves me. Isn't this what you do for the ones you love?

This is the happiest I've been since Pike, but I think knowing he's back in town has me on edge.

At home. Migraine hit me hard - Aubrey

Aw, babe. Did you take anything? Some coffee might help - Caleb

He's right, a coffee might help my headache.

The Tuxedo property is in an older neighborhood further into Indianapolis, but at least there is a drive-thru Starbucks on the way. I can pick up some lunch on my way back.

Be there in 20 - Aubrey

After saving my progress, I grab my keys, laptop, and two of my leather bags full of samples for different projects. At least while I'm out I can get some other work done. There's a whole-sale company nearby I've been meaning to check out.

With the stop it takes me half an hour, and when I arrive the crew is loading up a dumpster that is occupying the drive-way. Some days I wonder how Caleb does it. He's juggling seven projects right now, is under contract for three more homes, and is constantly searching for new ones. Lately he's been branching out into areas further away, though still on the Northside of town. He's pretty much completely abandoned working on the Southside where he started.

Add in his rigorous workout regime, and it's a wonder he's as collected as he is. Getting him a coffee is nothing in the grand scheme of things, and it shows him how important he is to me.

I've got my high-heeled boots on, which catch on nearly every space between bricks on the front patio. One causes my ankle to turn and I nearly fall, but hands grab onto my waist and arm.

"Whoa, you okay?" one of the workers asks as he steadies me.

"Yes, thank you."

He stays close, and I make it through the door without any more mishaps. There is nothing to get my heel caught on inside as the flooring has been stripped down to the floorboards. In the center of the large, newly demolished main living area is Caleb talking to the project manager, Scott.

"What was that about?" Caleb asks when I reach him.

"What?"

"Why were his hands all over you?"

I glance back to the man who caught me. "He was helping me. My ankle turned, and I was falling." Sometimes Caleb's jealousy is so outrageous I have to roll my eyes. However, I force myself not to because I can tell he's in a bad mood.

"Coffee," I say, holding the venti cup out like a peace offering.

He takes the cup, making a noise of appreciation before taking a sip. "Thanks, babe."

"How is it going?"

"No structural issues," Scott says.

"Finally some good news."

Caleb nods and takes another sip. "Another kitchen to figure out."

I glance over and groan. The house is older and has been added on to over the years, much like the house in Carmel. However, the kitchen is original and is more like a hallway between the older section and the new. A small galley kitchen that, for the size of the home, really needs to be larger.

"Another bump out?" I know Caleb will hate the idea because of the money he will have to cough up to flip the project, but it's probably the best option.

"We're going to get through demo and take a look at things then."

I nod. It's day one, and they've already removed the flooring and demolished the half bath, working their way to the kitchen.

"Any updates on the Carmel house?" I ask. "I've had a few more ideas."

"The engineer is coming this afternoon. We'll wait to see what he thinks."

I nod. "Okay."

"Let me walk you out," he says, his hand on my lower back like usual.

I'm a little taken aback by him practically shooing me out, but I know it's a busy day and I'm in the way.

"How's your head?" he asks once outside. His hand slips into mine as we walk and I soak in the affection. My headache drained me and I need the recharge.

I shrug. "Getting better, but still bothering me."

"Have you taken your meds?"

I roll my eyes. "Of course."

"Thank you for bringing me coffee," he says with a smile.

That smile is everything I need right now. "You're welcome."

When we get to my car, he pulls me close, his nose running up the column of my neck while his lips pepper kisses. "You know, I was thinking that tonight after dinner we could try out that little package I got you for Valentine's Day."

My first thought is the pressure cooker, but then I remember the other gift he gave me—a set of furry handcuffs and a butt plug. While the handcuffs excite me, the butt plug does not. Lately he's been pressuring me into anal, but I'm just not ready to try it.

"I am definitely down for being restrained," I say with a smile.

He presses his lips to mine, nipping at my bottom lip as he reaches behind me to grab the door handle.

"Zionsville after three?" I ask, just to clarify how much time I have.

"And then dinner at your place at seven. Some steak and those roasted Brussels sprouts. Pick another lower-carb side. We overdid it the other night, and you've got a goal to hit."

Another thing to add to my ever-growing to-do list. "Sounds good," I say as I slide into the driver's side. "I'll think of something. Maybe more of an appetizer."

He leans down for another kiss. "See you soon."

I try to busy myself with visiting some of my suppliers to look at products for all of my open projects, but I'm having a hard time concentrating. I do manage to push through and find a few possibilities to show Caleb, and something that may work for another aspect of the Walker project.

I grab lunch at Panera and homestead a booth for just over an hour as I work on my laptop. There is so much to do and I feel like my brain is all over the place, which for me is the worst feeling in the world because I am all about organization. Every project has its own bag, and each bag is tagged with the name so they are easily distinguished from one another. Each client has a folder on my laptop, and I have spreadsheets for everything.

It's the only thing that keeps me sane with so many projects.

By the time I arrive in Zionsville, it's after three and an unfamiliar, dark grey Jeep sits outside. My bag with the Zionsville tag digs into my shoulder, weighed down by a large batch of samples from countertops to a dozen paint options and cabinet styles.

I think nothing of the unknown vehicle and head through the door as Miguel, the project manager, steps out.

"Afternoon, Aubrey," he says with a smile.

"Hey. Checking in?" Miguel manages three different projects and is constantly driving all over the city every day.

He nods. "We've been talking to this new engineer. Looks bad, but it's gotta be done."

Ugh. Caleb is not going to be happy. "So, you're saying I should go hide the fifty-dollar-a-square-foot marble in my car."

The corner of his lip twitches up. "Might not be a bad idea."

"Oh! Before you go." I dig through my purse that seems like it's had an expandable charm put on it, fishing through everything until I produce a container of cookies. "For the bake sale."

He lets out a sigh as he reaches for it. "Thank you so much. I completely forgot."

"Anytime." I grab his hand. "Really. I'm happy to help. How is she doing?"

His lips seal together into a thin line. "She has her moments.

The drugs are hitting her hard, and chemo brain is a real thing. It took her five minutes to remember Celia's name the other night."

"It will be worth it when she's better. And she will get better."

He gives a nod, but I can see how hard it is on him. I can't imagine how difficult it is to watch someone you love be consumed by a devastating disease and not be able to do anything to help.

"Thanks. I…I can't thank you enough, Aubrey. For everything."

"If you need me to take the kids one day, just give me a call. I'll take them to Dave and Busters and wear them out."

He smiles at me and nods. "I'm going to hold you to that."

I wrap my arms around him, giving him a squeeze before stepping back.

With a wave he steps away, giving me a "See you later," as he goes.

I've only known him for a year, but from the very beginning, the love he has for his family was very apparent. Of the many men in Caleb's employ, Miguel is one of the nicest guys and best crew heads.

The bang of a sheet of plywood being dropped makes me jump, and I continue my path into the house. There are voices and air hammers and two men standing by an even bigger hole.

"Is that safe?" I ask as I take even greater care walking around the now giant and deep hole, especially after my near fall earlier in the day.

"Oh, hey, babe." I look up and stop short at the blue eyes staring at me. "I want you to meet someone. This is—"

"Pike." My expression drops, and I freeze.

You have got to be kidding me. My heart flutters in my chest, beating like a hummingbird's wings. What is he doing here?

Caleb's brow scrunches, his smile dropping at my reaction. "Yeah. How did you know?"

"We know each other," Pike says with a smile as he looks back to Caleb.

Caleb's jaw ticks. "Oh?" It's a motion I know, the first sign of agitation that leads to outbursts. It's a situation I need to defuse. His temper is swift when it comes to me.

"We went to high school together," I elaborate as I continue my way around, and that seems to make Caleb relax. "It's been a long time. How are you?"

It's a conversation we just had, but I'm still reacting to him being in front of me.

"Happy to be out of New York and back home."

He stretches the word home out, sparking another memory.

"I'm going to be so homesick without you."

"And then you'll get busy with new friends and school."

"You're not getting it, Bree. Without you, I'm a nomad. Every bed is just a place to lay my head, because you're my home."

"Good ol' Indiana. That's a big change," I say and let out a breath.

"That's quite a ring. When is the big day?" Pike asks, smiling extra brightly at Caleb. It's his fake smile. The ultra-kill-them-with-kindness kind. It was his weapon of choice when he verbally smacked down some of the jocks in school when they were picking on people.

Caleb pulls me close and takes my hand. "October. When the leaves change."

Pike looks between us. "That sounds beautiful."

"Caleb found this beautiful venue just outside the city that has all these huge maple trees. It's going to be gorgeous."

Caleb squeezes my hip. "It sure will be."

"So, what's going on here?" I ask as I turn my attention back to the gaping hole, then look to the plywood beneath my feet. "And is it safe?"

Pike lets out a chuckle and nods. "The floor over here is fine."

"What about over there where I just walked?"

"Fine. The floorboards under that section are fine, and the cross piece is oddly on a slab."

I blink, then glance over. "Why would there be a slab?"

"I think it was a breezeway they closed in and incorporated with the space," Caleb says, his body rigid next to mine. "But the floorboards are only part of the problem."

I look up to Caleb. "Oh, no."

"There are two rotten footers and the house needs to be jacked up, so we can't get a header in for this wall until all of that is done."

"Crap. How much time is that going to add?"

"I don't know yet, but a few weeks at least."

I let out a groan. The two mishaps are causing hiccups in my schedule. "I'm two for two this week on these projects."

"Well, Pike here is meeting me tomorrow at the house in Carmel to see what our options are."

I look to Pike. "I'll be there."

"Great," Pike says with a smile, then glances to his watch. "I'm sorry. I have another appointment to get to."

"Sorry for keeping you," Caleb says as he holds out his hand.

"No problem at all. I'll see you tomorrow." Pike looks to me, and I give him as good of a smile as I can under the conditions.

I can't help but watch him go. A stabbing pain hits my chest, the image dragging up memories that mirror the action, and I have to force back a strange desire to call out to him.

"Maybe you shouldn't go tomorrow," Caleb says once Pike is out the door.

"Why not?" I ask, turning to him. The house is a major project, and the engineer's insight is a huge step in the direction and design.

"There's just going to be a lot going on with workers and everything."

"And that's different than any other day?" Something is off in his reasoning.

"I scheduled too much tomorrow, and it's just best that you stay away."

"Caleb." I don't understand. Why is it that suddenly I can't go?

"Work on the Westfield house."

"You haven't closed on it yet." There are still two weeks, and the financing is pending.

"So? Go do a showing and get some inspiration on what to do there."

My gaze bounces between his eyes. "What's going on?"

His jaw ticks, and he glances toward the door, then back to me. "I don't like the way he was looking at you. You got weird around him."

"I was just surprised to see him. That's all."

"Is it?"

"Yes. It's been ten years."

I can see the anger simmering beneath his calm exterior. "Just friends?"

My body tenses as I try to figure out how to defuse him

again before he blows up. "He was my high school crush. I guess some of that hit me when I saw him again. It was nostalgia, nothing more."

We were so much more than that, but with Caleb's jealousy, he would fire Pike on the spot and who knows when we'll get another engineer in. Plus, the last thing I want to do right now is fight.

"Nothing more?"

I shake my head. "Caleb, really?" I stroke my hand up his chest, then down. His muscles are tense, but after a couple of strokes, they relax. "Why are you acting jealous? I love *you*. I'm marrying *you*."

He blows out a breath. "Can't have any man stealing you away." His hands wrap around my waist and pull.

I collide into his chest with a squeak. "Never."

Another flash of a memory, of a promise to another man that I swore I would never stop loving. I don't let Caleb see, but it's hard to keep myself in check.

Every part of me is a wreck, and all I want is to stop the onslaught of a seventeen-year-old girl's emotions.

chapter 4

Pike

THE PEN GLIDES ACROSS THE PAPER, SOAKING UP MY thoughts. I don't write these often, but I need to today. It's therapeutic, in a way.

I rest the pen down on the paper and relax back into the hammock as I stare out across the backyard. The air is cool, but it's the only place that calms me.

Seeing Aubrey not once, but twice in just over twenty-four hours reignites my reasoning for moving back. It's been two months since I returned and I had yet to seek her out, even though she is the sole reason I came home.

To see her.

To feel her.

To stop her from making a mistake.

Shock invaded me, and I was unable to react. I *felt* her before I even noticed it was her. That feeling, that overwhelming, consuming buzz radiated from my skin through my blood and deep into my chest.

When she turned, her golden-green eyes peeked from behind her too-blonde hair. I missed that shy look of hers and the saucy little smirk she would throw me.

When I saw her this afternoon, I got the full effect of the "new" version of the girl who was my whole world, and it didn't feel right. It felt like she was putting on an act, trying to be someone or something she just isn't, and that worries me.

She's bleached her dirty blonde hair to almost platinum, losing the softness of her natural color. Her makeup is too much, and her clothes too pretentious. What happened to casual Aubrey? I've kept tabs on her via Facebook over the years, so I know her style was pretty much the same until she met him.

The drive to find her when I got back was overshadowed by doubt and fear, but the moment I had her in my arms, it all hit me. All the happiness, love, and peace I'd ever known crashed down on me.

Aubrey is what my life has been missing, and I was an idiot to ever think anything else.

There is something about Caleb that rubs me wrong. I certainly don't like him, regardless of whether he is with my Bree or not, but his flare of jealousy was plain as day this afternoon.

He didn't like that we know each other, and he especially didn't like her reaction to seeing me. His handshake at the end was meant to intimidate, and Aubrey still has the same "shut the fuck up" expression she had at seventeen.

Which makes me wonder more about their relationship. It's obvious she's become subservient to him, something that shocks me. Aubrey always had the desire to please people, but she had a strength in her. We had arguments like any other couple, but I feel like his word is law and she's not allowed to have an opinion.

Maybe I'm reading too much into it, but from what Mom told me, I'm not far off.

My phone pings with a text message, and I jump up with the name that pops up on the screen. "Shit!"

Landed. See you soon! ;) - Kate

I jump from the hammock, my foot catching on the edge and nearly sending me tumbling down to the deck as I race to my car. The airport is over half an hour away.

I fold the paper as I jog and stuff it into the envelope. Once in my office, I pull the false book down from the shelf and scramble to slip it under the red twine that holds the stack together, then slide the book back in place.

It's not the best timing for Kate to come out, but I haven't seen her in two months.

By some small miracle, I make it to baggage claim at the same time she steps outside. Her smile is beaming as she waves me over, but I notice something very un-Kate like.

"Hey, stranger," Kate says, a huge smile on her face as she throws her arms around me.

"Hey, you pain in my ass." I press my lips to her cheek. "Where's your bag?"

She pulls her carry-on in front of her and gives me a shy smile.

I look at it, then to her. "You're kidding me."

"What? It's less than four days," she says.

"I once watched you pack two large suitcases for a two-day conference." I wonder how long she'll keep this up before admitting what happened.

"That's different. This is vacation," she argues.

Kate is high end, high maintenance, and it's all bullshit. "Are you telling me you fit all your cosmetics in only carry-on sizes?"

"Give me some credit."

I quirk my brow at her. "They lost your bag, didn't they?"

She straightens her spine. "No."

"No?"

"Not *technically*."

Aha. "What *technically* happened?"

"It went to La Guardia."

My brow scrunches as I look at her. "You left from JFK."

She nods. "And it went to La Guardia for some reason. They're going to deliver it hopefully tonight, if not first thing in the morning."

I toss her roller bag into the back while she climbs into the front with her shoulder bag.

"I can't wait to see the house. What are we doing first?" she asks.

"I've got an appointment in Carmel."

Her lips turn down into a pout. "I thought you were off today."

"Just a quick consult. It won't take long. Promise," I say as I pull out of the line and head toward the interstate.

"It better not. I spent the whole flight thinking of things to do."

"What did you come up with? Besides some shopping for essentials."

She waves her hand in her *"Don't worry about it"* way. "I'll just use yours. Have you heard of this place called Conner Prairie? It's supposed to show what life was like in the old days."

"We used to go on school trips. I'm surprised you want to go there."

"Why?"

I shake my head as I check my blind spot and merge onto the interstate. "Because you are a born-and-bred city girl."

"And this is me exploring life outside."

"What else?"

"The Indianapolis Motor Speedway. I want to see what all this racing stuff is about."

"That's a possibility. We will be passing the exit for that in a minute."

"There is supposedly this fantastic children's museum." My smile falters, something that doesn't go unnoticed. "What?"

I shake my head. "Just memories."

"Come on. Tell me."

"I remember being there with Aubrey, sitting on this spinning bench and looking up at this blown glass installation. One of those perfect moments."

"You had a lot of perfect moments with her."

"And."

"Have you run into her?" Kate asks, and I can't tell if it's excitement or trepidation in her tone.

Finding her was never the issue. One word to my mother, and I'd have every bit of contact information the FBI has on her. "I ran into her the other day." I shake my head. "It was completely unexpected. My new client is her fiancé."

"Wow."

"That's where we're headed now."

"To see her?"

"No, my client—her fiancé."

We pull off the interstate and work our way through each intersection, which have almost all been replaced by roundabouts.

"I wish you didn't leave New York."

"I had to."

"You didn't *have* to. I miss you."

I take her hand in mine and squeeze. "I miss you, too."

"Dinner better be worth this interruption."

A chuckle leaves me. "What does the princess want?"

"Surprise me."

"You won't regret it later?"

She makes a squeak. "Mr. Warren, I do believe you are insinuating I'm pretentious."

"Because you are, sweetheart." I park the car on the street at the end of the driveway. "I'll be back in a few minutes."

"Hurry back, baby," she says in a sickly sweet voice.

I shake my head and listen to her laugh as I shut the door and walk away.

Most of the crew is gone, if there were even any on site. One man stands in the garage looking over the stacks of materials. Normally I would just head on in since I've already met Caleb, but the man looks completely worn down and in need of a friend.

"Hello," I say as I step inside. "I'm looking for Caleb."

He looks up from his clipboard and blinks at me. "You are?"

"Pike Warren from CTW Engineering."

"Ah, yes, hello." He holds out his hand. "I'm Miguel, the project manager. Nice to meet you."

I shake his hand. "You as well. Didn't I see you at a house in Zionsville yesterday?" I ask.

"Yes. I'm sorry I couldn't stay. I had to get home."

"I hope everything is okay."

He gives me a strained smile. "Thank you. Caleb is inside."

"Thanks," I say and head in. "Hello?"

"In here!" Caleb calls out. I walk around the staircase that is taking up the entire center of the home and find him looking over some blueprints. "Pike, good to see you again."

"Same. What's going on?"

Caleb relays his dilemma, and we take a look around. They've demolished everything they can, and even taken drywall down. When he gets to the staircase, I understand the issue. Its placement is pretty bad with the way the house is laid out, creating small rooms.

"I wouldn't move the staircase. You'd have to get rid of the fireplace, and it would cut into the doorway from the garage, plus the clearance for the stairs leading to the basement."

"Shit, I forgot about those," he says with a sigh.

"An expansion of this back section would require a steel I-beam and a post at the edge of the dining room extension, but you would have a huge kitchen and it will really open up this first floor. You'll need a footer for the load as well."

"What if I just took this wall out?" he asks, motioning to the line of two-by-fours that was once covered in plasterboard.

I shift my flashlight upward, and it's clear. "It's load bearing, so you'll need a beam there if you decide to take it out, regardless of an extension."

"You've got no good news for me."

"It's not easy to hear, I know. In my opinion, this area is hot. This is an older neighborhood close to great schools, and people will pay top dollar for a large house like this with a pool. It's worth it to expand for a big kitchen."

"I'll give it some thought and have some plans drawn up."

He moves to the door leading to the garage, and I follow. "Sounds like a plan. If you need me to look at them, you've got my number."

"Will do. You know, it's so funny that you and Aubrey know each other," Caleb says, and I can tell he's fishing for information.

"Amazing to bump into her. Small world, right? It's been so long I hardly recognized her."

"She's changed a lot over the last year and a half."

"Really?"

He nods. "Anything to please me."

The temperature of my blood spikes up as I take in his smug smile. "How nice that she wants to be what you want."

"It is. She's great, and with some guidance, she's becoming perfect."

She is already perfect, I think, but refrain from saying it because I might deck him. "You've been together for a while?"

"Almost two years."

"Awesome. Congrats on your engagement and all." The words taste like acid as they spill from my mouth. This man is trash, and he's treating Aubrey more like a dress-up doll than a person with thoughts and feelings.

I hold out my hand and Caleb shakes it, using more strength than necessary to squeeze my fingers. A challenge? A warning? It's odd, seeing as Aubrey isn't here, but I wonder if something happened. Maybe she told him, but his friendliness makes me suspect not.

As we walk to my car, we find Kate leaning against the car looking way too posh for the area. Her hip is sticking out, accentuating her small waist.

"Who is this?" Caleb asks, and I can't help but note the way his eyes take in every inch of Kate.

All it does is solidify the off feelings I've had since our first encounter, and I'm not sure I'd be surprised to find out he's cheating on Aubrey. I hope that isn't happening.

"Hi, I'm Kate," she says with a smile.

"Lovely to meet you," he says and takes her hand, placing a kiss on it.

"Oh, you've got competition," Kate says with a wink.

Caleb laughs. "What are your plans for tomorrow?"

I glance to Kate, who raises an eyebrow. "Nothing planned. Why?"

"I just had a client cancel our dinner meeting at Filet. It's nearly impossible to get a reservation there right now since it's a hot spot, but I had an in and thought maybe you and your girlfriend might like to go on a double date with me and Aubrey tomorrow?"

Before I have the chance to say anything, Kate wraps her arms around mine and tucks her body against my side. "We'd love to."

"Perfect. We'll meet you there at seven."

"Sounds good." I wave and climb into the car. "Why did you do that?" I ask as I pull away. What is she thinking?

"If you think I'm missing the opportunity to meet the woman you're still infatuated with, you're stupider than I thought."

"Hey!"

"Don't 'hey' me. For years, no woman has ever come close to measuring up to her, not even me."

Sad but true. Aubrey is the only woman I've ever loved.

chapter 5

ALL AFTERNOON I'VE BEEN RUSHING AROUND. FIRST, I spent way too much time with a client shopping for furniture, and then was completely lost at the grocery store trying to find another side for dinner. A woman caught me staring at the vegetables in contempt and we struck up a conversation, which led me to look up mashed cauliflower recipes.

It's turned out to be a little more work than I anticipated, and I'm hoping Caleb likes it because I have no backup. At least I know he loves the roasted Brussels sprouts.

The good thing is that dinner is at my place. We spend most evenings at his house, and it took a while to get used to his kitchen and where everything is located. However, it seems I'm now having that same issue at home, unable to locate the utensils I need. Items I've probably taken to his house.

It isn't often he stays overnight at my house, mostly because he has no clothes here and almost every day starts at seven. I've had to split my wardrobe in half and buy a second set of toiletries while carrying my makeup around in a case.

The plan is for me to move into his house, but we've both been so busy that it hasn't happened yet. I'm ready for it. The back and forth, trying to remember where a shirt is only to find later that it's in the laundry at my house, has gotten old.

Not only that—I'm ready to start our lives together.

Caleb's house is beautiful. It was a house he flipped two years ago, just before we met, and he decided to keep as his own, moving his Greenwood business to the north side and expanding. It has four bedrooms and an office, making it perfect for our future family.

The thought of children robs me of my breath as another memory of Pike slams into my conscious mind.

"I'm so happy my period came," I said as I snuggled into Pike's side. An oops in the form of a torn condom left us both sweating in the days until my period arrived. When it did, we both sighed in relief. My cramps were bad, but I gladly suffered through them as Pike made soothing strokes up and down my back.

"I want babies, but I was thinking once we both graduate college at least," Pike said as he kissed the top of my head.

I craned my head to look at his face. "You want babies?"

"Yeah. I mean, not now, but I want to have babies with you."

"What else do you want?"

"A big house with a back porch where I can hang a hammock."

"And a swimming pool," I added. If we were dreaming, I was going to dream big.

"And a swimming pool."

"A big kitchen with lots of counter space."

"A wood-burning fireplace," he added.

Another cramp hit, reminding me what would feel good. "A big soaking tub and huge shower."

"What else?"

"I want the kitchen open to the family room, and a basement."

"Definitely a basement." He nodded in agreement.

"Tall ceilings and lots of windows."

"And?"

I thought about it, trying to think of anything else. "You. You're all that's important. All of those are wants, but all I really need is you."

The memory guts me and I try to will it away, but like everything else with Pike, it lingers just outside my grasp like he has for the last ten years.

I make my way to the refrigerator to pull out the wine I bought for dinner. After popping the cork, I pour myself a glass and take a few long sips.

This isn't right. None of it. I shouldn't be thinking about Pike in any way. I shouldn't be having these feelings for another man. But since I bumped into him, I'm assaulted multiple times a day, ignited by the most inane things, reminding me of the time in my life that I was happiest.

I'm happy with Caleb. I am.

But I can't deny that Pike was the love of my life. And now he's back, and I don't know how to process the long-buried emotions that keep bubbling to the surface.

It's like I'm being attacked by another form of myself, and in a way, I am—the seventeen-year-old girl who cried daily and fell into the deepest depression when he left.

The sound of the front door opening and slamming shut causes me to jump, and I glance at the clock. It's seven on the dot, and I step out of the kitchen to get a view of Caleb stomping toward me.

My brow furrows, and my stomach drops. He's angry, so something must have happened today.

"Caleb? Is everything okay?"

He doesn't respond, only grabs my arm, spinning me around and pushes on my back, leaning me over the couch. The burn of denim across my hips stings as he drags my jeans down to the floor without undoing the clasps.

"Ow," I hiss, then cry out again as his hand slams down on my ass. The sting isn't pleasant. "Caleb, please." Tears sting my eyes. "What's wrong?" I ask, trying to get through to him.

The only response I get is him lining up and shoving his dick inside me. I cringe as he pushes into me dry, the cushions of the couch clamped between my fingers.

No words, no prep. Nothing.

I've never seen him like this, and I don't know how to get through to him. He's never taken his anger out on me before, but he is now and there's nothing I can do but take it and wait for him to be done.

His fingers knot in my hair, forcing my back to arch up. "You're fucking mine," he growls into my ear before shoving my head back down. "I fucking own this ass." He pulls out, and relief floods me, but is immediately replaced by fear as he presses against my asshole.

A scream leaves me and I slap at him until he pulls out, only to slam back into my pussy.

His hands grab onto my ass as he slams in hard, a roar leaving him as he finally finishes.

He's breathing hard as he comes down, then steps back. I don't move for a moment, then slowly straighten up and turn to him.

His chest is heaving as he stares at me.

"What the hell was that?" I shout as I slam my hands against his chest. His eyes are blank, hollow, and he grabs my hands to keep me from hitting him again. "What is wrong with you? Would it fucking kill you to warm me up a little first so that maybe I can enjoy it as well?"

"You should always be wet and ready for the man you love, right?" he spits out.

A tear rolls down my cheek, and I yank my hands from his grip. "You should always be caring to the woman you love, remember? Because that was fucked up, Caleb." I slap his chest again. "How was what you just did any different from rape?"

There's a flash of recognition in his eyes and the anger seems to finally fade from him, replaced by regret.

He lets out a deep sigh and falls to his knees. "Fuck, baby." His arms wrap around me and pull me close. He's shaking, and I'm even more confused by his behavior.

"What is going on?"

He places a kiss just below my belly button before he stands. I'm tense when he reaches for my face to tip my chin up. His brown eyes gut me, so much sorrow and regret reflecting in them. "I'm sorry. I just…it was a rough day, and I took it out on you and I'm so sorry. I know that's not an excuse, but I promise it won't happen again. Can you forgive me? Please, Aubrey."

"I…" I stare at him, my chest tight. His eyes reflect his remorse, his brow crinkled, mouth lax, and I know it was a mistake, but I don't understand what set him off so badly. "Never again."

"I swear it," he says with a sigh and pulls me closer. I relax against him, my head on his chest as his fingers make soothing strokes up and down my back.

"You didn't wear a condom."

He pulls back. "And? You're on birth control. We're getting married. It doesn't matter. We've talked about this. I don't get your hang-up."

My hang-up… I step from his arms. "Is it too much to respect my wishes on this?"

"For fuck's sake, Aubrey, what is the problem? We're going to have kids eventually, and I'll have to come inside you for that to happen."

My body goes rigid as I stare at him. He hangs his head, blows out a breath, and closes the gap between us again, his hands gently pulling me close. "Can't we practice? Just a little?" His hand slides around to sit on my abdomen. "Practice me filling you, knocking you up?"

"Just until the wedding. Please. I don't want to have to find a dress to cover a pregnant belly. Birth control isn't a hundred percent."

He nods. "Okay, but on our wedding night, I'm bending you over and fucking my come deep into you."

My lips twitch up into a smile. "Sounds like a good night. I can't wait."

"Me either." His touch is soft, kisses light as he helps straighten my clothes.

"Are you going to tell me what got you so worked up?"

He shakes his head. "It wasn't just one big thing, it was lots of little ones." He sits down and pulls me onto his lap. "The basement in Carmel flooded. The financing fell through for the sale of the Fishers' house, so I have to put that back on the market. All the fucking structural issues. Then I got out to my truck to find some asshole sideswiped it, took out the mirror, and there are scratches all down the side."

I rub my hand around his chest and try to ignore the lingering pain between my legs. "I'm sorry."

"I'm sorry, too. I love you and I never want to hurt you."

My chest clenches and I lean in to press my lips to his. "I love you, too."

"Is dinner ready?" he asks. "I'm starving."

"Almost. I just need to grill up the steaks."

"Okay, I'm going to grab a quick shower."

I slide off his lap and watch as he heads toward the master bedroom.

There is an unsettled feeling in the pit of my stomach after what happened, but I believe him when he says it was a mistake. A mistake can be forgiven. Moved past.

Still, what he did rocked me. I was used to him being commanding in bed. Forceful, even.

But that is a far cry from what just happened between us. I've never felt pain like this from sex.

The grill is set to high and I head to the bedroom to change, unable to stand the moist feeling between my legs. There is a twinge when I bend over to push my jeans down, then again with my panties. I stare at them on the ground, at the pink-colored wet spot, and reach between my legs. It's tender, sore, and there's more red than pink.

I push it out of my mind and clean up in the spare bathroom before putting on fresh clothes and returning to the now-hot grill.

Caleb finishes his shower just as I'm plating the steaks, the table set with everything else.

He places a kiss to my temple before sitting. "Change of plans for tomorrow."

"Oh?" Maybe I can get together with Nora after all.

"Randy cancelled when I was at the Carmel house, which is another issue. We really need more money right now, and I'm tapped out thanks to that sale falling through. Anyway, I invited Pike and his girlfriend out for dinner tomorrow. Sound good?"

Pike? Girlfriend? The word is like a punch to the gut, and I nearly double over from the invisible force.

It's just a fraction of a second, but the pain that rushes through me feels like each wave takes hours. The hits of his return just keep coming.

Caleb seems to be gauging my reaction, and I attempt to make it as neutral as possible. I don't want to upset him. I force a smile and hope that he doesn't notice my internal turmoil. "Wonderful."

Spend the evening with the first man I ever loved and his girlfriend sounds like a perfect Friday night. In actuality, it sounds more like a living nightmare. All the girlfriends over all the years were just photos on a screen, but this will be in real life. A breathing, talking, fully three-dimensional person.

It doesn't matter, I remind myself. I'll be sitting next to Caleb.

chapter 6

I HAVEN'T BEEN THIS NERVOUS IN YEARS. IN FACT, I'M pretty certain I wasn't this nervous for my first date with Caleb. I'd never really dated an older man, and while Caleb is only six years older than me, every other guy I'd ever been with was in a three-year range of me.

My hand is shaking, and I flex it in an attempt to get it to stop.

I'm a mess. An absolute mess, and all of it is Pike's fault. I don't know how to act, and I'm walking on eggshells with Caleb anytime Pike is mentioned. It's obvious Caleb doesn't like our connection, and I hope that dinner will quell his suspicion and he'll see that Pike and I are veritable strangers now. That years apart created two people who no longer know anything about each other.

That's my hope, at least. The problem is I do know a lot about Pike. At least Pike up until the age of eighteen, and there are just some things about a person that never change.

I inspect my reflection, analyzing each angle. Are my thighs too big? I stare at them in the mirror, noticing for the first time that they are starting to slim out. The running is working.

The smile on my face is so big that it hurts. All of my efforts are finally showing the payoff. Now to keep it up.

The plum dress is fitted, with the exception of the trumpet hem, and I'm a little afraid of what will happen when I sit down. The dress fabric itself has a small amount of give, but the lining does not.

Hitting just above the knees, the sleeveless, scoop-neck dress is a good mix of sexy and conservative. It's the one I had planned to wear to meet with the investor, and it still seemed appropriate for the change of companions.

For two hours I primped my hair, noticing how dry it's become from all the lightening to the platinum blonde Caleb loves, and meticulously applied my makeup just the way he likes it. I also make sure to wear the black platform pumps he loves. I even top it off with the necklace he gave me for Christmas.

I was always a flats girl before I met Caleb, but he loves the heels. I just wish my feet did. Over time I've gotten more used to them, but every time I look at them my feet make a little whimper noise.

I smooth out the dress once again and blow out a breath. My palms are sweating, and I walk to the bathroom to grab a towel.

I hear the door as Caleb calls out.

"In the bedroom," I say back.

"Are you ready?"

"How do I look?" I ask as he steps in.

He stares at me, his head tilting, then narrows his eyes. Not the reaction I was hoping for.

"What about that black dress I got you?"

My smile falters, and I nod. "Okay." I move to the closet and unzip the dress before tugging it off, trying to ignore the sinking in my stomach and keeping a smile plastered on my face.

"You'll need that shaper thing underneath," he says from the doorway of the closet, his eyes scrutinizing me.

The high I felt plummets to the ground, and a knot forms in my stomach. "I've been working—"

"I know, and you're doing great, baby. Keep it up." He lifts my chin with his fingers and smiles at me.

I can't help but smile back at him, at his compliment. Every praise from him warms me. I've been working hard, and I'm so happy that he is noticing my hard work. He appears to be happy with all my progress, even if his praise is sparse and a little underwhelming.

Still, I hate wearing the shaper, though I do love the way it smoothes everything out, making me feel like a size six compared to a ten. The weight I've lost has taken me down from a twelve and I'm shooting for a four—a size I haven't been since my freshman year of high school. Caleb is pushing me toward a two, and he's right that I'll feel better about myself when I reach our goal.

The black dress hangs at the end of the rung, and my stomach knots as I pull it out. Every woman needs that quintessential little black dress, but I'm not sure this is mine.

It was a gift from Caleb, and I've worn it twice. The dress is short, leaving my massive thighs on display, and it is definitely more fitted than the one I was just wearing. The design was made to hug every curve. Then there is the top.

Low cut and cleavage for days.

Thankfully I can pull it off, but I always feel like I'm on display. In a way, I am.

Caleb dresses well and keeps fit, and he expects the same from his partner. I'm going to get there, become his ideal woman and be what he expects from his partner.

After a few minutes of jumping up and down to get into the shapewear, I pull on the dress and we head out. As always, Caleb holds the door open and I slide into the passenger seat of his Lexus. Usually he's in one of his wrapped company vehicles, but on nights like tonight, he can break out his toy.

"You look gorgeous."

"Thank you."

He brings my hand up to his lips and places a kiss on my fingers. "Everyone is going to be so jealous of me."

"How does that work when you get so jealous sometimes?"

"The men who look at you will want you on their arm, but only I can touch you. I want them envious of what I have, and what they can't have."

I suppose it makes sense to him, but I just don't see it. The dress has more of a slutty vibe than sexy, but maybe that is just my opinion. Maybe that's what guys find sexy.

Either way, I'm so happy that he is happy with how I look.

It's only fifteen minutes to the restaurant, and only a short wait for our dinner companions.

I stop breathing at the sight of Pike. He's even more handsome than he seemed just the other day, wearing black slacks and a gray button-down with the sleeves rolled up, and a slim black tie.

It is a very fashionable, very New York look and oddly enough, the opposite coloration of Caleb's outfit. If there was a *"Who wore it better"* panel, there would be no doubt that Pike is the winner, despite Caleb's best efforts. Pike makes it look effortless, and for him it probably is, while I know Caleb spent a lot of time on his look.

"Hi," he says.

An awkward silence hangs between us. "H-hi." There's a slight woman next to him with one of the largest smiles I've ever seen, and she's practically vibrating beside him, the waves of her cropped hair bouncing around her large eyes.

"Aubrey, this is Kate. Kate, Aubrey."

"It's so nice to meet you. Pike has told me so much about you," she says as she takes my hands in hers. Her smile is genuine and her manner warm. It takes me back a bit, because I really want to hate her, but I'm not sure I can.

I shouldn't hate her anyway, I reprimand myself. She's with Pike, and that's perfectly fine. It's wonderful. It's…

My stomach is in knots as I stare at her perfect pouty lips and button nose, wide eyes with perfectly winged liner that I bet she did in one pull, and the perfect body.

How many perfects is that? I can't stack up against her, so there's no use trying, and now I really want a breadstick. Where are the freaking breadsticks?

"What sort of things has he been telling you about my lovely fiancée?" Caleb asks from beside me, and I freeze.

I'm not keeping it from him, but I also know his jealousy. Caleb once punched a guy because he put his hand on my lower back as he leaned toward the bar to get the bartender's attention. Therefore, I'm saving myself the headache of him going off on Pike for simply being part of my past.

Kate stares at Caleb for a beat, then says, "Oh, that they lived in the same neighborhood and went to high school together. That type of thing."

Caleb's jaw ticks, and he looks to Pike before turning to follow the hostess. I move to step behind him when Kate slips her arm around mine. When I glance at her, she gives me a wink, then leans in.

"I know a lot more than that, but I can tell he's the jealous type," she whispers.

I stare at the back of Caleb's head, then turn to her and mouth, "Thank you."

The encounter is odd, and I'm not sure how to take it. Has Pike really told her all about us? And if so, why would she be so friendly about it?

I'm sizing myself up to the beauty whose perfect red nails contrast against the paleness of my arm, and find myself lacking.

The hostess leads us to a square table in the front corner. A long, cushioned bench seat follows the window and bends at the corner before ending.

Kate and I take the booth seats in the corner, while Caleb takes the chair next to me and Pike sits in the space across from me.

Silence falls as we survey the menus, and my mouth waters at the thought of the filet mignon.

Caleb wastes no time ordering an expensive bottle of wine for the table the moment the waiter arrives, and even orders appetizers.

"We'll start with the calamari and—"

"Oh, wait," I say, stopping Caleb and the waiter. "We can't do that one."

"Why not?" Caleb asks.

"Pike's allergic to shellfish."

"Squid is an invertebrate," Caleb says with a small chuckle.

Pike waves his hand. "Aubrey, it's fine."

"But your doctor…"

"Said I should avoid it, but I've had it in the past without issue." He looks up at the waiter. "Calamari is good."

Caleb's lips form a thin line as he also orders. "I suppose the oysters, shrimp, and crab are out, then?" I can tell he's a bit annoyed, only I know it's not just about him not getting the appetizers he wants.

"Those definitely not," Pike agrees.

"Fine. We'll have the charcuterie," Caleb says before setting the menu down.

"I'm surprised you remembered that," Pike says once the waiter leaves.

"How could I forget?" My eyes go wide as I recall the day I first found out. "We were having egg rolls and there was shrimp in them. Your face swelled up and turned pink, and you started having difficulty breathing. I was freaking out! Thank God you had an EpiPen in your backpack."

"You sure know an awful lot about a neighbor," Caleb says snidely.

I freeze for a fraction of a second before turning my attention back to my fiancé, who is practically glaring at me. He's obviously not happy. His posture is rigid, and I can feel the tension rolling from him.

"We were in the same circle of friends, and we were all out to lunch. It was just a moment that was profound and stuck with me. I've never witnessed something so terrible before," I elaborate for his benefit.

I *lie*.

It was a half-day at school, and the two of us went to our favorite little Chinese restaurant that had a lunch buffet. We weren't the only students to do so, but it was just us at the booth, in our own little world.

His reaction was fast and both scarred and scared me for life.

"It's late. You should go home," Pike said as I lay on his chest, his heart thumping beneath my head. His hand was wrapped around mine while the other held me close.

"No." I had to stay, needed to stay, to make sure he was okay.

"Your mom is gonna be pissed."

I snuggled in deeper. "I don't care."

"Well, I do."

I sat up. "Do you want me to go?"

His expression softened, and he reached up to push a lock of hair behind my ear. "Of course not, Bree. But I want to go out with you this weekend, and if you're not in by curfew, your mom is gonna ground you."

The wine arrives, pulling me from my memories, and I quickly take a sip to help calm my nerves. Every muscle is tense while I try to play relaxed, but I know it's not working by the way Kate reaches under the table and squeezes my hand. I glance over, her head stuck in the menu, before squeezing back.

Of course, the woman with Pike would be wonderful.

"Everything looks so good," Kate says with a smile toward Caleb. "Thank you for inviting us."

Caleb's lips twitches up, and the storm brewing begins to subside. "I couldn't let the reservation go to waste. It's great the turn of events worked out so well."

"They steak is wonderful here," I say. "And the mac and cheese is the best I've ever had."

Kate's eyes are wide in excitement. "Well, I know what I'm getting. Just give me the mac and cheese and a fork. You all can fend for yourselves on the side, but that one is mine."

A laugh leaves me, as does some of the tension.

The waiter comes back and takes Kate's order, then turns to me, but before I can order the steak that my stomach is growling for, Caleb speaks up.

"I'll have the steak Collinsworth with the balsamic Brussels sprouts, and she'll have the peppercorn kale salad."

My stomach drops and cries out in revolt. I hate kale and

was really looking forward to a good steak and some of that mac and cheese. I catch Pike's gaze and his raised eyebrow, but quickly turn my attention back to folding the menu and handing it to the waiter.

Pike places his order last, and the waiter leaves.

"A kale salad at a steak place?" Pike asks.

I open my mouth to speak, but Caleb beats me to it.

"We're working on Aubrey's ideal size," Caleb says as he takes my hand in his.

I hate the way he draws the word out, making me feel like I'm about to bust out of the shapewear that is holding me to-gether. Still, I force a smile.

"I think she looks perfect as is," Pike says, but I can't look at him.

I just want to crawl into a hole. Pike doesn't know he's egg-ing Caleb on and making the situation worse.

An uncomfortable silence falls over the table, and I can't bring myself to look at Kate or Pike. Instead, my vision is locked on the glass of wine, while in my head, I calculate how many calories are in each sip. Not seeing them doesn't dull the change in atmosphere at the table. It's a palpable force.

"It's been a week for you two, huh? One house with a bad layout and another with serious foundation issues," Pike says, turning the attention away from me and onto work.

Work is always a topic that gets Caleb going, and the awk-wardness fades away. Pike and Caleb talk about the projects, and I interject when possible while Kate listens with vested interest.

The appetizers arrive, and I watch with bated breath as Pike spears a piece of calamari with his fork and pops it in his mouth. It's then I realize how the buildup to this moment is one thing that has my nerves so tightly wound as I count the seconds.

"See? Fine," Pike says after a moment of me staring.

I nod, but before I can get a piece for myself, Caleb has moved some of the meats and cheeses along with olives from the charcuterie.

"No fried foods, babe."

"You're right." At least the appetizer I can enjoy is savory.

"So, how did you two meet?" Caleb asks, spreading the conversation to include Kate.

My stomach knots again, a feeling I'm getting tired of experiencing. I don't know if I want to hear about them as a couple, but at the same time, I'm dying to know.

"I work for an architectural firm in New York, and Pike was part of the engineering team that came to check out our plans."

Caleb stacks a piece of cheese with a slice of the salami. "How long ago was that?"

Kate glances over to Pike. "Three years ago?"

He nods as he finishes his bite. "Just about. It was that freak day in May when it snowed."

Three years? They've been together for *three years*? I know now that this is the woman Pike is going to marry, and take another large sip of wine, finishing off the glass.

"Oh, yeah, it was snowing that day. Anyway, here he comes, sticking out as the youngest by half. He was kind of hard not to notice," Kate says with a giggle. "Pike was wearing jeans and steel-toed boots and a heavy coat complete with hard hat and electric yellow vest, while the others were in slacks and pressed shirts. It was obvious he was an on-site engineer."

"All that for a consult?"

"In New York, I worked with steel structures and I'd just come from a job site. They also failed to mention the consult was in an office and not a site."

"Nobody seemed to care anyway, except Nancy when you tracked dirt in."

We all laugh, and I find I am completely enamored with every morsel of information about his time in New York. From favorite restaurants, to his job and what he did in his free time. Each minute I missed, each event I didn't get to witness, each moment I wasn't there.

"Why did you move back home after so many years?" Caleb asks.

The question has my stomach clenching in anticipation. Pike's gaze locks with mine, and I feel my heart speed up.

"I missed home so much and knew if I didn't come back now, I'd never have it again."

I draw in a quick breath and rein in my composure, but I can feel the heat flood my face. In my periphery I catch Caleb staring at me, but I can't seem to break away from Pike's eyes.

"You talk as if home is a thing or a *person*," Caleb says.

Pike looks to Caleb and smiles. "It's a feeling. One I can only find here."

My heart races in my chest, and my hands are shaking so badly it feels like my whole body is vibrating.

"It took you this long to miss home?"

"No. I missed it from the moment I left, but there were opportunities in New York that I just couldn't pass up. I interned for companies, and I learned more from that than many of my classes, getting real, hands-on training."

"Did you and Aubrey keep in touch?"

"Sadly, we lost touch after high school, besides the occasional update from my mother."

"Your mother?" Caleb presses.

"She and Mrs. Hart are very good friends."

Caleb turns to me. "Did your mom do the same?"

"Occasionally," I say, not sure where he's going with the line of conversation, but I'm thankful that Pike is keeping things neutral.

"She didn't tell you he was moving back?"

I shrug. "She never mentioned it. I'm not sure she knows."

"Surely his mom told yours."

"Even so, it's not like she tells me everything about her friends' children," I say.

That seems to shut him down on the line of questioning.

"Well, we should have a toast to your return," Caleb says with a smile as he refills my wine. We all raise our glasses. "To new friends."

"To old friends," I add.

"To love," Kate says.

Pike raises his. "To home."

We all take a sip and lower our glasses.

"I think we're going to need another bottle," Caleb says. The waiter hasn't been back in a while, and Caleb turns toward the bar. "Jason is here."

I glance over and sure enough, one of Caleb's investors is at the bar.

"If you'll excuse me for a few minutes," he says as he stands. "I need to go say hello to someone."

When he makes it over, Jason greets him with a warm smile and a handshake before introducing him to his companions.

As I turn back around, I notice the stares from men in nearby tables. It makes me uncomfortable, and I cross my arms over my stomach, holding my glass of wine across my chest to cover myself some.

"I'm going to go the restroom," Kate says before standing

and walking toward the back of the restaurant, leaving Pike and me alone together.

I draw my arms tighter as I force myself to ignore the tingling that spreads across my skin from his gaze.

"You look…uncomfortable," he says after a moment.

I blink at him, a weight settling on my chest as he points out exactly how I feel. Tears sting my eyes, and I bite down on my lip. "Caleb's favorite."

Pike clenches his teeth, a habit he's kept after all these years. It's his version of holding his tongue—if his teeth are mashed together, he can't speak. "I'm sure he just wants to display your beauty," he says after a minute, but I can hear the strain in his voice.

"Or my boobs. I haven't figured it out yet." I try to lighten the mood, to play it off.

He chuckles. "You do have a fabulous rack."

I roll my eyes. "Thanks."

"But in all seriousness, you are stunning this evening," he says, his eyes never leaving mine. I have no response but to stare back at him. "You're stunning in anything, or nothing at all."

"Pike," I hiss, my eyes wide as I look around.

"What?"

"Don't let Caleb hear that," I grind out between clenched teeth. He had been doing so well.

His brow scrunches. "It was a long time ago, Bree."

In all my life, Pike has been the only one to call me Bree, but that was when we were together. "Don't call me that."

"There seems to be a lot of things I'm not allowed to do." The annoyance is strong in his tone, and in the curl of his lip. "Can you make a list for me?"

"Caleb gets jealous easily."

He glances to where Caleb is, then back to me. "And you're afraid of that? Does he take it out on you?"

My eyes go wide at the accusation. "What? No. He's just hard to calm down."

"And what does he do to you? How do you pay for it?"

I scrunch my brow, unable to comprehend what he's saying. Caleb's jealousy sparks angry outbursts, and he does have some violent tendencies in that regard, but not with me.

I push down the other night as an example, because that was an accident. He didn't mean it.

"You're being ridiculous, Pike. It's not like that."

"I'm not convinced."

"Well, it's not up to you to be convinced," I hiss. "You have no say in my relationships. You have no clue what my life with Caleb is like, and you're basing some pretty nasty accusations on a few minutes together."

He gives a nod. "You're right. I'm sorry."

I raise the glass up, and I watch as recognition sparks.

"Your ring," he says.

My eyes widen and we're caught, our eyes locked. Before I can form a thought or response, the seat next to me scoots back.

"Sorry for the wait," Caleb says.

Kate also returns, and any conversation about what is wrapped around my right-hand ring finger is squashed.

I didn't even think about it when I put it on, because I've worn it daily for ten years. It's become a habit to slip it on my finger before leaving the house. And now, Pike can't take his eyes off it.

Because he gave it to me.

It's just a simple, thin gold band, but on the inside there is an engraving—*Forever*.

The evening continues on with Caleb in a better mood. The food helps, and Pike and Kate gush over their meals until everyone is stuffed.

Well, everyone but me. The peppercorn dressing on the kale made it palatable, but not that appetizing, and I failed to finish it. When Caleb made a bathroom run Kate shoved a forkful of the mac and cheese into my mouth, and I couldn't be mad about it because it tasted so good.

At least with a few glasses of wine in me I'm feeling nice and relaxed, and not bothered by the cold when we step outside.

"Thank you for a wonderful evening," Kate says as she wraps her arms around me, and while we are close, she whispers into my ear. "You can reach me through Pike. Do you have his number?"

Her? Through Pike? Do I want any of that? A way to contact him?

No, I don't. I can't have that kind of connection to him.

However, that doesn't stop some part of me from shaking my head or handing her my phone when she asks. There's just something so genuine and sweet about her that I can't say no.

"I hope to see you again," she says with a smile.

"Yes, we should do this again," Caleb says with his business smile.

My stomach drops, knowing that look. He means what he says about doing it again, but not for the enjoyment of their company. I'm not sure why, though, or what has suddenly spoiled his mood.

I watch as they walk toward a now-familiar Jeep and climb in as we turn toward the other side of the parking lot.

Caleb never drops his doting appearance and holds the door open for me, but I can tell he's not happy about something.

Silence spreads as he slides in and starts the engine. I reach out and take his hand in mine in an effort to soothe him. "What's wrong? I thought it was a nice dinner."

"What were you two talking about?"

I'm taken aback and stare at him. "Who?"

"You and Pike."

I scrunch my brow. "We talked about a lot. You were there."

"When I was at the bar," he clarifies. "You two were talking, whispering."

"We were just talking about when we were younger. What is so bad about that?"

"Because you are going to be my wife. I'm not going to sit there and be disrespected by you flirting with another man at all, let alone in front of me."

Flirting?

"I wasn't—"

"You were. You were practically eye fucking him all night." There's a tremble in his voice as if he's straining to control himself.

"I-I'm sorry. I didn't mean to do anything like that," I stammer. "I don't even remember doing it."

"You were fawning over him."

"I was just curious about what he'd done with his life."

My answer seems to calm him some. "I'll let it slide this time, but don't you ever flirt with anyone ever again."

I nod, thoroughly scolded as I go over the evening, retracing where I went wrong. I failed him, and I need to make it up to him.

He takes my hand and places it on his crotch, over his hard

length. "You know how you can say you're sorry." Deftly his fingers pull his belt out and draw down the zipper.

The shame of disappointing him burns, so there is no delay in adjusting my position to lying over the center console to take him into my mouth. If I get him off before we make it home, maybe he'll calm down and we can enjoy the rest of the night together.

chapter 7

THE NEXT MORNING, THE COLD AIR BURNS MY LUNGS, and I expel a wisp of cloud with each exhale. I've never been a fan of running, and especially not in the cold. The early peek of spring left as quickly as it came. The temperatures dipped with the cloudless night.

Light crests the horizon, reaching out into an endless rainbow. People bustle around open curtains, the glow leaking out, but it's still early. Fine by me. All I need is a beat, and I go, lost in music and thought, though my mind isn't filled with normal thoughts.

With each footfall on the asphalt, my mind produces a new image, running through them like a flip book.

All of Pike.

The striking angle of his jaw, the slight stubble lining it perfectly. Bright eyes that always seemed to be searching for mine. He's aged perfectly. Even his smile, the one that made my heart skip, has increased in brilliance.

Last night tore me up in unexpected ways. He has a girlfriend, but there was something off about the way they interacted. She was great, though. I could even see us being friends, but it won't happen.

Being her friend would mean seeing Pike more, and I just can't do it. Each time I do is filled with this torrent of emotions that shut my whole system down. I tried to relax last night, to push past it, but it didn't happen.

It was like he was this light, this beacon, and I was drawn to it, to the warmth.

Those emotions didn't go unnoticed by Caleb. When we got back to his house, he stripped me and pulled me up to the bedroom. Sex was a bit harsh, but I deserved it for the way I acted. Caleb is my fiancé and I spent the night giving my attention to another man.

He was right. I may not have thought I was flirting with Pike, but I evidently was. I woke up prepared to be a better fiancée. The first step to that is to stop thinking about Pike.

In a few hours, I'll be at Nora's house, and I haven't even gotten to tell her all that's happened. I'm not sure I want to, only because I know she and Caleb only get along for my sake, so bringing up Pike will only get her riled up. Still, it's not something I want to keep from her.

A zing moves up my spine, pulling me from my head. I scan the street but don't see anyone, though I feel like someone is close. I decide to speed up, flipping to a faster-paced song to shake off this feeling. I've still got another mile to get back to the house, and it's barely light out.

My thoughts unconsciously move back to Pike and the way he looked at me when he told Caleb why he was back. It confused me, because there we were with his girlfriend, and he was saying I was the reason. Well, I was the only one who understood.

A hand clamps down on my shoulder, and my heart jumps. A scream erupts from me as I turn, my hand grabbing my chest while my wide eyes find my attacker. My footfalls slow and I stop, swatting at the man beside me.

"Pike!" I cry as I pull out my earbuds. "What are you doing? You scared the shit out of me."

His breath is hard as he bends over. "I called your name, but you couldn't hear me, then you sped up."

"You could have just let me go."

His eyes meet mine as he straightens. "I tried that once. Never again."

I purse my lips and look away, knowing he isn't talking about jogging. "What are you doing here anyway?"

Clouds of moisture erupt from our mouths with each pant.

"I live a couple blocks away."

"You're kidding, right?"

He shakes his head. "I had no idea you lived so close."

"I don't. Caleb does."

He knits his brow. "You don't live together?"

I shake my head. "Not full time."

"Huh."

"What?"

He shakes his head. "Nothing. It's nothing."

"It's something."

"How do you know?"

"Because you've made that sound as long as I've known you. It's your equivalent of saying something like 'that's curious.'"

"I can't just make a noise and it not mean something?"

"No."

"Fine. I find it weird that you haven't moved in together, especially with your wedding closing in." His eyes scan me up, then down, and I can't help but bite down on my bottom lip. "I mean, I'll need you in my bed every night long before we get married."

"Considering those are two things that will never happen, I'm completely floored as to why you would point those out."

"Aubrey."

I cross my arms in front of me. "No, Pike. You can't just suddenly show up and say those things."

"Why not?"

"It's wrong."

"How so?"

"Because it makes it sound like there's something between us when there isn't."

His eyes bounce between mine. "There used to be."

"A long time ago."

"Some things never change."

"And some things do."

"Then why do you still wear the ring?" he asks.

I freeze. "It's just a piece of jewelry."

"That you still wear."

"It's a classic. It goes with everything," I say as I try to defend my reasoning. Try to make myself believe it when I know it is more than that.

"Has Caleb seen the inside?"

I shake my head. "No, and this is over. I have an appointment to get to."

"Aubrey, wait."

"Why? I don't understand what it is you're trying to do. What is your goal?"

His lips form a thin line, and he reaches out, linking his pinky with mine. There's a shot to my chest, a shock that sends my heart into overdrive.

Image after image, memories of long ago. It started with a pinky promise when I was twelve.

"I'm scared," I said, my teeth chattering as the line crept forward a few more feet, screams cutting through the air.

We were at Kings Island with a group from school, in line for my first coaster ride, and I was chickening out.

"It's not that scary," Darcy said with a roll of her eyes.

"It really isn't," Pike agreed.

I shook my head, not believing them in the least, especially with the new round of screams from the train that just went over the first giant hill.

"I've got an idea," Pike said. He looped his pinky finger with mine. "I pinky promise that if you don't like it, you can punch me in the stomach. Okay?"

I let out a small laugh and wiped away a tear. "Okay, but you can't let go of me."

"Done." Our arms relaxed beside us, pinkies linked.

He didn't let go, and in the end, I loved the ride. After that, everything was a pinky promise, and later an unspoken show of emotion. Before we started dating, we would just be watching TV and he would grab my pinky. I don't know if that was his way of saying he liked me or just wanting that connection, but whatever his reasons, it always made me feel special.

When we were together, it was an unspoken "I love you." But now, here in the middle of the street, years later, I am dumbfounded by the meaning.

"I missed you," he says.

Another shot to my heart, to my senses. "Go home to your girlfriend." I pull my hand from his and take off, not even waiting for a response.

Tears spill from my eyes while I hold back choked sobs. He missed me, but doesn't understand that I never stopped missing him. He was my whole world, and even when I was with Jack, I thought of him.

Jack was funny, and he was persistent. He liked me and I needed to move on, so I gave it a chance. It had been almost three years since I'd last seen Pike. Three years without a word, and someone was paying attention to me, someone wanted me, and I desperately needed to be wanted again.

It wasn't the same. I tried to love him, tried to gain his love, but my tries were never good enough. In the end Jack could never measure up to the feelings I had for Pike, and I was never good enough for Jack. Shortly before finals the following spring, he broke up with me.

Once again, I wasn't good enough. Once again, I was left trying to mend the fissure in my heart that Pike left.

I'm not good enough for anyone. That's why I try so hard to please Caleb. I can't have him leave me, too.

It only takes a few minutes to get back to Caleb's place, and I pace out front to gather myself before heading in.

When I reach the bedroom, the lights are still off, meaning Caleb is still asleep. A quick shower helps to hide the evidence of my crying, and I quickly dress and head back down.

I have two hours until I'm meeting Nora, so I busy myself with making Caleb his favorite breakfast and force myself to stop thinking about Pike by listening to an audiobook. For once it helps, and my mind is Pike-free.

I'm nearly done cooking when Caleb pads into the kitchen and stops my book.

"Good morning," I say with a smile.

He looks around to the meal I'm finishing up, his expression neutral. I'm not sure if he's still upset about the night before or not.

"This is quite a spread."

I nod as I direct him to sit down. "Fresh-made biscuits,

fresh-squeezed orange juice, and your favorite spinach, parmesan, onion, and mushroom omelet with a side of turkey sausage."

I make a plate and deliver it to the charger in front of him. When I move to leave, he takes hold of my wrist and pulls me down.

"You did good." He pulls me further and presses his lips to mine.

Warmth fills me, pushing out the disappointment in myself for the previous night.

"Thank you." I'm happy he is in a better mood.

"Are you joining me?" he asks as I head back over to the sink and begin soaking some of the dishes.

"No, I'm sorry. I'm headed over to Nora's. She has a lunch date, and I promised I would help her find an outfit."

"When will you be back? We were going to do wedding planning stuff."

"I'll be back before lunch," I say as I glance at the clock. It's already eight-fifteen. "Shoot, I have to go." I run over for a quick kiss.

"I'll probably go work out. Text me when you're on your way back."

"I will," I say with one last kiss on my way out the door.

chapter 8

It's just before nine when I hit the doorbell to Nora's condo, which is just on the other side of the complex from mine but still four miles from Caleb's.

"Coming!" I hear from the other side of the door just before a crash followed by a "Motherfucker!" and the stomping on one foot before the lock flips and the door swings open. Curly brown locks are everywhere, her shirt is on backwards, and her golden-olive skin is washed out from the layer of foundation she has on.

"That kind of morning, huh?"

"That coffee better be super strong."

"Quad venti skinny vanilla latte," I say as I hold the cup out. She greedily scoops it up from the carrier and steps back. I hold up the bag in my other hand. "Cinnamon rolls, biscuits and gravy, and chocolate croissants, topped with extra crispy bacon."

"Oh my God," she says, her eyes wide as she practically drools on the spot. "Perfect." She takes one of the bags and ushers me in. "Have I told you lately that I love you?"

"I love you, too, boo," I say as I give her an air kiss.

Nora and I met in our sophomore year of college, thrown together as roommates, and it was the best thing ever. From then on, we were inseparable, and roommates until we graduated.

She is the keeper of every secret, of every fear, and I am the same for her. So, of course when the time came, we bought condos in the same complex.

I also know she is a tidy person who keeps a meticulous closet, unlike mine, and that's why I stop in my tracks.

"Holy moly," I say at the entrance to her bedroom.

"I'm lost. Help me," she begs.

It's a very un-Nora-like scene. Like someone murdered her closet in a brutal fashion. There are clothes strewn everywhere. The closet is almost empty, every article of clothing looking like it shot out in an explosion. I feel like I'm in someone else's house.

I blow out a breath and clear off the seat at her vanity. "But first, breakfast."

Her hands clap together. "Yes!" She runs to the kitchen for some plates and silverware before digging in, pulling out the top container and tearing open a biscuit, then pouring some gravy over it. A contented sound at the first bite leaves her and she collapses to sit on the edge of the bed.

She points to the plate with her fork as she chews. "This is what I needed."

When the smell hits, my stomach rumbles, but I try to quiet it with my coffee.

"Indulge with me," Nora says, staring me down. "There is way too much here to eat on my own, so you're going to splurge this morning."

"I can't."

"Yes, you can. Your body is fucking perfect."

"No, it's not."

"Yes, it is."

I don't want to continue this constant battle, so instead I pick at a croissant, wondering just how many calories are in it.

I still have at least fifteen pounds to lose before the wedding. At least, that is how many I figure I need to get my thighs to stop touching.

"If he doesn't love you as you are—"

"Stop," I cut her off.

Her brow furrows. "Aubrey, I hate to see you so obsessed about your body. You are so beautiful, your body is beautiful, and your soul is beautiful. I just wish you could see what I see, what so many other people see."

"What I see is an imperfect woman."

"Every woman is perfectly imperfect, and that's what makes us beautiful." She purses her lips. "Question, and I want a real answer. What attracted Caleb to you?"

"My smile."

"Did he have a problem with your body?"

I shake my head. In the beginning, it was hard to keep Caleb off me. He was always so hungry for me, and I drowned in his touch. It felt so good to be wanted again, to be desired.

"When did this change happen, then?"

Change? I think back, trying to remember a specific point, to see if there was one, but there isn't. Small comments made, but I do remember the first.

"I love thigh gaps on women."

"You know that's not all that realistic, right?"

"You've got the hips for it. I bet a little bit of weight off and you could do it." A groan leaves him as he arches his hips, pressing his hard length against my center. *"That would be so sexy."*

I want to turn him on, to have him always that excited for me. I *want* to be his *perfect* woman.

"When did it become wrong to want to make your partner happy? To be desirable to them?" I ask.

"You should already be desirable to him."

"I am. *I* want to be more desirable to him, and he's helping me with that."

"How?"

"By not letting me indulge in excess calories, by encouraging me to exercise more. He's helping me become a better me. I hate running, but I feel better when I'm done. I may not like it all the time when he has me eat something I don't want, but I know it's because he wants to help me."

Nora's head hangs. "I'm sorry, I just see you changing so much for him, and I'm afraid he's pressuring you into it."

"He's helping me, Nora. Sometimes his help just isn't the most tactful."

"You can say that again," Nora says with a laugh.

"All right…" I take a big bite of the croissant. "Happy now?"

"I will be when you stop spitting crumbs all over my floor."

We both laugh and take a few more bites before Nora jumps up and finally fixes her top. "Okay, so he is meeting me at the restaurant."

"Good on the meet up."

"We're going to The Melting Pot in Castleton."

"Intimate, fun with food." I nod in approval.

"What do I wear?"

"Fun and flirty? Casual?"

"Both?" she more asks than says with a grimace.

"Remember, it can be cool in there," I point out.

"True, so definitely a cardigan."

"Or a sweater in general. The high is fifty today."

"Right. No tank tops." She nods, seeming to be happy one possibility is scratched off her list. She throws a sweater dress over her head that ends a good six inches from her knees.

Instantly, I'm jealous. Nora has thick thighs and hips but a tiny waist, and she looks gorgeous. Her confidence is so much higher than mine, and I can't wait to one day feel good in my own skin the way she does.

Nora is my body positive idol.

"Ugh, this isn't going to work," she grunts as she pulls it back off.

"Why not?"

"It's a button-down. A little too flirty for a first date. I don't want him to think I fuck on the first date."

I almost spit out my coffee, barely containing it in my mouth with the help of a napkin. "Warn me next time."

She laughs and pulls another dress from a pile she's created on the floor. It looks like it's the maybe pile, but at this point I haven't figured out her system.

If there is one.

I chew on my bottom lip as she immediately discards the item she just picked up in favor of another. This is the right time, the right place, to tell her, but I know what road it will lead down. But if I don't tell her and she finds out another way, she'll be hurt I didn't confide in her.

It's not that I don't want to tell her, it's her reaction that worries me.

No time like the present. My stomach is in knots, and I take a deep breath to prepare me for the conversation I've been dreading but also dying for.

"So, you'll never believe who I ran into."

"Yeah?" she says as she pulls a flowery dress over her head.

"Pike."

She stops, the hem sticking out the top, keeping it from falling down. It hangs from her breasts, the back flowing. "Did you just say Pike?" I nod while she stares back at me. "Pike? Pike, Pike? The guy you were madly in love with in high school who left to go to college in New York? The man no man will ever compare to?"

I roll my eyes at her theatrics. "Yes, that Pike."

"Wow. What was that like?"

"It was…weird." I take a sip of my coffee, the same coffee I ordered that day. My skin tingles at the memory of his hands on my waist, his chest firm and pressed against my own. "It was terrible."

"Terrible? What happened?"

"All those old feelings surged to the surface. I felt like an idiot while he held me, and I couldn't move."

Her hand flies up in the air. "Wait, he was holding you?"

"My legs gave out."

Her mouth forms a perfect O. "Oh, my God, he made your knees weak after all this time?"

"From my run!"

She claps her hand down on my shoulder. "No, girl, not your run."

"Nora."

"Seriously, it sounds like there's still something there, yeah?"

I shrug my shoulders, the flash of heat and tingles from his touch surfacing again, but I push them back down. "He was a long time ago."

"Then why are you trying so desperately to convince me it's nothing?"

"I am not!"

"But you will be," she says with a grin. It's that evil, mischievous one that causes my hackles to rise. "The perfect man is back in town and he wants to see you again."

"I never said that."

"I bet he did, though."

"If he really wanted to see me, wouldn't he have sought me out sometime over the past few months?" I don't want to get her on this train of thought, and on mine, reminding me that he's home and he's real.

"You think you'll see him again?" she asks.

I blow out a breath. "Unfortunately, yes."

"Why is that word before yes? It's just yes. 'Yes, Nora, I want to and will see him again.'"

"Turns out, he's the new structural engineer Caleb is working with on a few projects."

A gasp leaves her, eyes wide, mouth open. "No! How did that go down?"

"No clue, and on top of it, we had dinner with him and his girlfriend last night after the investor cancelled."

"Shit, he has a girlfriend?"

"And I can't even hate her because she's wonderful."

"That sucks."

"You're caught up. I had a terribly awkward dinner with my ex last night. Now I want to hear all about this guy and your plans."

She quirks a perfectly arched brow at me. "I'm not letting this Pike thing go."

"I didn't think so," I grumble.

"But I will for now." She lights up, her smile beaming. "His name is Jared, and he's an engineer from Cincinnati. Total nerd and cute as can be."

Nora is absolutely glowing as she talks about him, and I remember when I was like that with Caleb. He hired me for a project, and after a few weeks and some sparks, he asked me to dinner.

For weeks I was hoping he was interested, because he seemed interested, but I couldn't tell. He was everything I wanted in a man—good looking, intelligent, hard worker, driven. Caleb is picture perfect.

Or at least he is everything I thought I wanted in a man. The resurgence of Pike reminds me that once upon a time, everything I was looking for in a man was all that Pike was—caring, strong, handsome, loving, and fierce in his convictions. A man who thought about more than himself, and treated me like I was his sun.

I shake my head to clear it and focus back on my friend and her current fashion dilemma.

A few more hard nos, a couple of possible yeses, and she finally lands in the Goldilocks zone.

A pair of dark-wash skinny jeans paired with black pumps and a wine-colored, fitted, off-the-shoulder sweater.

"Stop. That's it."

"Yeah?" she asks as she inspects her reflection, takes a twirl or two, and tilts her head making her curls bounce.

"Casual, but still dressy. Flirty, but still conservative. Good mix."

She nods her head and smiles. "I think you're right."

We switch places, and she sits at the vanity to finish her makeup, which is still on the base foundation.

I watch as she expertly applies her makeup. More than once she's been my teacher, showing me the ropes. She has the perfectly shaped, full, cupid-bow lips from her mother, and the blue eyes of her father. A beautiful mix that makes her such a stunning beauty.

"You're so beautiful," I say as I stare at her reflection.

"Aww," she smiles and blows me a kiss. "I love you, too, gorgeous."

The alarm on her phone sounds, and she curses as she hurries up, putting on her eye shadow and finally, false eyelashes.

"How do I look?" she asks as she stands and turns in a circle.

"Like a goddess."

She smiles, then hops around the room gathering up her purse and essentials she'll need for the day. "What are you doing later?" she asks with a hopeful edge to her tone.

"I'm not sure. We're doing some wedding planning."

"Can I call you after?" We head to her front door, and she's still frantically making sure she has everything.

"You better."

"Just didn't want to interrupt your couple time."

"Interrupt away." I wrap my arms around her, giving her a big hug. "Go knock him dead."

She beams at me and blows a kiss as she climbs into her car. Watching her drive away, I'm left with a twinge in my chest. The happiness and excitement that radiated from her is gone, and I find myself envious of her. I miss that feeling, and it's been a while since I felt it.

Probably when Caleb proposed, or it should be, but it's not. For some reason what comes to mind first is a different ring, placed on a different finger by a different man years ago.

I glance down at the simple band on my right hand.

Caleb's proposal was on a trip to Chicago just after New Year's. He was up there talking with another investor, and that was when he bought me the black dress. It was for a special dinner, he said, one that we were having with the investor and his wife.

The view from The Signature Room at the 95th was the most spectacular thing I've ever seen, sitting next to the window staring out at the bright lights of the city in contrast with the black darkness of Lake Michigan. The whole evening was beautiful, the food fantastic, and I was having a wonderful time.

After multiple bottles of wine, appetizers, and our entrees, but before dessert, Caleb produced a small box from his pocket and sat it in front of me.

"I have another business proposition to discuss," Caleb said with a smile.

I looked from Caleb to the box before picking it up and opening it. I drew in a breath at the large diamond ring nestled inside.

"Aubrey Hart, I'm completely in love with you. Will you be my wife?"

My mouth went slack as I attempted to process his words. We'd only been together a year and a half, and I was blindsided. Never in my life did I imagine someone other than Pike proposing, but there was Caleb, smiling at me from across the table. Waiting. Expectant for my answer.

There was only one answer to give.

"Yes."

He kissed me from across the table. No one knee, no putting the ring on my finger. None of the cliché sayings or gestures I've seen time and time again on TV, movies, and the Internet.

Then again, I wasn't sure any man would be able to top the video of the whole choreographed proposal to Bruno Mars's *Marry You*. That man created standards that I'm sure make men cringe.

I pull out my phone and text Caleb.

Nora is off! Are you back? - Aubrey

Be home in 10. Pick up the wedding binder and the invitations on your way - Caleb

It may not have been the proposal my romantic heart was looking for, but that didn't change the fact that the man I love asked me to be his wife. That is what is important.

chapter 9

OR TWO HOURS I'VE STARED AT THE CEILING, watching as the sunrise began to slowly creep in. I've listened to Caleb's slow, steady snore. It's low, thankfully, but once I woke up, it kept me from falling back to sleep.

Though that's not entirely true. A little worm crawled into my brain and refused to leave. Tall and more handsome than he was at eighteen, all I can think of, all I can see, is Pike. Even though it's been over a week since I've seen him, it seems no matter how hard I try, I can't stop the memories from flooding in.

I know I shouldn't, and I try not to, but I can't help it sometimes. All the good times we shared, from scaring off some guys who were picking on me in junior high, to when he asked me to homecoming my sophomore year.

God, how awestruck I was. Sure, we'd known each other, had the same circle of friends for years, but he was always the older, cute boy with the sexy, lopsided grin and dimples.

Those blue eyes and the way they would sparkle in the light would send my pulse racing with just a glance. He was my sunshine and happiness. With him, the world was truly a wonder. Colors were deeper, more intense and brighter, almost like the sun never shined until he was near.

A dark cloud covered me when he left, my heart broken. When we parted, I believed there would be a minimum of five years that we would have to survive without each other. After all, with the thousands of miles between us, it wasn't practical to expect that we could survive long distance for so long. Yet, I would always dream of him coming home. Returning to me. He would pick me up, spin me around like the hero in a movie, and our love story would continue as if we had never parted.

But it never happened. After college, he didn't come home for me.

And it was like I lost him all over again. I waited, I counted down the days, but he never came. The whole summer was spent in a spiral of depression eating and I gained fifteen pounds, which only made me feel worse.

Then the news came—he was staying in New York.

It gutted me.

A glance over to Caleb shows him still deep in sleep. It's going to be a busy week. Between the wedding growing closer and me finally moving in with him, we really haven't spent much quality time together in the last few weeks.

The clock shows it is finally after six, and a reasonable time for a run.

Quietly I pull my running gear from the dresser and move to the bathroom. Caleb usually sleeps in late on the weekend, and I don't want to disturb him.

By the time I make it outside, the sky is a beautiful orange and blue as the sun crests the horizon. I can't wait until the sun is up earlier so I can run in the light. While I know the neighborhood is safe, there is just something about running in the dark that unnerves me a bit.

With every beat of the music and my steps, I try and shake

my thoughts of Pike away, to redirect them, but I just can't seem to. Having him back in my life gives him a tangibility distance couldn't.

Pike was my first everything. After giving him my V-card, I truly thought that he'd be the only man I'd ever be with. Even when he left, I held onto that, saying that if I dated other boys I wouldn't give them my body.

But as time and distance grew, that expectation slipped away with reality.

It was a reality I hated, and one he knew would happen.

"You're saying you want to be with other girls!"

"No, I'm not! What I'm saying, what I'm trying to do is be a realist. I can't ask you to put your emotions on hold for five years."

"So this is for me? That's bullshit, Pike, and you know it!"

"What I know is I'm going to NYU and you're going to Purdue, and that's five years of barely seeing each other and…I don't want to say these words, because it kills me to think them, but the reality is a lot of things can happen in five years, and I don't want either one of us getting hurt because of them."

"So we're breaking up?"

"No… yes… I don't know. Fuck, Bree! Why does it have to be like this?"

"We don't have to."

"Life is splitting us up. This isn't something I want."

"You want to go to NYU."

"Something I've been planning since long before we started going out. Long before I ever knew I could love someone so much." His fingers brushed back a strand of hair as his forehead fell against mine. "Nothing will ever stop how much I love you. Not time or distance. I'm yours forever."

My throat feels thick, and my eyes sting. I knew he didn't

want to separate. I knew it was hard on him. But it felt like he was choosing to leave me.

I try to switch my brain over to work, to thinking about the designs I have meetings for this week. There's so much on my mind all the time lately, and I hate that it keeps being diverted to Pike.

Fuck!

I nearly trip at the figure running down the side street. His blue eyes meet mine, and his lip twitches up as he slows. I mimic him and slow as well, until he turns and jogs beside me.

"We have to stop meeting like this," he says with a smirk.

Each breath is hard from my faster pace. "Smooth. You know, I'm beginning to think you're stalking me."

"Stalking? No, I wouldn't call it that. Chasing, maybe."

I laugh and shake my head. "Chasing?"

He nods. "I let you get away, and now I'm trying to catch back up."

I slow down more as I turn toward him. "I'm with Caleb."

"I know."

"Do you?" I shake my head. "What about your girlfriend?"

His brow furrows before shooting up. "That. Well, I have to tell you something. I'm not with Kate, Aubrey. I never have been."

I stare at him, my heart soaring. I want to laugh, and I want to cry. Once again, he's made me a complete mess. Even I don't understand myself, my reactions. I'm actually happy he's not with her, but that emotion is mixed in with confusion and a twinge of regret.

"She is a friend from New York who came to see how I am settling in. Caleb assumed we were together, and I asked her to play along. She flew back on Monday."

"Why would you do that?"

"It wasn't on purpose, but I went with it. I know that I let Caleb operate under the assumption that I was with Kate by not correcting him, but I never intended to present you with a falsehood. I'm not playing games, I promise. It wasn't until dinner that I realized how much I wanted to see your reaction. I needed some sort of recognition from you that I wasn't the only one who thought about the other."

"I never stopped thinking about you," I admit. "But that doesn't change anything."

"You seem to be running a lot," he says, changing the subject. "That's new."

"Yeah," I said, my lips pursing. "Trying to get these massive thighs down before the wedding."

I've always had thicker thighs. They've been my bane and impossible to thin out. Even with the weight I've lost, they've stuck around.

"Your thighs aren't massive," he says, his gaze down, running along my legs.

"Yes, they are."

"Is that him talking?" he asks as he catches my arm and pulls me gently to a stop.

The disdain in his tone throws me off. I thought they were all buddy-buddy, but there's a fire in his eyes that makes me question it.

"Him?" I ask, trying to feign ignorance and draw more information out.

"Your fiancé."

I stare at him, wondering how he could know that. It was an aspect of my body Caleb didn't particularly like, especially since they rub together. What started as Caleb's initial comments about how sexy he found thigh gaps led to his outright admitting he disliked my thighs rubbing together. It hurt to hear and I've been trying to please him since, but nothing I do seems to be working fast enough.

I swallow, and it doesn't go unnoticed by Pike.

"Your thighs are perfect. You don't need to do anything."

I glance at him, and he's completely serious.

"Oh, come on." Heat begins to flood my face, which thankfully is masked by the redness from running.

"He should be kneeling down every night praying to those thighs."

"Pike…"

His eyes lock with mine. "I would be."

I'm transfixed as more memories flood my mind unbidden. I don't want to remember his head buried between my legs, of fisting his hair as my hips ground against his mouth. Still, they come, and I'm lost in long-forgotten sensations.

"I've never stopped thinking about you. I always assumed that we would never settle down with anyone but each other, that one day we would be together again. But Bree, did I mess up?"

"What do you mean?" I ask.

"Should I have come back five years ago? Did we lose those five years?"

His brow is knitted and his tone genuine. I'm caught between calling him a fucking idiot and screaming "of course!" but I manage to pull myself back. "Obviously! If you wanted to spend your life with me, you should have come home sooner. I get staying for an internship, but why not after that?"

"What does your head say?"

"Well, my head says my heart is stupid."

He lets out a chuckle. "Oh, I'm very familiar with that."

"You are?"

"It's why I didn't come back."

"Your head got in the way?"

He nods. "And my heart. I was scared. A lot was going on in both of our lives at that point. Would coming back mean fucking things over for both of us? Were you in an emotional position to see me again? Or would Jack still be on your mind?"

My mouth pops open. "Oh, wow, Jack…that's right, we broke up right before finals."

"I used that as an excuse. Well, that and you needing to find your way and not be distracted by me."

"You think you're that distracting?" I ask with a quirk of my brow.

"I know there was no way I would let you go for weeks the moment I had you in my arms again. And the head spoke up and reminded the heart that it wouldn't be good for either of us. Things were going well for me in New York career-wise, and I couldn't logically throw away the opportunity."

"These convictions of yours are very strong, but ten years changes a person. You don't know me anymore."

"Maybe not the particulars of the last few years, but I know you, Bree. I always have."

"Stop."

He sighs and runs his fingers through his hair, and that's when it catches my eye. It's weather worn, the braided leather straps no longer as supple as they once were. Etched into the stainless-steel clasp is two names with a heart—*Aubrey and Pike*.

My mouth drops open as I stare at it. There is no doubt it is the exact bracelet I gave him for his eighteenth birthday. It cost me a lot, but I'd saved for a long time. It had to last the years he would be gone, and it had and then some.

"Open it," I said with a smile covering my face.

"You already got me a gift." He pointed to the framed photo of the two of us that sat on his bedside table.

"That was just to throw you off the scent."

"The scent?" he asked with a laugh.

His mouth dropped open as he looked at the thick leather straps, then snapped closed when he saw the stainless-steel clasp. "Bree…"

"Do you like it?" I asked, my stomach a mass of butterflies. I hadn't been that nervous around him in a long time.

"I love it," he said as he pulled it from its box and worked it onto his left wrist.

"Just a little something so you don't forget about me," I said with a sniffle. There was a smile on my lips, but tears in my eyes.

"Fuck," he cursed before lunging forward and throwing me down onto my back, his lips crashing to mine. "I'll wear it every day and never take it off."

I follow the movements of his hand, transfixed and unable to believe that he's worn it for this long. Did he wear it to dinner last week? I try and recall. The memory is fuzzy and clouded by how good he looked, but I do remember something dark around his wrist, next to his watch. I remember the same when I bumped into him running the following morning.

"Your bracelet," I say, unable to form any words past that.

His other hand clamps down on his wrist, and he draws in a deep breath. A moment passes, then another before his hand relaxes and he reveals it again, fingers playing with the clasp that holds the inscription.

"I told you I'd never take it off," he says. His smile devastates me. The pain there, the fear of my reaction.

Another stab to the chest. I hate that look on his face, the vulnerability there. Why does he wear such an expression?

"Every day?"

He nods. "All but a sparse few, but most of that was for a minor surgery and they made me take it off. Not having it on was more nerve-wracking then the actual surgery."

Surgery? "What happened?"

"Do you remember when I dislocated my shoulder?" He rotates his right shoulder back, and the image of it out of socket makes me cringe.

"How could I forget?" My lips creep up into a smile despite the memory. "That was the day I fell in love with you."

"That day? Really?"

"I was thirteen, and you got hurt saving me from falling. How could I not? You, however, were completely blind to it."

"I was not."

"You were. You were a high schooler and didn't have time for us babies."

His lips form a thin line, but one corner is turned up as he suppresses a smile. "Maybe, but from the day you moved in, I liked you, even when I didn't understand what kind of like it was. And that day I realized I loved you too."

"So much love we didn't understand."

"You were crying because I was hurt. So upset, and it upset me. I hate seeing you cry. I'd be the worst hostage because all they'd have to do is make you cry, and I'd tell them whatever they wanted just to get them to stop."

"Are we getting abducted soon?" The ease of our conversation, the flow—I can't believe I'd forgotten how easy it is with him.

He shrugs. "You never know. Anyway, I dislocated it twice in high school."

I nod as the memories come back. "When you tripped

at that cross-country meet, and then the last winter when we crashed while sledding."

"Well, those compounded, and it happened a few more times and the doc finally said I needed surgery. It created an instability, so they had to go in and fix the ligaments. Haven't had an issue since."

"How long ago was that?"

"I pushed it off as long as I could and finally caved the summer before my last year of college. I had to cut my internship short, but thankfully they understood. Mom flew out and took care of me. About six years." He twists the leather around his wrist. "I made Mom wear it to keep it safe. Made her promise she wouldn't take it off."

"Why?"

"Because it means the world to me." His gaze moves down to my hand. It's empty of the ring at the moment, but he didn't forget. "Why do you wear the ring? It's just you and me right now. The truth."

My heart slams in my chest. I want to blow it off and say it's habit. It's a pretty and simple ring that goes with everything, but with him standing in front of me, I know that's a lie I've been telling myself for a long time.

It's precious to me. I wear it because he gave it to me. I wear it because it's the remnants of a promise, of a love I've never forgotten. There's nothing simple and everything is complicated about the ring I have worn every day since my seventeenth birthday.

As his eyes beg me for an answer, for the truth, it's a truth that is breaking a piece of me apart. The reality of that lie causes an ache in my chest. Part of me crumbles away, and I don't like what is exposed.

I wear it because I still love you.

It's a feeling I can't face, so I turn, refusing to answer him. I run full out, even as he calls my name, even as he chases.

I run.

There is no way I can face him with that realization. It has me unhinged, and I head through the yard to sit on the back porch as I calm down.

My heart is racing, and I struggle to regain my breath after running faster than I have probably ever run before.

I ran from him.

A few minutes of cooling off and I'm able to go inside.

"I'm back," I call out as I enter the kitchen, but am met with silence. As I climb the stairs, I can see light coming from the master bedroom.

"Where have you been?" he asks when I enter.

"On my run."

He glances to the clock. "It took you longer than normal."

"Sorry, I ran into one of the neighbors and we got to talking." Not a lie, but my omissions are piling up.

"On your knees," he says as he pushes on my shoulder. He flexes his hips, pressing his hard cock against my face as I slide down. "Make me come."

He pulls down the waistband of his boxers, freeing himself, while his other hand knots in my hair.

I say nothing, do nothing but comply as he chokes me, pushes me down to the point of pain, and slaps me with his dick. After a few minutes of fucking my face, he pushes me all the way down to the base, holding onto the back of my head. I have no breath and I press against his thighs to get away, but he holds me tighter, his hips making small movements before shooting forward and finally coming.

When he's finished, he lets go of me and I fall down to the floor, coughing and sputtering as I attempt to draw in a breath. Cum and slobber drips from me as tears stain my cheeks.

"Fuck, that was good, baby," he praises me.

I hate the way I feel, but one sentence from him and I'm happy I've pleased him. He smiles at me, and I'm happy.

Bending over, he helps me up and walks me to the bathroom. It's quiet as he turns on the spray in the shower, then helps me undress, tossing my clothes into the laundry hamper.

"The laundry is full," he says, noticing the overflow of clothing.

"I'll do it today."

He presses his lips to my forehead. "Good girl."

The spray feels good against my skin, warm and soothing. Immediately I put my head under to rinse off my face and wet my hair.

"You're joining me?" I ask as he steps in behind me.

"I want to fuck you now."

I glance down to see him fully hard again. "Already?" He rarely bounces back that quickly.

"I woke up so fucking horny." He wraps his arms around me and pulls me close, one hand kneading my breast. "And if I remember, it's your job to keep my balls drained."

I nod and crane my neck, giving him room to kiss his way down my neck to my shoulder where he bites down for a quick second. His hand is cool contrast against my water-warmed skin as he presses on my back, bending me forward as I press my hands against the wall.

"Condom," I say, earning a growl from him. He steps out of the shower to grab one and slips it on.

When he steps back in, he wastes no time entering me. I

make the sounds he likes, but I derive little pleasure from the angle and simply bounce back at him. Pike flashes into my mind, and suddenly I'm reliving the time we had sex in the shower. A shudder rolls through me, spreading like fire through my veins. The way he held me, the way he touched me, and the sounds he elicited from me.

The echoes on the tile wall suddenly aren't fake, but the feelings fade away as Caleb's hips slam against me and a deep groan resounds.

"Damn, that was good, baby," he says.

We resume showering and I lather up, desperate to get the grime off me—to wash away the feelings of regret that are surfacing.

"Don't forget, we have dinner with my parents tonight," I remind him.

"Shit," he curses.

"What?"

His head is shaking. "I can't make it."

My stomach drops, and I turn toward him. "Caleb, you promised."

"I'm sorry, I forgot. I've got an appointment at six, and then I'm meeting Dan and Trey to watch the game."

"Can you come over after the meeting? Please?" I hate that I'm begging, but this isn't the first time he's backed out.

"It's more than just watching a game. Trey is only in town for a few days, then he's going back to Nashville."

I nod in understanding. "You're right." Trey has only come to town a few times since we've been together.

"Hey," he calls and lifts my chin until our eyes meet. "I'll make it up to you, I promise. I love you."

"I love you, too."

The words fall from my lips like a practiced speech, but at the moment I'm not feeling their meaning.

I do love him. Even as I think the words, my chest clenches as that crumbled section I'd buried away exposes a deeper truth.

I love *two* men.

That knowledge scares me more than anything.

chapter 10

THE WEEKEND WENT BY IN A FLASH, AND THE WEEK is already half over. It feels like the days are flying by— all but today, which completely drained me. All I really want to do is go home and become one with my couch. Maybe a little Netflix, then maybe some chill with my little vibrating friend.

Instead, I head over to my parents' house after my last appointment, knowing if I go home it will be hard to get myself going again.

Pulling into the driveway of my parents' house is always filled with nostalgia. I still remember the day we moved in, and it's hard to believe it's been seventeen years. Every time I walk inside, it's like I never left. Then again, I only bought my condo right before I met Caleb and had been living with them before that.

"Hello," I call out. The TV is on in the living room, and I find my dad relaxed in his recliner.

"Hey, pumpkin," he says as he sits up and lowers the volume.

I lean down and give him a hug. "How's tricks?"

"Good, but your mom keeps trying to put me on this keto diet." He rolls his eyes. "A man and his carbs are not to be separated."

"What did she say to that?" I ask as I fight a giggle.

"Shut up and eat your celery and cheese."

I let out a laugh as I shake my head. "Where is she?"

His head ticks in the direction of the kitchen. "Making some keto concoction she found on the Internet. Don't tell her I went to Olive Garden for lunch and stuffed my face with pasta and breadsticks."

"Tsk-tsk, Daddy."

"This is your mother's doing. I'm just along as the guinea-pig taste-tester."

I kiss his forehead and let him get back to whatever he's watching, then go find Mom. I spot her standing in the kitchen. Her long blonde hair is almost silver now, and I applaud her not falling into the dyeing trap. It looks good on her, and instead of looking older, she looks younger.

"Hi, Mom."

"Hi, baby," she says, looking up from her tablet, then back down.

"What are you making?" I ask as I take a seat on one of the island stools. She has a bowl full of some meat mixture and a smaller bowl filled with what looks like cut-up string cheese.

"Some yummy cheese-stuffed meatballs I found on Facebook. I follow this keto video recipe blog, and some of it is really good. Just ask your dad." There is always an edge of elation in her voice, but even more so when she is excited.

I laugh on the inside while I nod at her. "Why keto?"

"Well, with the wedding coming up, we both need to drop a few pounds, and everyone is raving about this. It's helped Marcie Sharpe with her diabetes, and it's cured so many of her health issues. She went from twelve medications to two and has lost ninety-five pounds in a year."

Mom isn't big by any means, and Dad is rocking the Dad-bod, but they are both happy and healthy—that's all that is important.

"I think you look great. I'm the one that has to worry about my weight for the wedding, not you."

"Well, I think you look great and don't need to lose any more weight."

"My thighs are still touching."

"And? What does that have to do with anything? My thighs have always rubbed, and I was smaller than you when I met your father. He didn't care about things like that. Women today are bombarded by photoshopped images of thigh gaps that don't exist, and men that expect the unattainable."

"It is attainable," I argue. Once upon a time I had thighs that didn't touch, right?

She narrows her eyes at me. "But at what cost?"

"So, what's the latest neighborhood gossip?" I ask, desperately wanting to change the subject.

Mom lights up like usual, and she relays all that is going on in the neighborhood while she cooks. Once she has the meatballs in the oven, I pull out the salad fixings and while she cleans up.

Before long, we're sitting at the kitchen table with a large salad and a pan of meatballs.

"Oh, Aubrey, did you hear that Pike moved back?" Mom asks as she passes the salad around.

It's a strategic move. She didn't mention it earlier in the gossip update, which meant she was waiting to bring him up.

I heap a good portion onto the plate and set it back down. "Um, yeah, actually I ran into him."

"Wonderful!" she says, a little more excited than I feel she should be. "You know, I was always so sure that your dad would be walking you down the aisle to Pike."

"I used to think that as well."

She smiles at me. "He's back now."

My expression falls. "Mom." My parents like Caleb as far as I know, but they loved Pike.

"Pike is back. You don't have to settle for Caleb."

I snap my head in her direction, blood beginning to boil. "*Settle* for Caleb? What are you talking about? I thought you liked Caleb."

Mom's lips form a thin line. "I just want you to be happy. Is Caleb who you really want?"

"Yes, Mom. I'm happy with Caleb. Pike is…Pike is the past. We've grown up, and apart."

"Where is Caleb tonight?" Dad asks, piping up for the first time.

"He had a meeting he had to attend."

"That's three dinners in a row," he says.

I grind my teeth. "And?"

"Nothing, just noting it."

"He's a busy man, Dad." I look to each end of the table, then down again. "I don't get what is going on, but enough."

Silence falls over the room. I move the lettuce in my salad around on my plate but can't stomach putting another fork full in my mouth. It's not appetizing anymore, not that it ever really was, and it takes everything in me to choke down the next bite. Fed up, I pull a meatball from the sauce, break off a chunk, and pop it in my mouth.

A moan leaves me at the tang of the sauce mixed with the savory flavors.

"Oh, Aubrey, I had a thought about the table numbers,"

Mom starts once I've finished off the meatball and am reaching for a second, no longer caring about the calorie count. "We could get some of those wood block numbers and spray them with some glitter paint and glue them onto a board with a pretty background, like some of those scrapbooking pages."

I swallow my bite, then wipe my lips. "You've been looking at Pinterest too much."

"Oh, but it would be so easy and beautiful."

I nod in agreement. It does sound pretty, and there are so many beautiful scrapbooking prints. "I'll run it by Caleb and see what he thinks."

Mom's lips form a thin line as the tension rises again. "Why do you have to run everything by him? Aren't you allowed to make any decisions by yourself?"

"Mom."

"Look, we're happy that you're happy, but I feel like you've changed yourself a lot for this man."

"Where is this coming from? Suddenly Pike is home and it's time to dump my fiancé? He's not the fucking prodigal son returned from the desert. He left me and never came back. Why am I not allowed to move on from that?"

I stand, unable to continue the conversation, and ignore the calls from the dining room as I rush up the stairs. Just as when I was a teenager, I stomp into my bedroom and slam the door shut.

I fall back on the bed, the springs bouncing beneath me.

Anger simmers below the surface, and most of it is directed at Pike. If he hadn't suddenly come home, I wouldn't have to defend myself, my fiancé, or my wedding. I'd be blissfully ignorant of hidden feelings and happily ironing out wedding details.

I take a few deep breaths and relax.

The smell…it's so comforting. It's a little stale from the door being closed, but the scent is one that hits me on so many levels.

This was my space. This was where I feared nothing, loved hard, and broke deeply.

Safety and security were always found within these pink walls.

While I moved out years ago, there are still some remnants of my childhood. The extra bedroom in my condo holds my office, and so there were some things I had to leave here for a while.

The bedroom furniture I grew up with still decorates the space. Mom has turned it into another guest bedroom. There's still the stain on the floor from when I painted flowers on the wall, the wear on all the furniture, and the memories.

Even when I came home from college, I didn't change anything. It took almost two years until I was making enough to move out on my own, and when I did, I took almost everything but the furniture.

And my hope chest.

A hard piece to leave behind, but a necessary one.

I turn my head toward my childhood dresser and the wooden box that sits atop. It was too painful to take with me, and even now I'm reluctant, but still it draws me in. The metal clasp sticks when I push on it, but then it releases, moving through the loop.

Dried corsages lay neatly on top. Once bright and colorful, they've since dulled and are fragile, but I still remember which dance they belonged to. Pike bought me a different one for the two homecoming dances, and the two proms we attended.

A pile of photos beneath catches my eye, some of them taken with a small Polaroid camera Pike got me for my sixteenth birthday. My breath hitches as I stare at the boy in the photos.

His jaw wasn't as angular, his features softer and definitely thinner, but the muscles were still there.

The Pike in the photos doesn't resemble this new one. This Pike was carefree, loved to sing to the radio, and adored me.

It was the happiest time of my life. Ever since then I've been…missing.

Or maybe just missing him.

His smile is so brilliant, and once again I'm drawn in. All the history we have I've hidden away for years, but never thrown away. I couldn't, because that would mean truly letting go. So much time we spent together. I can't even think about high school without thinking of Pike.

It was right here I lost my virginity to Pike. In the heat of July while my parents were at work.

It was the small two week gap where we were both sixteen. My birthday is June nineteenth and his is July sixth. Sadly we weren't in the same class due to the cutoff from the school system I moved in from.

I still remember the day he got his acceptance letter to NYU. He was so excited, and I was so happy for him, but I also knew what it meant. He was going to leave me. It was a conversation we both avoided, even when I got my early acceptance to Purdue.

Every fiber of me wanted to make a long-distance relationship work. I know it hurt us both to say goodbye when he left that August, and I hated every inch that separated us both physically and emotionally.

It didn't matter how much we loved each other. The distance in both time and miles was too much, despite what my heart said. It was right. We needed to grow on our own. That didn't mean it didn't kill my soul to lose him.

When he touched me, the world melted away, and I haven't felt that since. His kiss made me forget about the rest of the world. It was just the two of us with every caress, every exploration of our bodies.

Emotionally charged and electric highs that resulted in the most powerful sex I've ever experienced.

I've never had an orgasm with Caleb. I do everything to please him, but sexually get little in return. The same with Jack. It was all about coming and that was it.

There is more of that truth again, cold and ugly, and I hate that the simple fact adds another level of inadequacy in my relationship with Caleb. But as time progresses, the defects outweigh their counterparts. While I won't admit it out loud, I can't help but question if Mom and Nora and even Pike, who has been home two-point-five seconds, may be onto something

Before my thoughts can garner any more traction, a knock on the door draws my attention. "Come in," I call.

The door slowly opens to Mom standing in the doorway. Her brow is knitted, highlighting every line on her face. "Aubrey, I'm sorry."

"It's okay."

"It's not. It was selfish of me. I just…I remember what you were like with Pike, how happy you were. I haven't seen you that happy since."

"I'm happy, Mom."

She sits down on the bed next to me. "I know, but I also know you've never smiled as big as you did when Pike was around. The way you lit up like the sun."

"I've seen him, Mom. We've talked."

"And?" She's expectant, eyes wide and lips parted, and I know she's hoping for something I won't give her.

"And at the end of the day, he's just somebody that I used to know."

Her face falls in disappointment. "Oh."

I bump her shoulder with mine. "Wedding dress shopping is coming up. Can you please help me find the perfect dress?"

She runs her hand over my hair and smiles. "Of course, baby."

"Good." I lean forward and pull her in for a hug. Mom hugs are the absolute best, and it isn't until her arms wrap around me that I realize how much I need it right now. "It's been a long day. I think I'm going to head home."

I walk back over to the chest and start putting everything back in. As I shuffle things around, I stop at one of the Polaroid photos. It's of the two of us. I remember when it was taken. We were in his room, and I was leaning against the chest. His arms were around me while I held the camera away. His lips are pressed against my temple as he stares up at the camera, a sparkle in his eye.

"One day I'm going to marry you," he whispered into my ear.

I turned against his chest and met his lips with my own. "One day can't come soon enough."

I stroke the photo with my finger before placing it in with the others, then top it off with the corsages.

"You should take that with you," Mom encourages.

I shake my head. "No. Not yet."

With a hug and a kiss to my father and another to my mom, I head out. I text Caleb but get no response right away. There's a knot in my stomach as I pull down the driveway, and I don't know why.

When I see the house just down the street, I slow down. One that is almost as familiar as the one I just left. Playing in the yard, riding our bikes on the sidewalk, soft, slow kisses before finally parting and heading home—Pike's home.

The lights are off, the inside dark, but I remember when it was full of life and love. His parents still live there, but it's obvious they're not home, so I just mildly look like a creeper stopped in front of their house.

I can't resist the urge to look up toward the corner window and imagine him standing there.

I don't know why I do it, but I snap a photo of the empty window. Before I can comprehend it, I've got my text messages up and am sending him the photo.

Why does this make my chest hurt? - Aubrey

I don't really expect a reply, and especially not within seconds. **Because you miss me - Pike**

I can admit that I very much did miss him, but even though he is back in my life, I can't admit that I miss him just as much now.

I did, and now it's so strange knowing you're back and your window is dark - Aubrey

I can go turn it on if that would make you feel better - Pike

Stay home. It doesn't matter - Aubrey

Just as I put the car into drive, a light flickers, catching my eye. I look back and find the light on and a figure standing in the window.

It does matter - Pike

I jump as the phone begins to vibrate in my hand, Pike's name flashing across the screen.

"Why does it matter?" I ask him.

"Because your feelings matter to me."

I close my eyes and blow out a breath. The way he says it makes this feeling worse. "What are you doing there?"

"Dinner with the folks. What brings you over?"

"Same."

"How did it go?" he asks.

I pause and lean my head back against the headrest. "Not good."

"Want to talk about it? We could go for a drive."

For a brief second, I contemplate saying yes. "I'd like that, but I already told Caleb I was headed home." And I shouldn't be alone with him. I don't trust myself or my feelings.

"To his house?"

"No, to mine."

"Where is he?" Pike asks.

"He had a meeting, then went out with friends."

There is a pause. "Then what does it matter when you get home?"

"I just…I have to text him when I get there."

"So?"

"He knows how long it takes me to get home."

"Just tell him you ran into an old friend," he says with a chuckle, and I don't miss the double meaning.

"Ha ha." I blow out a breath. "It's not a good idea anyway."

"Why not?"

"Don't ask questions you know the answer to," I say.

"But I don't know the answer. I have an idea, a hope, but I can't read your mind."

"I…" I trail off. Why did I do this? Why did I initiate contact? "I have to go."

"Bree, wa—"

I end the call, cutting him off and speeding away.

Running away. Again.

chapter 11

Pike

"FUCK," I CURSE WHEN THE LINE GOES DEAD AND SHE speeds off.

For a split second, I thought I'd broken through to her. Thought maybe, just maybe, I could get her alone and we could finally talk.

Still, there was progress. Admission that she missed me, that a stupid empty window affected her so much she had to contact me. It gives me hope that I can wake her. Make her see what is glaringly obvious, that Caleb isn't just not right for her, but bad for her.

I've known guys like him, and I know what he's capable of, but he's blinded her. Used her insecurities against her to keep her on a leash.

Again, I kick myself. Regret settles deep in my stomach, an open pit that threatens to swallow me. I never should have doubted coming home years ago. I should have just done it. Fear never should have kept me from Aubrey.

But that's what fear does. It infects you, makes you unable to move, unable to think of anything of anything else. Fear slithers in like ice in the veins until you're frozen, unable to make a move. For a long time, it manifested in the thought that after so long apart, my memories were just a fantasy. Built up as time went, putting her on a pedestal above everyone else, and that in the end our relationship was nothing but that fantasy.

The second I saw her, held her in my arms, I knew that fantasy was real. It wasn't an apparition following me around.

It was *real*. Aubrey is *real*, and so is every minute that I've loved her.

It was crippling, choking when the memories flooded back, every bit as strong and not those of a boy holding onto the past.

There's never been anyone else for me. If I'm able to break down her walls, if I can just get the chance to be with her again, I'm never going to let her go.

I love her. Never stopped loving her.

I blow out a breath and push against the window, making sure to turn the light off as I leave the room and head back downstairs.

"What was that all about?" Mom asks as I slide back into my seat at the table. Their plates are empty, but I see both their glasses are topped off with wine.

"Aubrey."

Like always when Aubrey is mentioned, Mom lights up like the Christmas tree in Rockefeller Center. "Aubrey called?"

"Sort of."

"And?"

"And nothing."

"You moved a thousand miles, cut your salary in half, and after three months of being back, still nothing?" Dad asks. He, unlike Mom, wasn't happy about my sudden decision to move back. Nothing against Aubrey, he just didn't like me leaving the opportunities he felt New York provided.

But I'd never be happy there, and isn't that worth more than a few dollars?

"It's not easy to convince a woman who is engaged to another man that she should be with you. Have you tried it lately?"

He chuckles and raises his glass. "Fair point."

"It had to be something if you were talking to her," Mom says.

I blow out a breath and take a long sip of wine. "I can tell she's still angry, still hurt, and that makes it even harder trying to break through. She has these walls up, and I don't know if it's to keep me out or to keep the past out."

"Slow and steady wins the race." Dad raises his wine glass again, and Mom does as well.

But the race has been going for a while and I'm just joining, gaining speed. There's still a long way to go to catch up.

chapter 12

THE TILES IN FRONT OF ME HOLD NO SHAPE OR color. They are simply an object before me, occupying my spatial sight.

I've lost track of time. Minutes may have passed, or maybe only seconds.

I'm lost to the war between my head and my heart. The past and present collide like asteroids, exploding into a million pieces.

Layers peel back like wallpaper, exposing an older, different pattern, a different version of myself. Left to wonder when I became this spackled version of myself.

It's been over three weeks since Pike slammed back into my life. Weeks of spontaneous run-ins and heartaches. In that time, it's odd how much my life has been altered. Nothing feels right, and time is moving faster and faster while nothing is being accomplished.

Life has stalled, the tank dry.

Why can't I focus?

"Yo, Hart, you alive?" a voice calls out, breaking me from my trance.

I blink hard and turn to find a tall man with brown hair, blue eyes, and a killer smirk. The muscles that bulge from his sleeves don't hurt with his overall hotness.

"Hey, Briar," I say, finally comprehending visual stimuli again.

His navy-blue T-shirt with *Done Right Construction* printed in large letters across his chest is splattered with white, but I can't tell if it's paint or mud.

"I've been calling your name for a while."

"Sorry." I shake my head and smile up at him. "A lot going on up there."

He shrugs. "Better than nothing going on."

"True."

"Everything okay? You seem a bit off."

"Yeah, fine. How's Ivy doing? I saw Iris last week, and she was headed out for a visit." Briar is a few years younger than me, but I was in the same class as his twin sisters, Iris and Ivy.

"Ivy's doing great. She got a new job a while back. Boss is a real asshole, but she likes the challenge."

"She's so strong. I wish I had some of that."

Briar's brow scrunches. "You do. I've watched you go toe-to-toe with some big dudes on job sites. Seen you find peace for arguing couples."

"Thanks. I'm just feeling off lately."

"How's the wedding planning?" he asks.

"Good. So much to do that I feel like I'm constantly falling behind in some aspects of my life."

"I get that," he says with a shake of his head. "Hart, I gotta say something, and I'm gonna be blunt here."

"Okay…" I trail off. Briar is always blunt, so if he's softening it by giving me a warning, something is seriously wrong.

"My allegiance is to you. I think we have a great working

relationship, and I appreciate each and every referral you send my way."

I'm becoming nervous as to where this is headed. "I love everything you're saying, but I feel a 'but' coming."

"But if I'm working with you on a project, I'm working with you, not Caleb."

Briar is practically vibrating in front of me, and I can tell from the way his teeth are mashed together that he's angry. It's a stark contrast to his normally friendly and charismatic personality. "I don't understand. Did something happen?"

"We just clash personality-wise and I can see myself over-bidding future projects so I don't get the job."

I stare at him. Briar's attention to detail, the pride he takes in his work, the fact that I can count on his timeliness, and above all, that he won't cut corners to pocket more profit—these are the reasons I love working with him. Every project I work on deserves that kind of attention, so not having him would suck. That is something that is a very real possibility as Caleb and I intertwine our companies more and more.

"I don't do shit just to save a buck, and I refuse to do something just to get it done. Permits are a necessity, and I get every single one. And I don't use cheap, bargain-basement materials and warped fucking lumber."

"I'm so sorry, Briar, I had no idea he was doing that."

"I just wanted to let you know that projects you have with him, I'll turn down."

Briar's confession has me completely shell-shocked. His integrity is high, and Caleb's is as well, so I'm confused as to why he would ask Briar to cut corners. I know a couple of big issues have come up, but are the finances that bad?

"I hold you in high regard and would never ask that of you.

It's one reason I always recommend you. Done Right isn't just a name, it's a brand, and you and all your guys do just that. You make certain everything is done right."

He gives a hard nod and relaxes. "Now that the bullshit is dealt with and you see what a badass you are, what's up?"

"And just like that, you flip?"

He shrugs. "I've told you how it's going to be, and now onto why you hunted me down. I mean, I like it when a girl chases me, but you're pretty much married now. Not that I'm opposed to married chicks. They need dick just like everyone else."

"Really? Oh, come on!" A laugh leaves me. "Way to remind me you're a manwhore in your spare time."

"Equal opportunity lover."

I roll my eyes. "Sure. Anyway, the Hummingbird project just had a huge hiccup."

His brow quirks up. "The house my guys are tearing apart right now?"

I nod. "Turns out the laminate flooring is backordered, and they only have half the amount of the tiles we need for the bathroom in stock."

He steps back. "I may be your knight in shining armor."

"Really?"

"I was just talking to Jim in the back about a couple of things for another project. The flooring is this waterproof laminate in almost the same driftwood grey color I think you were using there."

"Do they have a sample?"

He motions for me to follow him. "Yeah, come take a look. They just got two pallets in. I know one is spoken for."

We push through the employee's only section to an area I

have rarely seen. The owner, Jim, is going through their delivery, but waves when he sees us.

"Here it is," Briar says as he pries open the box and pulls out a piece.

My eyes go wide as I stare at it. Immediately I dig through the twenty-pound bag on my shoulder and pull out the laminate sample we originally selected.

"It's almost the same color."

"I'm not sure anyone would notice," Briar says.

I glance down at the price and do a mental calculation. "It's about five hundred more than the flooring they picked out."

"Beggars can't be choosers. Besides, this is covering the main floor, right?" I nod. "You'll need the water resistance in this product. We're putting it into a basement tomorrow. Great for moist areas."

I heave a sigh and nod. "Ideas on tile?"

A grin spreads, and while the laminate may be more expensive, my worries will be over.

"You're a lifesaver, Briar," I say twenty minutes later.

"Your savior, even?" He grins at me.

"Savior." I wave at him. "See you later."

"Later, Hart."

I'm stewing as I walk out to the car. I don't like that Caleb is alienating Briar, someone I've worked with for years. We helped build each other's businesses by recommending each other, and it's been a great partnership. One that Caleb is trying to ruin, and I don't like that.

The second I'm in the car, I've got my phone out and calling Caleb.

"Hey, babe," he answers after the second ring.

"What is going on?" I ask.

"Sorry I didn't fill you in. A storm last night split a tree in half and it went through the roof."

Crap, I forgot he had to run to a house this morning, skipping out on breakfast.

"That's not what I'm talking about."

"What are you talking about, then?" The crew in the background starts hammering something.

"I just saw Briar, and he isn't happy," I explain.

"So?"

No pause, no nothing.

The noise level has lessened, but still there. "So, he's a good contractor I don't want to lose."

"He's just a contractor. I don't get the big deal."

"The big deal is he and I have a great working relationship and you're spoiling that."

"It's *my* money, *my* property, and it will be done *my* way," he grinds out.

"That's it? Your way or the highway?" I ask.

"I think you know that by now."

My teeth mash together.

That's the nail on the head right there. It's always his way or not at all.

Everything I do is for him. He's not perfect, but he's been there for me and he proposed, indicating that he wants to keep me.

But is that all I am? Something to keep?

"Besides, shouldn't your great working relationship be with me?" he asks. I can hear the jealousy in his tone.

"Are you honestly jealous of Briar?"

"That's not it. What were you even doing with him?"

"I ran into him at a supplier, not that I need to explain myself," I huff.

"Anytime you're with a man who isn't me, you need to explain yourself."

It's one thing to be jealous in our romantic relationship, but it's entirely out of line when it comes to our professional business.

"I can't believe you're trying to turn this situation against me because of *your* jealousy issues. Briar is a friend, and he runs a great company."

"He runs a company that doesn't listen to its clients."

My blood is boiling. I don't get his issues and I have no idea what to say or how to get through to him.

"Dinner at seven?" he asks like he didn't just upset me. "My place. You could make some lasagna."

"Or we could order in," I say, more than a little annoyed. "It's been a long day, I could use a break."

"What the hell is wrong with you today? I'm not going to fucking apologize for not agreeing or bowing to everything your fucking precious Briar has to say." He's angry and I don't have the energy to try and placate him.

I rub my fingers across my forehead. "I'm overwhelmed, Caleb, and I could use a night off."

"Fine, stay home and I'll see you tomorrow."

What the fuck? "That's the alternative? If I don't cook dinner, I can't see you?"

He lets out a deep sigh. "What do you want from me, Aubrey?"

"Say '*Sure, babe, let's order in and binge Netflix.*'"

"Sure, *babe*, order some Italian and I'll be home at seven," he says, but it's completely forced and with a biting tone.

"I'll see you at seven."

"Aubrey."

"What?"

"I love you," he says, all the anger and annoyance gone.

"I love you, too," I reply, even though I'm just not feeling it.

The conversation took a turn I wasn't expecting. Caleb can be set in his ways, but I am shocked at his reaction and his tyrant-like demands. Maybe we've just been working too much and not spending enough time together.

Our talk covered the near half an hour it takes to get over to the restaurant I'm meeting Nora at for lunch, and I luck into a spot right next to her car.

My phone goes off with a text letting me know she's seated to the right and I head in.

"Hey, girl," Nora says as I sit across the booth from her.

"Sorry I'm late," I say with a sigh. "So happy you had a half day today."

"No problem. What's going on?"

"Projects delayed, parts issues, wedding, ex-boyfriends, and a fiancé to take care of."

Her brow quirks as she passes her mojito my way. "There's a bit of annoyance at the end there with all that other stress stuff."

I greedily take a couple of large gulps before passing it back. "We just argued on the phone and I'm irritated. There's just so much going on, and I just found out that instead of helping to cultivate relationships with companies, he's pissing some off."

"Caleb is?"

I nod, my jaw clenching. "I have no clue what happened but Briar Prescot just told me he's never working with Caleb again after the current contracts are up. Apparently, he wanted Briar to cut corners." I shake my head. "I just don't get it."

"Maybe it was time related?"

"In flipping, it's always time related, but things should still be done right."

"Agreed."

"I'm just exhausted with everything. How's work?" I ask, wanting to change the topic to something that won't piss me off. "Are you seeing Jared again soon?"

She shrugs. "Work is work. I've gotten to that two-year point, and now I'm itching to change jobs."

"You just got settled."

"I know. It's just become monotonous and there's no challenge left. I need a new challenge."

"Can Jared be your new challenge?"

"That's a whole other challenge. It's only been a few weeks and a couple of dates, but I really, really like him."

I reach out and take her hand. "That is so great. I'm so happy for you. If things work out, though, you can't leave me."

"Sorry, girl, I'm out."

I shake my head. "Hos before bros. No moving to another state."

"You would deny me love?" she asks in mock incredulity.

"He could always move here, right?"

"Who knows if it'll even get that far?" She lets out a gasp. "Oh, my God, they have fried pickles."

"Have fun. Enjoy them for me."

"Come on, Aubrey. A few fried pickles won't make you explode."

The peer pressure is real, and I'm in no mood to fight it. "One pickle."

After scanning the menu, I decide on my own mojito, and I offset the drink and the pickle with a small steak and a side salad.

"I need details," I say after we place our orders. She made my mouth water with the bacon cheeseburger and fries she ordered. Maybe I can steal a fry or two…or three.

"Details?"

"Yeah. It's been a few dates and I haven't heard any dirty details. Have you kissed? Is he a good kisser? Were there sparks? Have you gotten to second base? Gone past second base?"

She throws her head back and laughs. "What's second base again?"

"Boobs," a familiar voice says as a body slides beside me in the booth. I'm so distracted I didn't even notice the flames of his presence as they lick at my flesh. "Hey."

I turn to him, my head shaking. Great. Just what I needed today. The man who keeps reminding me what I don't have. He's every-fucking-where I go. "You're just going to slide in with a 'hey'?"

The corner of his mouth draws up. "Hey, beautiful."

A sigh leaves me as I scrunch my eyes close and shake my head. "How is that better?"

"Hello, beautiful. What brings you to this establishment on such a fine day?"

"It's not a fine day," I say, pointing to the grey sky and the raindrops hitting the window.

"Any day I see you is a fine day."

I let my head fall forward and land on the table. He's laying it on thick, and I hate how my body responds to him.

"Not the reaction I was going for," he says, but I ignore him. "Sorry about that. I didn't mean to crash your lunch."

"Oh, you're good. I've never seen her like this, so I'm getting a kick out of it. I'm Nora."

"Pike."

My head snaps up to find Nora wide-eyed, her arm stretched out, hand in his. "You're Pike? *The* Pike?"

He leans back, wary of the demonic look in her eyes. "What does it mean if I say yes?"

"It means hand over your damn phone so I can get your number."

"Nora!"

"Oh! No, not like that. I didn't mean…" She looks quickly at me, then back to Pike. "Hi, I'm Aubrey's best friend, so I know who you are and what you are to her."

"He's nothing to me," I grumble, knowing she is going to gush about him the second he leaves.

"He's something to you, that's for sure," Nora says.

"Can this day be over?" I grumble.

"Not until I get the man's digits," Nora says as she snatches his phone from his hand and away from my swat.

"What for?" Nora getting his number spells nothing good.

She ignores me as she types away on his phone. "Nothing you need to be concerned about."

"No canoodling."

"I like canoodling," Pike says, his shoulder bumping against mine.

My eyes go wide, and heat floods my cheeks as I look away in embarrassment. "Colluding! I meant colluding."

"I think someone's not getting enough canoodling at home."

I send my best death glare in her direction. The last conversation I want Pike to be a part of is about my sexual life with Caleb.

I can't look at Pike, but I can feel him. It's been more than just a hard day, but a hard few weeks and I'm mentally and spiritually exhausted. The warmth rolling off him is inviting and intoxicating, and all I want is to be wrapped up in it. To lay my head on his chest and use him as a human body pillow. The worst part is I know I wouldn't even need to ask. He would let me and not move until I was done.

Another glaring difference between him and Caleb.

"Pike!" someone calls his name from across the restaurant.

He waves at them and turns back to me. "Lunch is over. Lovely bumping into you ladies, but it's back to the grindstone."

"And just like that, you're gone again."

He grins down at me. "Not for long. Catch you tomorrow?"

"You wish," I say, but my lips are creeping up into a smile.

"I do wish. The stop sign at Laramie and Avian? Six-thirty?"

I roll my eyes. That's where he always seems to ambush me. "Sounds about right."

"Nice meeting you, Nora."

"Fantastic finally meeting you." She grins at him.

I can't help but watch him walk away, watching his somehow perfect ass walk away. Did he always have such a perfect ass? My heart stops when he turns to look back at me, a smile creeping up on his lips when our eyes lock.

I don't know how many beats pass, but there are enough that a burning sensation invades my chest before he turns back and continues.

Nora is staring at me, her eyes wide, lips sealed, muscles tense. She leans forward, her expression dead serious. "As your maid-of-honor, I insist that man be your groom."

"Nora!"

Great, another one on the Pike wagon.

It may be a shitty day, I may have fought with Caleb, but that doesn't change anything. I still love him.

chapter 13

I DON'T KNOW IF IT WAS PMS OR EXHAUSTION, BUT FOR the first time in days, I feel better. Maybe it's because the sun is out, but I want to keep the positive momentum.

The problem is I can't keep my mind off Pike. Not that I should find that shocking or any different from recent events. From the moment I ran into him at Starbucks, he has been in the forefront of my thoughts like a boulder I'm unable to move. It's become apparent, if I'm being honest with myself, that he's unlikely to stray from my thoughts anytime in the near future.

Things are changing, and I'm doubting my relationship with Caleb. We don't seem to be on the same page since Pike returned.

Pike and I have moved on from each other. We are different people than before. I'm engaged, but still… There is no stopping the butterflies that erupt in my stomach when I see him or the way my skin buzzes in excitement when he is close.

Last night Caleb came home a bit contrite with a bouquet of flowers, and made good on ordering in and taking the night off. He even apologized, saying we both needed a break and ended with talks of taking a long weekend to just get away for a few days.

I'm not sure if Pike was serious about meeting this morning, but just after six-thirty I spot him ahead of me, just past the intersection he talked about. It wasn't a conscious effort to leave the house in time to cross paths with him, but I'm thinking maybe I did it subconsciously.

I pick up the pace and get up beside him. "Hey!"

He startles and pulls his earbuds out, and chuckles as he slows. "I can't shake you."

"Excuse me? This was a planned rendezvous. And anyway, you're the one that keeps jumping out at me from the bushes." I bump him with my elbow. I say it in jest, but inside I'm a bit mad. Every time I turn around, there he is. "Seriously, do you have it timed out?"

He laughs and shakes his head. "I'm not that dedicated of a stalker. It's pure luck most of the time."

"Good luck or bad luck?"

His eyes lock with mine and my heart skips. "Definitely good."

"And why is that?"

"Because I get to start the day with you. What better way?"

There goes my heart again, double timing it. "Not running is a better way. Snuggled in bed is a way better way."

"I would *love* to start the day snuggled in bed with you. Can we start tomorrow that way?"

A laugh leaves me and I bump his elbow again. "Incorrigible."

"You said it."

"That's not what I meant."

He makes a humming sound. "Race you to the stop sign," he says before breaking away.

I blink at him before pumping my arms to give chase. "You didn't say go! Cheater! Come back here!"

It is so out of the blue there is no way I can catch up to him. Pike has been running pretty much his whole life, and I just started this year.

When he reaches the stop sign he turns, his grin wide and blinding. It's so carefree and without pretense. He's simply happy with his victory, and the time between us melts away. We're teenagers again, if only for a moment.

"Not funny," I say through pants as I punch his arm.

He laughs. "I'll give you a head start next time, how about that?"

"Mm hmm, who says there's a next time? Maybe I'll change my route."

"Maybe I'll just have to wait outside until you go running." He's smiling, but the way he says it, the way his eyes connect with mine, I'm not so sure he's joking. Stalking is too extreme a word, but the implication that he's been searching me out lights a flame deep in my chest. "Plus, I thought maybe, since we seem to have the same route, we could become running partners."

"Only if you slow your roll, because I'm not as fast as you, Mr. Cross-Country-State-Champion," I say.

"Deal."

"What's on the docket for today?" I ask, a little more curious than I should be.

"I've got to go into the office this morning and look over some blueprints that were delivered yesterday, then I've got a couple of afternoon appointments."

"Is that how your days usually are?"

He nods. "Sometimes. I've got a larger project that's breaking ground next month that will keep me busy. The architects are attempting a structure that's definitely different and they hate me shooting stuff down."

"Wow."

"What?"

"You are so by the book. Where is carefree Pike?"

He shakes his head, and that blinding smile draws me in. "When it comes to work, the safety of people is so important I have to be rigid. But in my personal time, I'll still jump off a bridge into a river."

"And scare the shit out of me."

"I'd done it a dozen times before," he says in defense.

"Yeah, but right before you jumped, you said, 'I hope it's deep.'"

He grins down at me. "I just like knowing you care if I live or die. Is that such a bad thing?"

"When it practically gives a fifteen-year-old a heart attack, yeah."

"What are your plans today?"

I go through my mental calendar and am relieved that the day is lighter. "An appointment at ten, then home for designing."

"Your home?"

I nod. "My second bedroom is my office."

"Is that where *Designs With Hart* is located?"

"Yeah." I heave a sigh. "One day I'd love a real office space."

"At home or out somewhere?" he asks.

"Home, I think. I would love a guest house or garage apartment. Something that is separate from the main living area."

"Hmm."

"What does that mean?"

"Nothing, just agreeing."

"That was a thinking noise," I say. Even after a decade he still makes the same sounds.

"Okay, just thinking. Serious question here."

"Yeah?"

"Can I tempt you with breakfast?" he asks.

I stop, my muscles firing off in little twitches. My head says no, but my stomach says yes and my heart just likes the idea of spending more time with him, though I remind it that it shouldn't. "I should say no, but I'm hungry. Tempt away. Where do you want to go?"

"My house."

"Pike."

He holds his hands up. "No sneaky intentions. Just breakfast."

"Okay."

We jog side by side, turning down a street that leads to an adjoining neighborhood. The homes are a little bit older and a little bit smaller than Caleb's neighborhood, but they are still large. After a while we turn down a street, a cul-de-sac.

"Hi, Pike!" a boy calls from the end of the street. He looks to be around ten. There's a basketball hoop set up, and he's taking shots.

"Hey, Mason," Pike calls back as he claps his hands together. Mason turns and passes the ball, and I watch in awe as Pike catches it, stops, and expertly shoots it into the net with a swoosh.

"Nice!" Mason says with a fist pump.

"Waiting for the bus?"

Mason nods. "Who's she?"

"Ah, Mason, this is my friend Aubrey. Aubrey, this is my neighbor Mason."

I smile at him, my heart clenching at the way he's interacting with this boy. "It's nice to meet you, Mason."

"Same. Are you his girlfriend?"

I shake my head. "No, we're just old friends."

Mason's expression drops. "Too bad, 'cause you're really pretty."

"Aww, thank you, that's so sweet."

"Are you gonna be home tonight?" Mason asks with a hopeful glint in his eye.

"Looking for a rematch?"

Mason's head nods vigorously.

"I should be home before five."

I follow Pike to the left of where Mason is playing and I'm surprised at the two-story home in front of us. It's not what I expected, even though I knew we were in a larger-home neighborhood. This is a very family-oriented area, and the house in front of me has to be close to four thousand square feet.

There's something about the exterior that is just so inviting. Nothing in particular stands out, but it's not as new as the adjacent neighborhood and the architecture is somehow softer, not as angular.

"That's so sweet of you, hanging out with him," I say as we reach the door.

"He's a good kid. His parents are going through a divorce, and all the fighting gets to him. They're using him as a bargaining chip to get what they want."

I shake my head. "That's awful. I've never understood why people do that."

The entryway is the full height of the home with a large chandelier hanging above, highlighting the surrounding staircase leading to the second floor. To the left appears to be an office, and a dining room to the right that holds a stripped table.

"Wow, that's a beautiful table," I say, noticing a large rectangular table that appears to be made of reclaimed wood.

"Thanks. It's a work in progress. I started it a few weeks ago."

"You stripped it?" I ask, trying to figure out what he started.

"I built it."

My eyes widen as I stare at him. "You built it? I didn't know you built furniture."

He nods. "It's a hobby I picked up in New York, but I never had the space to make anything larger than a side table or a chair," Pike says as he leads me back to the kitchen.

"You made a chair?"

A laugh leaves him. "Four of them. Took me six months."

Despite its lack of design elements and being pretty bare, there's a familiarity about the home as we pass through on our way to the kitchen. Not in that I've seen it before, but more of a feeling. It has a comfortable feel about it. A warm feeling.

It almost even smells like home, if the feeling of home were a smell. Home where family and love reside.

It's a stark contrast to Caleb's house, which often feels more like a museum.

While it's obvious that the house is in the process of being updated, some areas are more complete than others.

The kitchen fits the others category.

The cabinets are missing their doors and the boxes have been sanded down. New quartz counters top the lower banks of cabinets, and the new flooring matches well.

"You've been busy," I remark as I look around. There is painter's tape around the windows and a couple of buckets full of supplies sit by the back door. Past the door is a screened-in porch with a hammock crossing the space.

A small laugh leaves me. He always talked about having a

hammock, and there it is. There's even a large, in-ground pool hidden under its winter cover, making me wish it was open.

"Trying to get it just right," he says as he pulls eggs, cheese, and bacon from the fridge and sets them on the island. The kitchen is quite large and nicely laid out with both an island and a peninsula.

"What are you doing with the cabinets?" I take a seat at one of the stools at the peninsula. My designer side is in full-on curiosity mode.

He purses his lips and glances over to a stack of swatches. "Yeah, that." I'm left with no time to ask what that means when he sets the stack in front of me. "They've been bare for weeks. I just can't decide. Any ideas?"

There are a few swatches of stains and the rest are paint colors. I spread them out over the counter, comparing the colors to them and the dark stain of the laminate floors.

"What are you thinking for backsplash?" I ask as I notice the patched drywall hidden in shadow under the upper cabinets.

He grimaces before leaning over and pulling out a bag of tile samples. "I'm good at the hard labor. Not so good with design."

"Guess it's a good thing I'm here."

He stops, and I can tell he's holding back from saying something, then goes back to cracking open eggs.

There are some decent, wide-ranging samples. From a basic subway, to penny tiles, glass and metal, marble and granite in different shapes. It seems the only thing he was certain on is the counters, which are white with a light grey marbling effect.

"Oh, I love this tile," I say when I come upon the Arabesque marble tile. The lines call to me with its lantern shape and marble attributes.

"You think that one would work?"

"It would work, but I'm not sure it's your style."

"You like it, though," he states for clarification.

"I love the movement."

"What would you put with it?"

The walls are patched and primed, but not painted. A few tests are splattered around the room, but no evidence anything has been chosen.

There are a few swatches that have been marked with a pen.

"In here? Is your favorite color still orange?" I ask, noticing the Summer Sunset swatch.

"I'm not painting the cabinets orange."

A hard laugh leaves me, and I slam my hand down on the counter. "Wow, not where I was going. That would be weird."

"Yes, my favorite color is still orange."

"It's a happy color," I say before turning my attention back to the colors before me. "I'd do a darker color for the bottom cabinets and white for the upper to help keep it light. Maybe a few glass panels on some of the doors with some interior lighting." There are some beautiful blues and greys, and I flip through the different samples. "This blue-grey with a hint of green is beautiful. You could ignore my white uppers with this one."

Pike brushes his hands off and steps over. "Wow."

"You like?"

He nods. "It's perfect."

"Add in a white subway tile and some chrome pulls, and you have yourself a kitchen."

"That just took you five minutes and I've been working on it for five weeks."

"I do it every day." I take another look around while he cooks. The ceilings are higher, probably nine feet, and the kitchen opens to a large family room sparsely filled with furniture. A large fireplace sits against the exterior wall and elicits another smile—a wood-burning fireplace was always a must-have for him.

"If you need help picking out furniture, I'd be happy to help."

"Thanks. The goal is to build the end tables, but I think I've bitten off a little more than I can chew."

"How so?"

"It's a fixer upper and then I got it in my head that I'd build the tables myself, all while getting stuck on design."

"How long have you been here?"

"Well, I bought the place in February, so roughly ten weeks."

"You've made progress."

"Thanks. I just keep picking at it, doing a little bit every day. It's mostly cosmetic."

"It's just you, so why such a big house?"

He shrugs. "Guess I was looking for something to grow into. It's a great house for a family." He walks over and sets down a glass and plate in front of me.

I blink at the plate in front of me, at the breakfast sandwich and hash browns that make my mouth water. It's way too many calories, but my stomach doesn't seem to care.

I flip the sandwich over and pop the bottom of the English muffin off to pepper the egg, but it's already been peppered. In fact, the sandwich is laid out exactly as I like it and the bacon is crispy, just how I like it. Even the hash browns have that perfect crispy exterior, and I salivate as he sets a glass of orange juice down in front of me.

It's my favorite breakfast, and it's been cooked perfectly for me.

"How…" I trail off as I look up at Pike, who has a mouthful of sandwich he's chewing on.

I'm taken aback and suddenly overwhelmed with a torrid of emotions I can't begin to describe. When was the last time a boyfriend cooked anything for me?

"Egg, cheese, bacon on an English muffin with the egg peppered, right?"

I nod. "How did you know?"

"It's what you ordered every time we picked up breakfast on the way to school. And every time we had breakfast together and they didn't have a sandwich, you always made the ingredients into one."

"I like sandwiches," I say in defense. It's all I can say as I'm still struck stupid that he remembered the way I like my breakfast after all these years.

"It's cute."

"It's weird."

"Maybe, but it's also completely you."

"How so?" I take my first bite and try not to moan as the flavors burst in my mouth, but it doesn't happen. I can tell by the way Pike's lip twitches that he heard me.

"You were never one to just take what the world gave you. You always made it your own. Whether it was breakfast or your OCD tendencies."

"My OCD?"

He quirks his brow at me. "You have got a dozen different totes in the back of your car, each with a color-coded tag attached to the handle. That way you keep your clients separate and things don't get mixed up. You did the same with notebooks and folders in high school."

I stare at him, my hands falling back down to the plate while

I slowly finish off my bite. In two years, Caleb hadn't figured out my system. It didn't even take Pike a month.

I quickly take a few more bites, making sure to savor it all, washing it down with the sweet tartness of the orange juice.

"What's the rush?" he asks as he wipes his mouth.

"I shouldn't be here," I say before taking another bite. Maybe I can take it with me…

"Why not?"

"All alone in a single man's home? I don't think you'd like that either if we…" I trail off, my teeth mashing together. "It's not right."

"There is a lot not right between us," he says, but it's meant more for him than me.

That doesn't change the fact that I heard it. "What does that mean?"

The napkin in his hand is discarded onto the counter, and he steps back and rests his hip against the farmhouse sink. "Ever since I got back, you've been angry. It's this living, breathing dragon between us. And I don't understand it at all… Why? Why are you so angry? Or is it not anger at all. Are you scared? Do I scare you, Bree?"

"I'm not angry or scared," I say, but I know it's a lie.

"Yes, you are. Your nose crinkles when you're lying."

There aren't really words to describe how I feel. It is there, simmering below the surface, but is anger the right word? Or is he right, and I'm scared?

"It's not anger."

"Then what is your problem with me? Because it's not always there, and then it's like this switch is flipped."

"Every time I look at you, I don't know, this feeling comes over me. I don't know how to describe it. You left…" I let out a deep sigh as I try to regain control over the volatile emotions that are churning inside me. "Now you're back, but you're injecting yourself back into my life like nothing happened, like you didn't leave me. But you *did* leave me. *You left me,* Pike. A decade later, you want to what? Just pick up as if that decade never happened?"

"I had to leave. It was college, and I had to go. For fuck's sake, I didn't want to leave you, Aubrey. That was the last thing in the world I wanted to do."

"I know, but it was really hard for me to watch your life change—on Facebook. Especially all your girlfriends. Knowing that the spot I once held was gone, and I was forgotten."

His eyes go wide, and he leans back. "Forgotten? Not for one minute have I forgotten about you over the last decade."

"Nice sentiment, but I saw it all unravel." Every single girlfriend comes to mind. Every smile that wasn't for me.

"Now you're sounding like a stalker." And humor is gone, his expression falls, and I know we're about to lay it all out. We rarely fought as a couple, and that is the warning sign. It's been coming on since that first day, but there is nothing and nobody to stop it now.

"What I'm saying is that you moved on with so little effort that it crushed me."

"You've dated, too, so don't throw that bullshit at me. Because if you're going to start that up, I can say that I *never* came close to asking any of them to marry me."

It's almost like he slapped me, and I stare back at him, completely frozen. His brow crinkles and he turns from me, fingers sweeping through his hair as curses spill from his lips.

It feels like my heart is breaking all over again.

"One day you'll be my wife."

"Your wife, huh? Think I'm going to marry you?" I teased, my bottom lip trapped between my teeth. It made my heart soar when he talked about our future, because he was the only man I ever wanted for my husband. He was the man I dreamed of walking down the aisle to.

"I don't think, I know," he said as he pulled me close. "No matter what, you're the only one I want to marry."

The legs of the stool screech against the tile floor as I slide into standing. The sounds gets his attention, and he turns back to me.

"Bree—"

I hold my hand up, stopping him. "You didn't come back," I say through clenched teeth. "You didn't contact me. Not once. Not for Christmas, not for the summer, not ever. It's kind of hard to save yourself for someone who can't be *bothered* to call you when he comes home for the first time in ten years, so, fuck you, Pike."

His eyes close, head in his hands. "It was too hard."

I fold my arms in front of me. "Too hard? That's why? Didn't you miss your home? Your parents?" *Me?*

He nods, his gaze bouncing around the room. "Despite your righteous indignation, you weren't the only one nursing a broken heart. I couldn't take it. My heart couldn't take being that close to you. I was afraid it would break all over again. Every day, I struggled to push through. I'd wake up each morning and struggle just to get out of bed."

"I waited for you. For any sign, but you couldn't be bothered to do *anything.*"

"And neither did you!" he yells. "This is a two-way fucking street. I tried. So many times I tried."

"So did I," I whisper.

"He's not right for you."

"Excuse me?" I step forward, my eyes narrowed on him.

"He's never been right for you."

"What do you know?"

He shakes his head. "It's not just me. Look at how you change yourself for him. If you choose me, I wouldn't ask you to change a thing."

I step around the peninsula to stand in front of him. Maybe then he'll hear and comprehend what I'm saying. "I'm engaged, Pike. I mean, damn it, I love him."

"Do you really love him?"

"What kind of question is that?"

His eyes bounce between mine. "Then tell me three things that you love about him."

"He's intelligent, he's a hard worker, he's handsome, he's… he's…"

"That's all you can come up with, so let me tell you three things about you." He takes a step closer, his eyes locked with mine. "You are the most beautiful woman I have ever met. Both inside and out, you amaze me. Your creativity blows my mind. You're so fun and easy to be with. I love your laugh and the way you tease. Your competitive streak that always ends in laughs because you usually tackle me to get your way. You're beautiful, you're timid…Aubrey, you are perfect."

I don't know what to say to that, how to respond, but my heart is melting in my chest. Pike is making everything more difficult. He's muddying my mind with memories of feelings that should be destroyed. After so long, they're gone, right? But I know they're not. I know part of me still loves him. He exposed it weeks ago. Part of me will always love him. And in this moment, it's the only thing I'm sure of.

"Tell me three things about me," he says, and it's there again. That reservation.

"You are always kind. Loyal. Always help me see the wonder and beauty of things even when I don't want to. Physically, you are so handsome. You're strong in body and in mind. You are someone I can lean on, someone who I can trust and… you never ever said anything bad about me or said I needed to change anything."

"And again, I ask—why are you with him? You've lost yourself, Aubrey. But I know you're still there."

"Am I?" Admitting it is the hard part. The self-introspection at what my life has become. I do everything to please Caleb, thinking it will make him look favorably at me. Foolishly, I've been thinking that if I am the perfect image, if I become what he wants, I will have what I want. What I want is happiness, but am I sacrificing my own to please a man who will never be happy with my effort?

It's a crushing realization, and I'm stuck in a tailspin. Especially because I know with Pike, there are no pretenses. There is no struggle to attain perfection, to be someone I'm not.

"You are. I see it, now and then. You're like a flower that starts to bloom, reaching for the sunlight, but then pulls everything back in when he's near. You're reserved, like you're walking on eggshells so as not to upset him."

I hate how right he is. How he shoves it all in my face and makes me look at it.

"And how am I with you?"

He takes another step closer. "An open flower stretching toward the sun, happy and full of life."

The overwhelming urge to jump on him hits me like a slap

in the face. That's when I realize just how close we've gotten. Barely a foot separates my chest from his.

I hate when he's close to me. When the energy circulates between us. The way he stares at me, unmoving, lips parted. I know he can feel it too.

It was subconscious, and now we're caught up in this pull.

Chemistry is a bitch. Cruel and unwavering in its torment.

But it's wrong.

Because despite my love, despite my commitment to another man, Pike has always had my heart. I gave it to him long ago, and he never gave it back.

The inches between us disappear as he pulls me close. One hand cups my cheek while the other tugs my waist.

The air between us is so charged I'm shaking. Everywhere he's touching me is on fire and pulsing through my body in waves. Powerful as it seizes control of every nerve to the point that all I want is for him to relieve this growing ache between my thighs.

Our attraction draws us in, and I can't even resist or protest.

He closes the distance, his lips crashing to mine and light off every cell in my body.

His lips…dear God, I forgot how perfect his lips felt against mine. I shouldn't want the kiss, shouldn't part my lips, my tongue searching for his and the scorching that burns through me when they touch.

A groan crawls up his chest as his grip tightens around my waist, drawing me closer, forcing me to feel every hard edge of his body.

This kiss is consuming me with each second that we touch, pulling me into a fantasy that I can't entertain.

"N-no!" I cry out as I push against his chest to gain space. We're both breathing hard, and I can feel my bottom lip tremble.

I refuse to hurt Caleb. Pike is my past, and that is where he needs to stay. My future is written, and Caleb is the man by my side.

My eyes meet his and everything is conveyed, but not a single word is said. The warmth of a tear draws a trail down my cheek.

"I love Caleb."

"Aubrey, I—"

"Don't! I can't do this, Pike. I can't go down this road with you. I won't."

I storm out and once again run like my life depends on it, because I know my heart does.

chapter 14

FOR TWO DAYS I'VE TRIED TO FORGET ABOUT THE kiss with Pike. I've tried to scrub it from my mind, erase it with new memories, anything to make it go away.

But it sits there, haunting me.

One kiss destroyed me.

Since then I've tried to be every bit the doting fiancée to try and make up for what I did. Including making him his favorite breakfast on a weekday.

"Why is your phone locked?" Caleb asks as he enters the kitchen with my phone in hand.

I scrunch my brow at him. "Why do you have my phone?"

"Why is it locked?"

"Because I was with clients who had a grabby-hands toddler yesterday," I say, but it's only a partial truth. There was a toddler playing with my phone, but there was also the guilt that infested me after texting with Pike.

"You have a text."

"Yeah?" I take the phone from him and unlock it, noticing how he looks over my shoulder at the text. There's a message from my pickiest client making sure I search for the correct fabric later today. "Why can't some people just let me design? If they want to be involved with every little minute detail, why don't they do it themselves?" I vent in frustration as I let the phone drop a few inches down to the counter top.

"When will breakfast be done?" Caleb asks, his curiosity seeming to have been satisfied.

I glance over to the timer. "About ten minutes give or take."

"Okay, I'll be back," he says and leans in, placing a kiss on my cheek.

I watch as he leaves, listen for his footsteps on the stairs, before picking the phone back up and looking at the other message.

Can we talk? Coffee? - Pike

I stare at the message on my screen. I've avoided Pike, altered my running route and time so that I don't bump into him.

No - Aubrey

I set the phone down and continue with breakfast, but it's seconds later when my phone goes off again. A whole lot of coffee is going to be needed for this day, I can just tell.

I'm not sorry I kissed you - Pike

The words nearly cause me to spit my coffee out. Thankfully Caleb is still upstairs.

Don't bring up that mistake again - Aubrey

It wasn't a mistake. Never a mistake - Pike

My fingers fly over the letters, the sound of footsteps on the stairs driving me.

Stop. Just stop - Aubrey

Don't message me about this again - Aubrey

Panic has me rushing around the kitchen to set Caleb's plate, then my own, before he makes it back into the kitchen. He smiles as he sits down and digs in.

"I have a meeting with Pike this afternoon at the Carmel house," Caleb says.

Thankfully I'm not mid-sip again, but I am half bite and I pause for a beat before resuming chewing.

"I thought that house was all settled."

"Other issues have come up and I need him to look at something. You should bring your layouts, see what he thinks."

I nod. "Sounds good."

"Good breakfast, babe," he says before pressing a kiss to my lips. A kiss that has no passion or fire or any of the heat I experienced with Pike. "I've got to head out."

"See you this afternoon," I say as I watch him leave.

I spend the morning going through fabrics for some custom drapes a client wants for their all-over design. It's not something I do often, normally opting for commercially made window treatments, but this client is very particular.

Later in the day, I pull up to the house in Carmel, but Caleb's truck is missing. The crew is still working, and also a familiar Jeep—Pike is here.

A Jeep is so fitting for him. I can still remember the old two-door Wrangler he had in high school. We would take it camping and off-roading.

Things were so much easier back then.

"Hi," I say as I walk up to Pike, my eyes scanning the space as I dodge tools and supplies scattered around the floor.

"Hi," he says in surprise, probably due to the way I ended our text conversation.

"Where's Caleb?" I ask.

"He got called away. An emergency at another project," Pike says as he straightens.

While I am used to things popping up that need Caleb's attention, it seems to be happening more and more lately. Also, he knew I was coming for this meeting, and he didn't text me. There are a few problem houses, but I am standing in one of them. One that I thought was figured out.

With Pike.

"Here. Got you one. Thought you might need it," he says, setting a coffee cup down in front of me.

"What's this?" I ask, staring at the cup.

"Caramel Macchiato. I hope you still like them."

"T-thank you," I say, completely stunned. Pike not only went out of his way to get me a coffee, but he remembered my favorite drink.

Warmth spreads through me, and tears sting at my eyes as my chest tightens. I didn't ask for one. He just knew I would be here and thought about me when ordering his own and got me one. Not because I expected it, but because he was being kind. Not only that, after nearly a decade he remembered my favorite coffee, which I hadn't had in almost a year due to the calorie count. Caleb had me switch to a skinny vanilla latte, which I tolerate so I can still get my caffeine fix.

"Are you okay?"

A small smile spreads as I look up at him. "You remembered. How did you remember?"

"You love caramel. In the colder months, you go for warmer drinks, and when it warms up it will be a caramel Frappuccino or an iced caramel macchiato."

I'm still in shock that he thought to get me a coffee, let alone that he remembered my favorite drink. "You were always simpler with your iced café lattes and black coffee, which I never understood. Blech!"

"Yours were always too sweet."

"But that didn't stop you from stealing sips or half my drink."

He grins and shrugs. "It's not that I don't like sweet things."

"So, if he's not here, why are you still here?" I ask, changing the subject.

He blows out a breath. "I'm trying to figure out how to keep this house standing."

Standing? Uh-oh, what idea did Caleb come up with? "Why?" I ask as I step around the makeshift table to scan the blueprints Pike is studying.

"He's looking at any avenue to move that staircase, but with each idea it causes a chain reaction of other issues, some with hefty price tags."

"Great, so my drawings are crap."

"Drawings? Let me see," he says.

I pull the rolled-up paper from my bag. "He'd settled on the bump out and opening up the space, so I drew up a layout based on the parameters."

"Opening up the walls is dicey."

"Why?"

"Location of the staircase."

I let out a groan. "Great." I heave a sigh as I look down at the blueprints. "That fucking staircase is killing me."

"Wow."

"What?"

"I just haven't heard you curse since I got back."

I purse my lips. "Caleb doesn't like it."

"Can I say something?" he asks.

"I don't know what's stopping you."

"It's not about the project."

I turn to him, then look around the room to the empty space. I can hear someone in the upstairs working, but everyone else is on lunch. "Okay."

"It's about us."

I freeze, eyes locked on his before looking away and back to the blueprints. "There is no us, Pike. Not for a long time, and not again." This is definitely not the time or place to have another conversation about past us.

"You weren't the only one hurting, you know."

I really don't want to continue our conversation, but he just won't let it go. "You expect me to believe you were crying about me in the pillow of your new girlfriend's boobs?"

He flinches. "When I left, I made no promises to you. It wasn't logical to string us both along."

"What does logic have to do with love?"

"Because sometimes the head knows what the heart doesn't want to face. Five years. A thousand miles. For fuck's sake, we were teenagers, Aubrey! Moving on was what I thought was best for both of us."

I snap my head to look at him. "Best for us? Finding out you were over me in no time because you posted a pic on social media with your new *girlfriend* was what was best for us?"

"I never…We weren't together."

"Maybe not physically, but spiritually."

"We talked. I thought you understood."

"I understood my boyfriend telling me he would always love me."

"That never changed."

I blink at him in confusion. "What?"

"I never stopped loving you. No matter how hard I tried."

"You're saying all the women you dated were just to get your rocks off?"

"They were all to help me forget you. To help me maybe have some semblance of normal. To give me hopes of finding someone, anyone, who could mean more to me than you do. But I never could. It was always you, Aubrey. It will always be you."

"You can't say that to me! You don't get to say that!" I shove him away, begging the tears filling my eyes not to fall. Not to let him see. "I get it. We were young, and the distance, and I understood, but that doesn't mean it didn't tear me up inside. That doesn't mean I didn't have fantasies of you coming home and swooping me up in your arms."

"I wanted to, so much. I may have been the one who left, but you always had my heart."

I shake my head. "Why did you move back? Really."

"I heard about your engagement, and I had this visceral response." I watch his jaw flex, his brow furrowed. "Something broke inside me, and I had to see. I had to find out for myself if he was truly better for you. If he was better than me."

"And what did you find?"

"A man that doesn't deserve a single one of your minutes. A woman who doesn't seem to know who she is anymore."

"How did you come up with that?"

"He ordered your food for you without even asking for your input. Deny it all you want, but I know you wanted a steak."

"How is that different than the other morning when you cooked me breakfast?"

"When was the last time he cooked anything for you?"

"That doesn't matter. We keep rehashing the same things

over and over, and no matter how many times we talk about it, nothing is going to change the past, so talking about it anymore is irrelevant."

"Nothing about my love for you is irrelevant. It's what gets me through the day, what makes me want to be a better man, because you deserve nothing but the best. I've messed up, I fucked up not coming home, but that doesn't change the fact that I love you."

"You love a memory."

"I'm *in love* with you, Aubrey. I've never stopped being in love with you."

It feels like my heart stops for a second before beating rapidly in my chest. Every fantasy of his return is exploding in front of me, and my heart can't take the joy of *finally* hearing the words fall from his lips. I stare at him in rapt attention and with bated breath, my knees weak as tears fill my eyes.

"Every time I see you, my heart skips a beat. Every time I see you, you're more beautiful than the last. And every time I see you with him, I want to punch his narcissistic ass to the ground. He's the one who doesn't know you."

Our breathing is matched, as hard as my heart is beating. The pulse is electric and familiar, pulling us closer together. It's the same as the other day in the kitchen.

I have to step back, to get some space, some breathing room.

"Pike…" Words evade me, and I'm unable to speak, but he's not done.

"I haven't had a girlfriend in four years. It was too exhausting. Easier to be alone than to be with someone who I was never going to love."

Silence fills the space between us. Everything is coming out. Rehashing the other day and digging in deeper. Opening old wounds and spilling out the deepest emotions that were buried away.

"Where did you go?" he whispers.

"What do you mean?"

"You've changed. You used to be so full of life, but now, you're timid and anxious. Like one wrong move and you'll be lost, unable to move. You're not the girl I left behind."

"People change."

He shakes his head. "That's not it. It's almost like you're hollow. Like Aubrey isn't there anymore."

"I'm not sure she is. I think I sent her to be with you, and she never came back. You're right. I'm not the girl you left behind. Life without you wasn't easy, and getting over you was impossible."

"Tell me about this Aubrey."

"Obviously, she's the shell of the girl you left behind. A shell that has been trying to figure out for years how to live without you, and…"

"And?" he presses.

"Has yet to succeed." I swallow hard. "I thought I had it figured out, who I wanted to be, but then you show up and I'm broken with no clue as to what I'm doing."

"When we talk, it's natural."

"It's because of our close past, isn't it?" I ask.

He nods. "I think so. But when you talk to *him*, it's different."

I cock my head to the side. "Different? How so?"

"Like you're walking on eggshells. You're stiff, unnatural almost."

"That's not true." It can't be.

"Isn't it? When was the last time you had that with him? The last conversation that was deep and about more than what he wants or the business or *his* wedding. When did you last voice your dreams, Bree? When has he done anything to support you or done anything selflessly? Do you remember how we used to just lie on the couch cuddled up together and watch nothing while talking about everything?"

A calmness floods me. Simple. Everything was simple and easy back then. There were no complications, no expectations. Just two people who loved to be with each other.

"He expects you to be someone you're not. While you looked incredibly sexy in that little black number, you also looked incredibly uncomfortable. It was his idea, and all I could think of all night was that I wanted to see what dress you picked out."

"It doesn't matter."

"Yes, it does. The whole night and every encounter with the two of you I've seen nothing but a Stepford wife wannabe. Is that what you want? To please someone who thinks so little of you?"

"He loves me. Do you hear me? He loves me, Pike!"

"He loves himself and the image he can create with you, but he doesn't love you."

"Shut up!" I smack my palms against his chest.

"You get up and run every morning to change a part of your body he doesn't like. Every part of you is perfect, and perfectly you, Aubrey, and if he can't see how special you are, how wonderful you are... Well, I already know he doesn't deserve you."

My hands fist into his shirt. "And you do? What do you want?"

He stares into my eyes, his hand reaching out to brush a lock of hair from my face. "I want to get up and make pancakes on a lazy Sunday morning. Spend the afternoon with our legs tangled on the couch as we both read. Come home to your smile. I want to breathe life back into you, to remind you of the beauty and wonder of the world. There is so much I want, so many little things, but I can't do any of it without you." He takes my hand in his and pulls it up, his thumb and finger spinning my engagement ring around. "This should be my ring sitting here, not this gaudy thing that isn't your style. You should be walking down the aisle to me. Having my babies."

I snatch my hand away, teeth grinding. "Why are you saying this?"

"Because this sham you're living is killing you. I'm not the only one who can see it. Don't lose yourself to him."

"Lose myself to him?" My body shakes in anger, replacing the pain. "I lost myself to you, Pike. It was you who put me on this path. Every girlfriend was tan and dark hair with exotic looks, something I could never compare to. And that's what I did. I compared myself to each and every one of them. What was I missing? What about me was so repulsive to you that you wouldn't come home even for Christmas? Did you not want to see me that strongly?"

His eyes go wide. "Aubrey…"

"When you got on that plane, I didn't think '*I love you*' were the last words I would say to you for a decade. You never called, you never texted. Hell, you didn't even attempt to contact me through your mother or social-fucking-media!"

"You didn't either."

"Because I needed…I needed you to contact me." Tears sting at my eyes as my darkest secret sits on the edge of exposure. "I needed *you* to reach out and remind me that no distance could lessen our love. But you didn't, and you moved on."

"I never moved on!"

"Yes, you did! When I needed you the most. When I was

crying on the floor of the bathroom. When I was bleeding and crying and *mourning,* you were off in New York, oblivious to it all."

He pauses and stares at me. "What are you talking about?"

"I'm talking about the day I lost our baby!" I cry out, letting loose my deepest pain. The one thing I've kept hidden for so long. Only my parents know, and Nora.

Pike's expression drops, his eyes wide as I watch the color drain from his face. "Baby?"

My breath hitches as tears slide down my cheeks. "It was the last thing you left me with, and it was gone."

"W-why didn't you tell me? I would have stayed."

I shake my head. "I didn't find out until you were gone. I didn't find out until the baby was gone. By then, you had started college. Maybe I foolishly thought that if we were meant to be, if we were so connected, you would feel my pain and call me. But you didn't, and then you had a new girlfriend."

His eyes widen, and his head shakes back and forth. "Fuck… Fuck!" I watch as he paces, his hands running through his hair. "How? When?"

"The camping trip," I say, but my voice is barely above a whisper. "That last morning."

"We ran out of condoms," he says as he finds the memory.

I nod as I fight to hold back the tears in my eyes. After a few years, after he didn't come home, I gave up hope of him ever knowing. "I was in so much pain and my period was really heavy. I went to the doctor. Only it wasn't my period. The doctor called it a spontaneous abortion. A miscarriage. I was about nine weeks."

As I speak, he becomes more and more distraught. He cups my face, his hands warm as his forehead presses against mine.

"I'm sorry I wasn't there," he whispers. "I'm so sorry you had to go through that without me. Why didn't you call?"

The purge of all that I've been holding onto drains me, and I have no energy left to fight. "Because by then, it didn't matter."

"Yes, it did."

"There was nothing you could do," I try to explain.

"I could have come home. I would have come home."

I shake my head. "Maybe that's why I didn't, because as much as it hurt, I knew New York was where you needed to be. And I knew you being here wouldn't help anything, despite how much I needed your comfort."

"You suffered," he whispers.

"I did, and now you know once upon a time we made a baby." I step away from his touch, unable to take it anymore. Unable to handle how much I need it.

"I'm so sorry, Aubrey. I should have come sooner."

"Then I ask again—why didn't you come back after graduation?"

He purses his lips, but his eyes never leave mine. "I wanted to, but…" He blows out a breath. "To be honest, I was afraid."

"Afraid of what?"

"Afraid that I would uproot my life, that I would lose this chance, that I would come back only to find that it wasn't there anymore. I mean… what I mean is I was afraid that what we had would be part of our history and not our future."

"You didn't think our love would still be there?"

He nods. "Our history as individuals is what we learn from, what we grow on, what we evolved and changed into as adults. Was what we had strong enough to survive the years apart? To survive relationships that had sex and intimacy and things that were reserved for each other? Would we be able to move past that and connect with each other, even though we weren't the teenagers we used to be?"

My mind whirls trying to keep up with him. "What?"

"When that wedding announcement came, all those fears? They ran away because they were replaced. They were replaced by the biggest fear of all, and that is never getting the chance to know if…if we could move past all that. If we could make it after everything."

My heart clenches as I soak in every word.

"After time, after relationships, after… and if we could move past all the *afters*, we'd have a chance. It didn't matter who I dated when we were apart because I always knew one simple truth—I wanted to marry you."

"But you didn't come back! Did you expect me to be waiting here forever? To never live? To always pine for you based on a teenager's promise after no contact for *years*?"

"You're right. I messed up. All I've ever needed was you, and I filled that void with people in my life, but that was just a lie because the void was never filled. I was always empty inside, just a pit of nothingness."

Everything is spilling out of him, and I know his fears because they were my own. I never filled the void he left, no matter how hard I tried.

"I had a career, I had friends, and I was totally and completely alone, and the thought of you marrying someone who wasn't me…it killed me. It ignited this flame, ignited this need. It ignited all the hopes and dreams and fears and…and I had to come back to you." He cups my face, his gaze boring into me. "I had to. I know you don't want to hear this, and I know you don't want to think about it, but after everything, Aubrey, I have been forever yours. I still love you. I always have loved you. I've never stopped, and I never will because you are the only woman for me."

I stare at him, my heart a kaleidoscope. Words I've longed to hear, and words that tear my world apart. They're every hope my heart wished for, longed for, and my elation is stagnated by one thing, one person. "I can't hear that, Pike. I can't process those words, I can't. I'm engaged."

"There's one last thing," he says, his lips inches from my own, and I have trouble keeping myself away from them. "I will love you until my last breath."

There is no stopping my hands from cupping his face, from stretching up on the tips of toes, or pressing my lips to his like my life depends on it. The electric pulse that moves through me is staggering, and only intensifies when his arms wrap around me and his lips part.

I can't tell if I'm shaking or crying. All I know is the warmth that spreads through me when his tongue moves against mine. The way I melt against his chest.

The way he feels like *home*.

chapter 15

I DIDN'T SLEEP. NOT A SINGLE WINK. AFTER PIKE'S DECLARATION, a loud noise from a worker outside brought me back to my senses, and I pulled away. I left on autopilot and proceeded to spend the rest of the day like that. A robot going through the motions with eight words on a loop playing in my head.

During the night I lay awake in the darkness, staring up at the ceiling. My chest clenched each and every time the words repeated, making it impossible to fall asleep.

All of our talks, our conversations, are draining.

Finding out he's still in love with me? Still desperately in love with me…

A pit forms in my stomach, and I feel sick. Not because he loves me, but because it's too late. I'm not a cheater.

Why couldn't he have just contacted me years ago? We were both single then.

I spend the morning catching up on some work and organizing my client bags. My dozen bags, all the same, with a color tag aligning it to a specific project. My OCD, as Pike called it. The only way I stay sane is what I call it. Either way, weird or not weird, it just works for me.

I try not to think about how Pike just glanced at them and

understood, while I've had more than one conversation with Caleb and he just didn't get it. Or how Pike remembers so many favorites of mine, while Caleb still thinks I like kale after telling him a dozen times that I hate it.

What is happening to my life?

I should be doing wedding planning stuff. There are invitations to address and bridesmaid dresses to shop for. Not to mention the entire binder full of lists of things that need to be accomplished. And I have no drive to do any of it.

I've never gotten back to Mom on the table numbers. Is it because I know Caleb will shoot it down?

Surprisingly, I haven't heard from him today. And he didn't even bother coming over for a quickie after whatever emergency took him from the Carmel house, which is weird because he always wants a quickie, but he said he was too worn out.

An unusual feeling flooded me after the call, one I can't identify, but it left me unsettled with all that happened during the day.

After a quick lunch, my head is splitting, but it's time to get Caleb. I can't even be bothered with dressing up, opting for jeans and a tee with some flats and a jacket. Fuck makeup. Fuck doing my hair. I still look cute with a messy bun and a little bit of jewelry.

I shoot him a quick text, then head out.

It's a short, ten-minute drive to his house, the sky grey and threatening rain. The garage door opens just as I pull into the driveway.

Caleb stands in the opening wearing jeans and a button-down, his brow knitted as he looks at me, the Lexus keys in his hand. Is he going to drive? That would be great.

"Aubrey, what are you doing here?" he asks.

My brow scrunches as I exit my car and walk over to him. "We have the cake tasting."

His eyes widen, and my stomach drops. I can tell he forgot. "Fuck. I'm on my way across town to the Avon house." The Avon house? In the Lexus and wearing a button-down?

"I put it on your calendar a month ago," I grind out. "I also reminded you last night on the phone."

"Well, shit comes up and I have to handle it," he snaps back. "Besides, it looks like I'm not the only one who forgot."

I fold my arms in front of me as I scowl at him. "What do you mean?"

"Have you looked at yourself in the mirror? I can't believe you're going out looking like that."

I glance down, not even giving a crap. "It's been a rough week, and I have a migraine." I'll stop at a convenience store on my way. Hopefully the pain can be tamed by an abundance of water and caffeine along with some ibuprofen.

"That's no excuse to be a slob."

"What does it matter?" I growl. "Why can't I be comfortable for once?"

My outburst seems to shock him a little. He pulls me to him by the arm and grabs hold of my jaw. "I'll see you at seven for dinner." There is no time to respond before his lips meet mine. "I'm sorry I won't be there. I promise I'll make it up to you. This just can't be helped."

I nod in response. "I'll see you at seven."

Another kiss, one that I can barely respond to. "Feel better," he says, then disappears back into the garage.

I run through the now pouring rain out to my car and head up to Noblesville on my own. Mom and Nora are meeting me there and I'm tempted to call Nora up, but then shoot that down. I don't want to talk about it right now. I just want to stew in the disappearance of my fiancé yet again.

"Are you okay?" Nora asks as she takes in my appearance.

It's a look I haven't worn in a long time and is a reflection of how I feel inside.

"Fine."

"Where's Caleb?" Mom asks as she peeks out to the parking lot.

"He got called away."

Mom and Nora look at each other, then back to me. "We should reschedule."

I shake my head. "There isn't another tasting that leaves enough time for making the cake."

"He won't have input," Mom says.

I shrug. "He said as long as one of the flavors was vanilla, he didn't care."

"He doesn't care what the cake looks like?"

"I'll take pictures, and we're going to decide later."

"Are you okay?" Mom asks this time.

I nod. "Fine."

I move past them toward the tasting room. Upon entering, three groups turn their heads to look at me, and it takes everything in me not to break down.

I'm not fine. I'm everything other than fine. A messy mass of swirling chaos and confusion. Nothing about me feels right anymore. Pike has infested my life, and everything is wrong. I've glitched.

Like the houses we work on, the foundation of me is there, but the layout and decor is in a constant flux. Every sense is completely consumed, and I'm losing the will to fight it anymore. I *want* to get lost in him, and the guilt of that crushes me.

Since the moment Pike came back, more and more and more of my life crumbles to the ground.

chapter 16

MY DAY HAS FINALLY COME. THE DAY I DREAMED OF so much as a little girl—wedding dress shopping.

The week has been long and trying, but for the last few days I've almost felt back to normal and I'm hoping the wedding dress shopping will be the lift I need. Something needs to get me back into the wedding mode, and my fiancé isn't helping with that.

Another bouquet of flowers was how Caleb apologized for missing the cake tasting. The last bouquet was still in the vase in good condition. Flowers twice in a few weeks when I've only received them on Valentine's Day in the past.

He also took me out to dinner and we went over all the photos and information I gathered.

I met Mom at her house and we drove over, Nora meeting us at the dress shop.

"Phone is fully charged, and I'm pumped. Let's find you a gown!" Nora says as she shakes her hips back and forth.

A laugh leaves me as I shake my head at my best friend. "How much coffee have you had?"

"Coffee? What coffee? Is there coffee here?" Her eyes are wide as she looks up and down the strip mall. Sure enough, there is one and she cries out in excitement. "More coffee!"

"There's a Starbucks cup in your hand," I say, pointing to the venti-sized cup in her hand.

She holds it up. "Oh, yeah. Quad venti skinny vanilla latte, baby! Lunch of champions."

"I hope you ate some actual food," Mom says, trying hard not to laugh at Nora's antics.

"Who needs food?"

"Nora Ann Johnson, you are going to crash so hard later."

Her lips pull back into a huge, almost manic smile, exposing her perfectly white teeth. "Just joking. I had brunch with Jared."

"Jared was here?" I ask as we head to the door.

She nods. "He surprised me last night. He's got some testing thing he had to go back for, but at least I got some time with him."

We check in and meet our stylist and go over what I'm looking for style wise, and begin the hunt. Nora is pulling dresses like a madwoman, earning a wide-eyed look of shock from the stylist.

"What are you doing?"

"You don't know if you'll like it until you try it on."

"Where's your coffee?"

She points to my mom who is leisurely going through the rack. When she finds one she likes, she takes it over to the rack outside the dressing area and comes back for the next one. Totally different strategies, and I decide to just let them handle it.

I take the coffee from Mom, head over to our area, and take a seat. I've got time, and my joy is trying them on, so I don't even have to look—they just keep bringing them over. Nora drops off a mountain of dresses. There are so many, they're slipping between her legs, and I almost spit out my sip of coffee watching her wrangle them.

"Wow."

"Options." She grins at me as she hangs them all up on the rack.

"I'm just going to finish off your coffee," I say before taking a large sip.

"All good. I've got the app. There's one a few doors down. We can order more."

I sit back and relax, because I know from Nora's strain those dresses aren't light and I'm going to need all the energy.

I'm excited, but there is still this trepidation sitting in my stomach, and I know why. If it were me marrying Pike, nothing could stop me from eagerly scouring magazines and Pinterest for the perfect dress.

I twirl my ring on my finger. Stare down at the large center diamond and its surrounding halo of diamonds and the band made of diamonds. It's made to look huge, and it is, but it's also meant to say that Caleb has money. It's a statement.

Pike is right—this ring is not my style. I prefer a dainty, vintage style. What kind of ring would he have bought?

"Why aren't you trying on dresses?" Caleb asks.

I look up to find him standing in front of me. "Caleb, what are you doing here?" I ask, my head tilted in confusion.

"You're shopping for your wedding dress."

"Yes. And tradition says you don't get to see it until the big day," I remind him.

He pulls me up and to him, his arms wrapping around my waist. "Well, fuck tradition. I want us to have the most elegant, stylish wedding this city has ever seen, and your dress is a big factor in that."

My heart sinks. "So, you're shopping with us?"

He nods and presses his lips to mine. "I can't wait to see how sexy you're going to be."

Sexy? In a wedding dress? Elegant, yes. Beautiful, definitely, but sexy isn't a word I've ever associated with my dream dress.

"Oh, Caleb," Mom says in surprise. "You're here."

Nora shoots out from behind my mom. "What are you doing here? Girls only."

"I want to help her find the perfect dress."

"You mean dictate," Nora mumbles, but thankfully Caleb doesn't hear. I don't want to deal with them fighting today.

Though in all my fantasies of this day, never did I envision my groom leaning against the wall, looking at his phone and giving his opinion.

The stylist comes over and helps me get into the first dress, which is even heavier than I thought.

The first couple of dresses are a bust. They just aren't what I'm looking for, and thankfully Caleb seems to feel the same way.

About seven dresses in, there's this feeling that takes over. It *feels* right, and I know just from that it's the dress for me.

I step out onto the platform and stare at my reflection, a gasp leaving me.

It is perfect. The trumpet shape accentuates my curves in all good ways. Ivory lace detail throughout with swag sleeves creating an innocent sexiness while keeping everything else modest. A smile spreads as I twist to look at different angles.

It is *the* dress. The perfect dress.

A flash of a vision hits me as I stand there. Walking down the aisle, my heart bursting, but it's Pike waiting for me.

"Oh, Aubrey…" Nora trails off.

My gaze catches hers, and my smile only grows. She immediately grabs her phone and starts snapping photos.

"It's perfect," Mom says, beaming at me. I swear I see a tear in her eye.

It's everything I want.

"Next," Caleb says, dismissing it.

My heart sinks as I find his reflection in the mirror. He is kidding, right? But there's no humor in his expression before he turns his attention back to his phone.

"Really?" I ask, turning to him.

His lip curls up. "I don't want you walking down the aisle to me in that."

My heart falls as I look at my reflection again. I'm in love with it. Absolutely in love with how I look in it.

"She looks beautiful," my mom argues. "The dress is perfect on her."

"This dress has your name all over it," Nora says.

"It doesn't have my name on it," I say, with a shake of my head. If Caleb doesn't like it, then it doesn't matter how much I love it. All the excitement drains from me.

"Is this the Caleb show?" Nora asks before looking toward Caleb, her jaw tight. "Does she get a say in *any* part of this wedding? If not, why aren't you the one doing everything?"

"Nora!" I hiss, and cringe, waiting for Caleb's response.

"It's *my* money paying for the wedding, Nora. And I'm going to have the final say on where that money is going. Understood?"

"You're not paying for the dress," Mom says. "I am."

My parents volunteered to go with tradition and pay for the wedding, but Caleb insisted he cover it. It's become very apparent why. Another way to control everything.

"If you want, but she's not wearing that one to marry me." Caleb walks off to continue the search, getting lost in the sea of racks while the stylist pulls others with his direction.

"This is your dress," Nora whispers as she helps me out of it.

I have no response, the wind completely gone from my sail. We keep it hanging nearby in hopes I can convince Caleb

It won't work. In the end, he'll make me wear what he wants.

The next few dresses are duds to everyone, and I look longingly at the other dress as I step back into the dressing room.

The stylist helps me out of the next dress, then grabs another. From first glance I know I'm not going to like it either.

The dress is satin, and sure to show off every single flaw in my body. It's definitely sleek, but the way the fabric is constructed resembles an unfinished base layer than a finished dress. The bow in the back is beautiful as is the button detailing, but the front is plain, boring, and easily wrinkled.

I step out and onto the stand in front of the mirror and shake my head. It looks worse under this lighting.

"Now that looks good," Caleb says, and I balk on the stand.

"What?" I ask as my eyes find his in the mirror.

"Finally, one that looks good."

I shake my head. "This doesn't look good."

"It's the perfect style to match the wedding."

"You can't be serious."

"Very. It is the perfect combination of sleek sexiness."

Sleek sexiness? Those have to be two words that in no way describe me. And when did that become the style of the wedding?

I pull the dress from my body, avoiding the look of pity from the stylist.

"I'm sorry," she whispers. Even she can tell how awful this experience is for me. A day that was supposed to be full of fun and whimsy, crushed by the man who says he loves me.

After a few more dresses, Caleb is still stuck on the satin

dress, while I want the lace one. The day turns out to be a stalemate.

"I have to go," he says.

"So, you're just popping in to dictate your opinion and then you're out?" I ask. My annoyance over the whole situation is at its peak.

His jaw ticks and he steps closer, wrapping his arm around me and pulling me close. "The dress is perfect for the look we're going for. So stop whining like a child and be happy that you are going to be the most beautiful woman in a hundred-mile radius."

I nod in agreement, but my jaw is still clamped down tight. It's all bullshit.

"Say it for me, baby. Tell me you're going to look so beautiful for me on the day you become my wife."

"That's all I want. To look beautiful for you," I say, but the words are like acid on my tongue.

His lips press against mine, and it takes everything in me to kiss him back right now.

"Come over tonight and we'll order in. Watch some movies and have a Netflix and chill night."

A laugh leaves me. "Chill, huh?"

He nips at my bottom lip. "Lots of chill." A smack to my ass and he's gone.

That's all I'm good for, huh? A doll to dress up, and sex on demand.

I fix my face, holding back the tears and the anger and the overall misery, and head back over to Mom and Nora.

"I guess the hunt is still on," I say with a sigh.

"Why?" Nora asks, and I can tell she's got an opinion.

"Caleb likes the satin one." I catch her typing and roll my eyes. "Now what?"

"I'm sending it to someone."

"Someone?"

"Just getting a second opinion," she says.

My stomach drops, because I have a bad feeling about what she's doing. "Nora."

"Where is Caleb?" Mom asks as she looks around.

"He had a meeting and had to go."

"Pike says that's the one."

My eyes go wide as I stare at her. "You sent the picture to Pike?"

She turns the phone toward me. **Thanks. Now all my dreams are going to be of her in that dress walking toward me - Pike**

What about the other one? - Nora

Hard no. That's not her. The lace is perfectly her. Soft and delicate, whimsical. Ethereal. - Pike

You still love her - Nora

Forever - Pike

Tears pool in my eyes. "Stop it." I slap the phone from her hand, sending it to the ground.

Her mouth drops open in surprise as she looks at her phone on the ground. "Aubrey!" She bends to pick it up, swiping at the screen, which lights up.

"Why did you do that? Why would you? I love Caleb. I'm going to marry him." Anger surges from me, but it's not really aimed at Nora. It's aimed at all these feelings, all these lies, at the upheaval inside me.

She stands back up. "Is that what you really want?"

"I thought you were on my side?"

"I am. And that side is wanting you to be happy and seeing what can make you happy even if you can't see it yourself."

"How do you know what I feel?" Tears sting at my eyes.

"Because I can see it." She waves her arm toward my mother who is staring at us, wide-eyed. "We can all see it. Caleb won't let you make a single decision about your wedding without his approval, and you always default to what he wants."

"Because he's right." Or is that another lie built up after months and months with him?

"No, not always. That dress he wants is awful and not you in the least. All it represents is his manipulation of you. How he's twisted you into this person who I don't even recognize half the time."

"I can't believe you're saying all this."

"I want you to be happy. That is all I want for you," she says and then sighs. "You're my best friend, and you deserve nothing but the greatest of loves. A man that worships the ground you walk on and wants nothing but your happiness and to love you with all that he is. Because that man deserves your love. That man will never know heartache or despair, because you will love him so fiercely."

"And you think that is Pike?" I ask.

Mom steps forward, finally speaking up. "It is. Honey, I know you have thought about him over the years. I know you never got over him."

"I'm engaged to another man!" I cry out. My outburst draws the attention from the other patrons, but I don't care. Everything is falling down around me and no matter how I grab at the rubble it crumbles to dust between my fingers. "I'm marrying Caleb, Mom. And that's the end of it."

Nora stands her ground. "No, it's not the end."

"Yes, it is." He won't leave me.

She shakes her head. "We've let you push back on this issue, try to convince us we're wrong, but Caleb is what's wrong. And if you're going to close yourself off and not *listen* to the truth, to what he's doing to you, then I…I can't be part of this wedding."

My eyes widen and my chest tightens. "Nora."

"I love you, so much, but that man isn't good for you. I've kept my mouth shut, but he doesn't see you as a person. You're just this thing with tits for him to play with. A maid to take care of his home and a whore to take care of his dick."

"What the fuck?" I cry out.

"That's all he sees you as. He doesn't love you. I've seen you with Pike. I've seen the way you two look at each other. There is real love there. Deep love."

"*Why* is everyone on Pike's side? Why is nobody on my side?"

"We *are* on your side, baby," Mom says. "That's why you need this intervention. You went through so much pain when Pike left and then he didn't come back. You didn't feel worthy of love, and men like Caleb pick up on that weakness, and he was able to twist you over time into this version that has never been you."

"It's who I wanted to be," I argue, but the truth slips out. I *wanted* that, but I'm not sure what I want anymore.

My slip doesn't go unnoticed by Nora. "He's a grown-ass man who saw he could use you," Nora says. "I know you don't want to hear it, but you need to. Aubrey, you need to leave him."

Mom takes my hands in hers. "You are worthy. You deserve the greatest love."

"I can't believe this. Caleb loves me!" I grasp at anything, to not give in to what they are saying. To believe the thoughts that have haunted me for weeks. Even when I know they are right, I cling to anything to save face.

Nora's eyes lock with mine. "But do you really love him? Or is your heart calling out for someone else." Nora takes my shaking hands in hers and catches my eyes. "Sisters for life. I love you, and I always will. My job is to tell you the truth, even when it hurts, because you need to hear it. You need to see it. I know it's hard because he's spent so much time warping your mind, but you need to."

She wraps her arms around me, and I do the same. My emotions are in an upheaval. "I love you."

"I'll call you later," she says as she pulls away. She swipes a lone tear from my cheek. "That lace dress is the dress for you, no matter what."

I nod and watch her walk out the door before turning to Mom. Her lips are pursed and there's a sadness in her eyes.

"What?"

"Nora said it all more perfectly than I ever could," is all she says as she gently takes my arm and we walk out to the car.

The drive back to her house is silent, for which I'm thankful.

Nora's ultimatum guts me. Not having her at my wedding is unthinkable.

Ever since Pike returned…he's like this little drop of snow that has just grown into a huge avalanche that I can't seem to get away from. Everyone in my life sides with him.

And deep down…I don't think they're wrong. I just have a hard time admitting it.

As we pass by the house Pike grew up in, I see the destroyer of my life standing there, hugging his mom.

I jump out of the car as soon as Mom has it in park and slam the door. My jaw is locked tight as I fight back tears. It's all his fault. Everything is his fault.

I stomp across the street, to the yard we once played on, to the house we spent so much time in. Mom calls to me, but I ignore her, my focus on the man who is the sole reason for my life falling apart.

The reason I question the ring on my finger.

chapter 17

Pike

I'VE SPENT THE LAST HOUR GETTING ALL THE DETAILS OF the house. Every sordid detail, information I don't need, to basically water plants for five days while my parents go away for a short trip, but they insist on telling me things like when the trash comes.

Their trash is empty. They came yesterday.

But I smile and nod and take notes—some information might be helpful just in case. Hugs, and finally goodbyes as I wave when their car backs out the driveway.

As soon as they're gone, a petite figure I know all too well is stomping a warpath my way.

I didn't realize there was a chance of tornados today, but one is headed straight for me.

She's angry, fuming, and I know we're about to have it out once more when all I want to do is kiss her again. Kiss her until she forgets all about that asshole.

"Why are you here?" she grinds out.

I blink at her and motion to the car that just pulled out of the driveway. She's shaking, tears filling her eyes, which means she's about to break down. "Why are you upset? What happened?"

"Why did something have to happen?"

"Why else would you be on the verge of sobbing?"

"I'm not—" She draws in a ragged breath that catches in her throat like she's trying to hold it back.

"Hey, it's okay," I say as I step forward to wrap my arms around her. Before I can, she swats at me and steps back.

"This is all your fault."

"What?" I ask, confused by her out-of-left-field statement.

"You had to come back."

Oh, we're back to that. "Yes, I had to."

"Why?"

"Because I…" I blow out a hard breath. All our talks come down to this. She's defeated, but that doesn't mean she's lost. Somehow I know this is the conversation. This is the make-it or break-it point. No holding back. "After all the years, after all the lies, after all the girlfriends, time, and space, it never changed."

"What's that?"

The only truth I've ever known. The thing that has kept me going despite the emptiness I've felt since I left you.

I grind my teeth and look to the sky. I know I have to lay it all out for her. That's the only way she'll understand, but it's hard to let go. There's so much pain shining in her hazel eyes, and it kills me to see it there. "That despite all the afters, I am *forever* yours."

She pushes on my chest. "Don't say that. You don't get to say that!" Her palms slam down on my chest again. It doesn't hurt, and I let her continue to get it all out.

It's a huge sign she's becoming self-aware again, not just some piece of plastic arm candy.

"Why not? Why can't I tell you how I feel, how I've always felt?"

"You know why."

"Because you're engaged?" I ask. Her face scrunches up as she nods. "Then it bothers you because it reminds you that you have feelings for me."

"I don't…"

"Come on," I say as I gently tug at her elbow and start walking toward the front door. She stares at me and I glance around, then back at her. "Do you really want to have this conversation in the middle of this nosy-as-fuck street?"

I take her hand and pull. She gives resistance, but it's more like a petulant child. However, her movement completely stops when we enter. When I look back, her eyes are unfocused and she's taking in deep breaths. The look clears just as quickly as it appeared.

"It looks exactly the same," she says.

"It does," I agree as so many memories of us being right here so many times before flood my mind. "Come on."

Her eyes go wide as I pull her toward the staircase. "We can talk down here."

I quirk my brow at her. "Are you afraid of my old bedroom?"

"Maybe."

"And why is that?"

Her brow quirks, and she gives me that sassy little attitude I haven't seen since before I left. The one she always used when she called me out on my bullshit. "Oh, you know why."

"It's just furniture," I assure her.

"It's a lot more than that, and you know it."

"Memories aren't a bad thing."

"Maybe, but they're powerful."

"Can I ask you something?" It's a question that's been nagging me, a *what-if* that guts me. I'm still reeling with the bomb she dropped on me a week ago. Still grief stricken from a loss I never knew existed.

"Sure," she says, though by the way she draws the word out, I know she's not really sure.

"If you found out you were pregnant before I left, would you have told me?"

Her mouth pops open, and she blinks at me. "I…I don't know. It wasn't something I ever really had to think about or contemplate, because by the time I knew, I wasn't pregnant anymore."

"What do you think you would have done?"

She pulls her bottom lip between her teeth. "If I knew before, I would have told you. There's no way I wouldn't, because we didn't…we weren't the type of couple to keep things from each other, no matter what. I would have been freaking out and needing you to calm me down. You could always calm me down."

"And if you didn't miscarry?"

Her arms wrap loosely around her waist as her gaze drifts to the floor. "I'm not sure," she says in a whisper.

"You just said you would have told me before I left, but you wouldn't have told me after?"

"Yes…I don't know. Your mom would have found out anyway and told you."

"But would *you* have?" I press.

"I don't know," she whispers. "You're asking a question about a possibility I never even had to think about. I was so depressed after you left that I didn't even notice I missed my period. In fact, I was still coming to terms with it when I found out you had a new girlfriend."

"New girlfriend?" I wrack my brain trying to remember, because my first date after we parted ways wasn't until my sophomore year. But it's the second time she's mentioned it, and I was just too consumed by her reveal that once upon a time we were pregnant to process it.

Fuck. My stomach drops, and some of the things she's said begin to make more sense.

"Shit."

"Did you forget?"

"No. Yes. It's not what you think." How could I be so stupid to think Aubrey wouldn't see those posts? That she wouldn't assume something that wasn't true.

"Not what I think? She tagged you in a pic with your arms around her, all big smiles."

"Tammi was a friend in my building. Nothing more."

"It said you were her boyfriend."

"But I never was, I swear to you."

"Why would she say that, then? And why didn't you correct her?"

Never did I believe helping Tammi out would hit me with repercussions years later. "She needed help with an ex who wouldn't back off, so we pretended to be a couple until he got the picture and left her alone. Kisses to the cheek and hand holding. Just a show. Only a show, and never more. It was over a year after I left before I dated anyone."

By the set of her jaw, I can tell I'm not getting through to her. She's believed it for so long it's hard for her to see any other truth.

"You seem to have a lot of fake girlfriends."

"I had a lot of friends who were girls. They knew I wasn't going to try anything and would protect them from other guys."

"Saint Pike."

"Four years."

"What?"

"That's how long it's been since I dated anyone. And she broke up with me because of you, because of my feelings for you that she could never measure up to. It was unfair of me, leading them on, though I didn't go out with that intention. I did date women who were different looking than you, because every time I saw a woman with blonde hair, all I could think about was you. And I couldn't stand wishing they were you."

"That's why?"

I nod. "You are so beautiful and so perfect, and I love you beyond reproach. I couldn't even stomach the thought of trying to replace you, let alone dating anyone who looked remotely like you. Every girl I met was a pale imitation of you."

"I thought…" she trails off. There are tears filling her eyes. "I thought I wasn't what you wanted. I compared myself to all of them."

I step forward and cup her cheek. "*You* are all I've ever wanted. There was no comparison to you, because you are perfect."

Her breath is erratic as I inch closer, and when I press my lips to hers, there is no resistance. Instead, her hands crawl up my arms, swoop over my shoulders, and up my neck until her fingers are sliding through the hair on the back of my head and staying.

Having her touch me like this after so long is worse than lighting a match. It's a blazing heat that takes hold, and suddenly I can't get enough. I need more to quench this thirst for her, because this is all I've dreamed of for a decade.

I deepen the kiss, devouring her mouth, needing more and taking it as I press her up against the wall. It's euphoria as my fingers find bare flesh at her waist. I slide my hand under the fabric of her shirt unbidden. Being as close to her as possible is as instinctive as breathing.

Her lips move against mine with just as much urgency. Her muscles tighten and draw me in closer. There's no space between us, but she's still too far away.

My dick strains against my jeans, harder than it's been in years, and I know it's all for her.

She draws in a ragged breath when I reach her ribs.

"Wait. Stop." Her voice is so breathy as she manages to pull away.

We're both panting, and my thoughts are sluggish. All I want is to continue, driven by the maddening need to consume her.

"You're messing with my heart."

Fuck. The tremble in her voice guts me, and my hand falls back to her waist.

I drop my forehead to hers and sag into her. "Because I want it with every fiber of my being. I'm better for you than him, and I will fight the heavens for a chance to prove it."

I will do anything to have a chance with her again.

"Why?"

I brush away a tear slipping down her cheek with my thumb. "Because you are everything I need in this world. Just you."

I just need *her*.

chapter 18

THE NEXT MORNING, I STARE AT MY REFLECTION AND cringe. My eyes are bloodshot, red from crying and lack of sleep. The latter has left me with a headache bordering on migraine that is attempting to split my skull open. Then again, I'm sure the crying also had a hand in it.

I stare out at the sky and the greyness of the day. It seems to match my insides. The fire in me is dying.

Nothing is right, everything is wrong, yet I continue on. Steady with the course, but I don't know the direction and the rudder is stuck, leaving me to ride the waves. The map has blown away and the stars have gone out.

The picture-perfect life I've sculpted lies in shards at my feet.

I'm lost in a sea of turmoil, drifting, my mast ragged and in shreds as I float aimlessly through the open nothingness.

I am broken, and I don't know how to fix myself. Left doubting everything I think and do.

Pike loves me. Pike wants me.

And me?

I made a commitment, and I've stuck with it despite everything. But why? Why does this sense of obligation hold me down like cement shoes in a flooding river?

I'm not sure about my love for Caleb anymore.

I'm not sure about Caleb at all, but I've fought against the feelings of those close to me. Fought against my draw to Pike.

For what? To be obstinate? Or was Pike right and I'm scared of how he makes me feel?

I wade through the day, spending the morning binging Netflix and eating whatever I have in the house. Nora is out with her sister and I don't want to interrupt her. I also don't want to talk about it. I don't want to hear any *I told yous.*

Caleb is…somewhere. Honestly, I don't really even care. That realization is just as powerful as any of the others I've been hit with in the past month and then some.

Sometime in the early afternoon I manage to gather myself together and head to a meeting on the Southside. Generally, I try not to schedule weekend meetings, but sometimes that's all a client has available, so I make an exception.

I also don't normally take on clients so far away, sticking mainly to the north side and suburbs, but Caleb referred them to me.

The sky is a light grey, but to the west I see the darkness of storms heading in. Just as I pull into my appointment, my phone goes off.

I'm out with the guys. When are you coming over? - Caleb

I blow out a breath. We hadn't made plans, but at this point, should we still be doing that?

In Greenwood. Be there in a few hours - Aubrey

By the time I leave to head home the storm is raging, and I get soaked running back to my car.

"Shit," I hiss when the fuel light pops on shortly after I start my trek. I don't want to go back out in the rain, and I know I have enough to get home.

This is going to make for a harrowing drive home.

It takes an hour of slow, methodical driving, the rain an almost sheet of water that the wipers can't keep up with. Rolling thunder and flashes of lightning are accompanied by the buffering of high winds.

Gotta love May in the Midwest.

The rain begins to let up the closer I get to Caleb's, but I'm still in no mood to get out in the rain, so I decide to leave it for now.

There's a station about a mile from Caleb's and I can fill up there in the morning.

Why am I here? I ask myself as I park in the driveway. The garage is reserved for Caleb's vehicles. The house is dark. Its angular facets and cool colors aren't inviting, and I don't want to go in.

All I want to do is go home and crawl into bed and *finally* finish *Lucifer*. Is it a sense of obligation? I know he's out with friends. I know all he wants is sex.

But what about what I want? Why it is always about him?

And why the hell can't he come to my place? Everything is *always* on his terms.

I make a break for it, dashing through the rain that is still coming down, though much lighter than earlier.

I stand in the entry as water drips down to the floor around me. My teeth chatter a little from the cold, but I'm stuck standing there. I feel like a stranger.

The house is quiet, echoing, and empty. It's devoid of all things that make it feel like a home. It's just something I'm going to have to get used to, because in a few months it will be my home.

My stomach sinks at that thought. This house is a temple of sterility. There's no warmth in the walls, nothing to make it feel like a home. It's a show. A display of opulence and emptiness.

That's how it makes me feel—empty.

That thought is enough to raise flags of warning, but the problem is they've been waving for over a month. Alarms go off in my mind, but are silenced like they're being snuffed out by a pillow. Ever since Pike arrived, I feel like I've been waking from a sleep I didn't even know I was in.

Smiles hide well-constructed lies. And I have mastered the smile. But it is crumbling, and the lies are spilling out around me.

Lies I've told myself. Lies I've made myself believe. Lies that became a shield to protect my heart.

They've become a barren sea around me, and a lone island of truth is all that remains.

What do I do with that truth? How do I change this path?

I sit on a stool at the kitchen island and set my purse down, lost in thought. Lost in the realization that Pike is so close. That warmth is so close.

I don't think about what to make for dinner. I don't think about things Caleb would like. I just sit and wait.

About a half an hour passes before I hear the garage door go up, and a few minutes later Caleb is literally stumbling in from the garage.

Shit.

"There you are," he says as he closes the space between us. Only inches separate us, and my heart begins to beat rapidly in my chest. There's an eerie calmness to him that makes the hairs on the back of my neck stand up.

"How much did you drink tonight?"

He shakes his head. "Do you love me?"

My gaze bounces between his eyes, trying to figure out where he's going with the question. "Of course."

"Do you love it when I fuck you?" He grips my ass, kneading it with his hands.

"Yes," I whisper.

He draws in a breath and leans in close, his lips ghosting mine. Our eyes lock, and the fear spikes.

"Liar."

"What?" It feels like cold water has just spilled down my spine. He's drunk. So drunk it's a wonder he made it home without hurting someone. "How did you get home?" I ask cautiously.

"It doesn't fucking matter!" The air surrounding him is vibrating. His eyes are almost black with the shadow cast from his tightly drawn brows. "I ran into someone today. Someone you went to high school with."

This level of anger I've never experienced and I find my chest is tight, my fight or flight instincts kicking in. All those alarms are screaming at me to run, but I'm stuck in place by his mere presence.

"What's fucking important is Trevor Albright."

My stomach drops, and I reach back for something to steady myself on, to give me some space from him. Trevor lived in our neighborhood and was in our tight circle of friends. I ran into him a few years ago, but we didn't stay in contact.

I know where Caleb's anger stems from now. Trevor wouldn't do it out of malice, but he knows all about my history with Pike. A history I'd only kept from Caleb to avoid this situation.

Caleb's lip draws up. "Are you fucking Pike? Has he shoved his dick in you?" he sneers.

"Stop being so crude," I snap. It's an attempt to draw out his more rational side, but instead a gasp leaves me as he grips my arm and yanks me closer.

"Answer me."

"No, I'm not fucking him." I turn my arm, trying to escape, but the moment I do he grabs me again and I cry out in pain. His fingers dig into my arm without mercy.

"But he has had his dick in you, hasn't he? Popped your cherry?"

I press my hand against his chest. "Stop. He has nothing to do with us."

"He has a *lot* to do with us. I've seen the way you stare at him, and I catch every look he throws at you."

Slowly, carefully, I pull my arm from his grip and step away. "You're drunk. Go to bed, and we'll talk about this when you have a clear head."

The feeling of my arm being yanked again hits me before the pain of his grip. His fingers dig in deeper, and he pulls me so that we're face to face. "You don't fucking tell me what to do. We're going to talk about it now."

My eyes are wide as they bounce between his—they're ice cold with no warmth at all. His lip is curled up, exposing his bright teeth. Waves seem to be radiating off him, and I can feel my strength crumble.

"Let go," I hiss as I pull back. My heart hammers in my chest so hard I fear he can hear it. Anxiety skyrockets through my veins when he doesn't let go, and panic surges again. I've never seen Caleb like this. He feels dangerous, and for the first time I'm truly afraid of him.

"I know all about you and him. Your *'high school friend,'*" he sneers.

"Stop."

"You want to tell me what the fuck that was all about? Hiding that shit? Just a high school crush, nothing more. That's what you said!" he yells.

I cry out in pain, his hand tangling in my hair as he pulls my head back and down. My back arches uncomfortably, my face twisted in pain.

"You're not going to talk to Pike again. If you do that, maybe I'll forgive you for being a lying, cheating, fat whore."

"I never slept with him."

"No?" His thumb runs roughly over my lips to the point of pain. "You kissed him though, didn't you?"

Without warning, pain explodes and I stumble backwards. A scream leaves me and blinding light covers my vision. I can't move, can't think, which gives Caleb an opening to take hold of me again.

Another strike with enough force that I fall to the ground. My head lulls, vision blurred from tears.

"Stop!" I cry out. The metallic taste of blood hits my tongue, and I can feel my lip already swelling.

"I've been nice to you, and you've been nothing but a disappointment, but I'll set you fucking straight."

Trails of tears slide down my cheeks as I'm forced to look at him again. His body cages me against the floor, his hand loosely wrapped around my neck while his other hand tugs my shirt up. He grabs my breast hard, kneading it as he draws in a long breath.

"I think it's fucking time I chained you up and broke you so you remember who the fuck you belong to," he growls. The pungent smell of alcohol from his breath makes my stomach turn. The hand around my neck tightens and my eyes widen. "I fucking own you."

Air becomes harder to gain, and there is nothing but a savage staring back at me in monstrous delight.

My heart is bashing against my breastbone. Fear and adrenaline battle for control.

I have to get out. I have to get away, because I no longer have any idea what he's capable of. What happens when I lose consciousness? My vision is already dimming. Will he be able to stop before he kills me?

There isn't much time left before that will happen and I do the only thing I know that will get him to let go. In a swift movement, my free hand is gripped onto his crotch, my nails digging in with every ounce of strength I possess. A howl leaves him and he lets go, tearing some of my hair out as he grabs my arm to break my hold.

I draw in a hard, gulping breath and turn on my side.

"You fucking bitch!" he screams as he holds his crotch.

I scramble to my feet, but before I can get away, he has my arm again and yanks me back, sending me tumbling to the floor again. The fall is enough force to free me from his grip, and I'm able to get back up and away.

"Where the fuck do you think you're going, whore?"

"The fuck away from you," I say as I grab my purse from the counter and head for the back door, pulling my keys out as I go.

Footsteps sound behind me, echoing, coming down on me in a thundering cascade.

chapter 19

THE AIR LEAVES ME AS I AM THROWN INTO THE EDGE of the granite island. My hair is knotted in his fist again and he lets out a yell, smashing my head against the counter. For a second, everything goes black. I can feel him grabbing the waistband of my jeans and trying to yank them down over my hips.

My vision is blurred but in front of me lies my open purse, and near the front is my stun gun. The stun gun he bought to keep me safe. For once, it is finally going to do its job. I grab it and switch it on as I realize he has my pants down far enough to get inside me. There is no more time to waste. I flip the rocker switch and swing my arm back, colliding with his side.

"Fuck!" he cries out, caught by surprise, and stumbles back, tripping on his own jeans sending him down to the floor. It gives me enough time to turn around and shove it straight at his chest.

He's drunk and it's probably not as effective, but still he howls in pain as I push it hard against him, holding past the few recommended seconds. I let go and he reaches for me, but the shock has left him disoriented.

I fix my pants as I stand, never taking my eye off him, his dick hanging out. I'm tempted to stomp on it, but I need to get away and I don't want to tempt fate that he'll grab me again, even angrier than before.

I grab my purse and run, fueled even more by the sounds of him getting up.

My hands tremble, making lining up the key to the ignition a near impossibility. Every fraction of a second I look to the house, waiting, expecting him to come crashing out the door after me.

Finally, it turns over and I step on the gas, getting away as fast as I can. I'm shaking as I speed through the neighborhood and onto a main road. I get a few blocks away before a red light stops me, but I'm still checking the rearview mirror every other second.

When the light turns green, I stomp on the gas. Another couple of blocks, then suddenly the engine sputters and dies.

"Fuck!" I cry out as I slam my hand on the steering wheel.

I've never run out of gas in my life, and at the worst time possible, I'm coasting down the road. Thankfully, there's enough momentum to get me into a nearby gas station parking lot, though not enough to make it to the pump.

I throw it into neutral and climb out. The tears are still flowing as I put one hand on the dash and the other on the wheel.

All thoughts of what to do are stifled by the need to just get away. I have no idea where I'm going, I just have to go. Put as much distance as possible between me and Caleb so I can think without fear.

Thankfully I have on flats instead of heels, but somewhere along the way I've lost one and the gravel bits of asphalt dig into my skin.

I hold it in, driven by my purpose. Get the car to the pump. Get gas. Go.

Go.

Go.

GO!

But the car is barely moving. I don't have the strength.

A scream of frustration and pain leaves me, and the sobs I've held at bay are churning in my stomach, threatening to spill out.

They can't. I have to go.

It's there, just on the edge, a sob so great that it will send me to the ground. I can't swallow it back as the weight of the evening presses down on me.

"Do you need help?" a voice calls out. I can hear footsteps coming closer and I shake my hair, settling it in front of my face in attempt to hide my injuries.

I try to settle myself, but inside I'm a crumbling mess.

"Aubrey?"

That voice…

I freeze, begging to be wrong, but the tingles that race across my skin tell me the truth.

I make every attempt to school my face to glance over at him. "Pike?" He's standing in front of me, brow furrowed. "What are you doing here?"

His lips part to speak, but he stops, his gaze narrowing on my face. I nervously draw a strand of hair forward, but it doesn't stop Pike from stepping up to me. I try to hide my lip in the deep shadow created by the harsh lighting, hoping he doesn't notice.

There's a pause as he looks at me, but I can't gather the courage to meet his gaze. It's only a few seconds, but it feels like time stops before he hooks his finger under my chin and gently tilts my head back.

I can't look at him. If I do, I'll fall apart and I still need to get out of here. His finger at my chin is shaking, and I can't stop from glancing up.

His jaw is locked down, his top lip curled up into a snarl. "Where is he?" he asks through clenched teeth. His thumb lightly moves over my skin.

"It was an accident." I don't know why those words slipped out, but they did.

"Like fuck it was. Where is he?" he asks, pressing forward, his gaze over my shoulder searching.

"Pike, no."

"I'll fucking kill him."

"Please! Just… please…" Every cell in my body begs for him, for comfort. He doesn't move as I wrap my hands around his waist, drawing them up his back until I'm clutching his shirt in both hands, my face buried in his chest.

The muscles under my touch relent, tension draining away. His arms wrap around me, pulling me close.

He presses his lips to the top of my head while his hands make soothing motions on my back. "Shh, I've got you. You're safe."

It's only when he says it that I realize how much I'm shaking and convulsing. That the sound filling my ears is the sobs pouring out of me.

"What happened?" he asks. "Bree, what happened?"

"He was so drunk and he found out about our past and he just lost it," I cry into his chest.

"How did you get away?" he asks as he pulls me closer.

"S-stun gun."

"Is he still there?"

"I don't know."

"You need to report this."

"Report?" I ask.

"To the police."

I shake my head. "What? No. I can't."

"Aubrey, he beat you."

"I don't want to!" I cry into his chest. "Please."

"The hospital."

I shake my head. "No hospital."

He blows out a breath. "Then let me take you home."

I shake my head. "No."

"You're right. If he's worked up enough to…" his teeth grind together "…beat you, then there's a chance he'll go there."

"I don't…I don't know what to do," I admit. Because I don't know where to go from this spot right here. I don't know anything right now, except that I need Pike.

He lets me go and reaches into the car to push it forward a few more feet into a parking spot. I hold onto his shirt with each inch, begging him not to leave me even for those few inches. After putting the car in park, he pulls out my purse and locks the car.

His gaze stops on my feet and he hands me my purse.

"Come on," he says before sweeping his arm under my legs and picking me up.

I let out a small squeak and wrap my arms tightly around him, my head tucked against his neck.

"Where are we going?" I ask.

"Home."

The way he says *home* sends a wave of calm through me. I feel safe, secure. I know Pike won't let anything happen to me, and with that knowledge, the adrenaline begins to crash.

He loads me into his Jeep and I tense as we head back in the direction I just fled, and I know Pike can sense it as well.

He threads his fingers with mine and squeezes, then lets go to change gears of the manual transmission as he turns down another street, taking a route I don't usually go.

He doesn't park in the garage but in the driveway.

"Stay," he says as he jumps out and runs around to my side.

"You don't need to carry me," I say, but he's already to my door and sliding his arm under my legs again. We enter through the front door, and he immediately turns left into the office, setting me down in the plush sofa chair before turning on the lamp sitting on the end table.

"I'm going to go get some things to clean you up," he says. "I'll be right back."

I reach out for his arm, desperate for him to stay, but unable to form words.

His eyes lock with mine. "I'll only be a few feet away."

I release him, my brow knitted as I watch him head down the hall toward the kitchen. The thumping of my heart increases with each second he's gone. The flash of headlights through the window makes me jump, and I freeze as they turn away and continue down the street.

Pike returns a few minutes later with a slew of things including a first-aid kit and a wash basin filled with water.

"I need to do something you're not going to like, but if you're not going to go to the police, I'm going to make damn sure there is evidence."

"What is it?" I ask, my voice barely coming out.

"I need you to take your shirt off. I need to make sure you're not hurt anywhere else, and I need to take photographs."

There's an eerie, restrained calm emanating from him. He's upset that I'm hurt, he's angry, but first and foremost in his mind is my safety and security, now and in the future.

"What are you looking for?" I ask as he moves the light to what I assume is a better position.

"Any lacerations and any pink spots."

"Why pink spots?"

"They are areas that may blossom into bruises."

I nod and attempt to lift my shirt, but my body is on lockdown. No words pass as he helps me out of it.

As he takes some photos, even a few with me standing, I notice the set of his jaw and the trembling of his lips. His gaze lingers in areas, and his expression tightens each time it reaches my face. The anger simmers so close to the surface and wants to escape.

Every touch is gentle, every word spoken in soothing inflections. He's fighting against his need to protect me and the desire to avenge me.

After he's done, he picks up my bare foot and sets it into the basin. A hiss leaves me as dozens of stinging points light up. I must have broken a lot more skin than I thought.

Another hiss leaves me when he presses the towel to my lip and I pull away, brow furrowed. "Sorry," he says while lightly dabbing, washing the blood away. "I'm trying not to hurt you."

"I know," I whisper.

This situation, being beaten and terrorized, is one I never thought I would be in. I never thought I'd be in that type of relationship, but here I am, being cleaned up because the man I'm with hurt me. He physically beat me in a jealous, alcohol-fueled rage.

And I know there is only one thing to do.

There's no salvaging our relationship, even if I wanted to. It's over. We're done.

"You were right," I say as I take hold of the ring on my left hand and slowly drag it up and off. "I can't marry him."

Pike stops, and the look of pity on his face…I can't stand it. Not from him.

My face scrunches up as a sob takes over. I don't know how I got here, how I stayed with Caleb and never admitted to myself who he really is, but in the end, it doesn't change that it did happen.

Pike runs his hands up and down my arms, and I can't help but cringe at a few spots. "You're okay. You're safe with me."

"You were right," I choke out.

"I didn't want to be right, Aubrey. I just want you to be happy. That's all I've ever wanted."

I sniff, and he hands me a tissue. "Thank you." I wipe my nose and swipe at the tears, but they keep coming. "Tonight just proves how messed up I've been. Mom said it, you said it, and Nora said it. And everyone was right—I was someone else for him. He manipulated me for so long, and I let him." I blow out a breath as I set the ring down on the table.

I stare down at it, the way it sparkles in the light, and just how, though beautiful, it was never my style.

"Wow," I say on a breath.

"Wow, what?"

"I just noticed how much of a weight that is. A few seconds off and I feel lighter."

"That just proves you did the right thing."

"It was more than a ring. It was a weight that held me down, made me walk on eggshells to make a man happy who never put in half the effort for me." Never any effort for my happiness. "Just some doll that he told how to act, how to dress."

"It was obvious from the outside how he was manipulating you."

Amazing how I couldn't see it when everyone else could. "He never really loved me, did he?"

Pike shakes his head. "He never knew you."

I reach out and brush my fingers through his hair. "You must think I'm an idiot."

He turns his head and places a kiss on my wrist. "Never."

"Why not? I do."

"Because unlike him, I know you. He fed off your sweetness, off your insecurities and your desire for love. He used that. Abused it."

"So much time and effort wasted. How did I not see it?" I ask, but it's more for myself.

"Guys like that don't start out that way. They hook you in before exposing what they're really like. By then, you're in too deep and can't see what's happening."

"That almost sounds like experience."

"Not to me, but my friend Amanda. The guy seemed great at the beginning, but slowly he pulled her from her friends and family and monopolized all of her time." He brushes against my lip again. "Conditioned her into thinking nobody would ever love her but him."

My head falls into my hands. "Oh my God."

"Are you okay? Did I hurt you?"

"You just described my life over the last two years."

It takes a few more minutes to clean up my wounds. He wraps my foot to make it easier for me to walk on. It's just some scrapes, but it's enough to make it tender.

"Are you hungry?"

I shake my head. "Drained. I feel like I've run a marathon and then tripped down a rocky hill at the finish line."

He gives a small chuckle and I watch some of the tension

leaves him. I glance to his watch and am surprised that it's just after nine. Somehow two hours flew by. And while I don't normally go to bed for another hour and some, I'm tired.

"Do you think you can stand?"

I nod and slowly push up, though my muscles do protest.

"Go on and start up the stairs. I'm going to grab you some water and ibuprofen."

Another nod and I head toward the steps. The bandage on my foot helps, but it still hurts. Everything is beginning to ache, and I'm scared of what the morning will bring.

By the time I'm halfway up the stairs, Pike is behind me.

"Where are we going?" I ask, though knowing full well the bedrooms are on the second floor. I just want to know where his head is.

"Turn to the right. The guest bedroom is the second door."

He passes me in the hall to open the door and flip on the light. Inside is a very beautiful but simple guest room. Very little decoration, but a soft greyish taupe color adorns the walls with an upholstered headboard with swooping lines. There is a matching style of dresser, chair, and nightstand.

"Kate picked this out, didn't she?"

He chuckles behind me. "Yep. I'm worried that means she might come and stay for longer periods or forever."

"She liked it that much?"

"Surprisingly so for a NYC girl," he says as he sets my purse down on the chair.

I sit on the edge of the bed and groan at the softness. It's exactly what I need right now. To just curl up and let the bed hug me.

"Here's a T-shirt for you," he says as he hands me a neatly folded white shirt before setting a bottle of water on the nightstand along with a small pack of pain pills.

The shirt is inviting and I'm ready to get out of these clothes, but all the tension has left my arms stiff. "Can you…can you help me get this off?" I ask as I look up at him.

He swallows hard, then nods as he lifts my shirt over my head and unclasps my bra. Using my arm, I cover my breasts as I slide it off while Pike pulls the shirt over my head and shoulders.

His fingers swipe across my skin just below my ribs, eyes narrowed on the spot.

"What?"

"It's like there's a line."

I lift the shirt back up and notice the very slight discoloration and press into it with my fingers. A groan leaves me and I know it's going to be a nasty bruise.

"What did that?" he asks in a strained whisper.

"Granite countertop. Just before he slammed my head into it."

His hands are shaking as he runs his fingers through my hair. "Thank you."

"For what?"

"For getting away. For not being afraid of me."

"I could never be afraid of you."

He leans forward and lightly presses his lips to mine. "We'll talk more in the morning, so get some rest. I'll be just down the hall if you need anything."

"Can you help me get my pants off?"

Our eyes lock and he swallows, *hard.* "Neither snow nor rain nor heat nor gloom of night will ever stay me from helping you get your pants off."

I giggle for what feels like the first time in years, my whole body rocking, and I lean into him. It is exactly what I need to relieve the weight of the evening's events. He helps me out, once again finding more red spots where my jeans basically burned my skin.

I crawl into bed wearing his shirt, and it somehow feels right. It also feels wrong, but only in the knowledge that he won't be lying next to me.

"Goodnight, Aubrey," he says as he places his lips against my forehead.

"Goodnight."

My chest constricts as I watch him walk out. The click of the door echoes off the walls, and all the warmth is gone. Quiet creeps in, seeming to silence everything to where all I can hear is my own breathing.

I lie back and stare at the ceiling in an attempt for any possibility of sleep. The thumping ache on my face seems to intensify and radiate through my sore body, or maybe I'm just noticing it more in the void of stimulus. It's my focus, the demander of every thought. I can feel each place he grabbed me, every impact that is blossoming into a bruise. There is barely a part of my body that doesn't feel a level of pain.

Tears well in my eyes and one lets loose, sliding down and around my ear. It's not the torrent I expect when thinking about the night's events. Maybe I got that all out when I sobbed into Pike's shirt.

Caleb was out of control, his anger greater than I'd ever seen before, and when he grabbed me, my entire body retracted. My mind reeled with confusion and a sudden clarity the moment he struck me.

He isn't the man I thought he was. We didn't have the loving relationship I craved, and never would. His true colors literally hit me right in the face, and I am no longer wearing blinders.

There should be a weight on my chest and my heart should

be breaking. In a way, it is breaking, but instead of weight added to me, I feel lighter. A sense of freedom I can't even comprehend.

Internally I've found the key and am undoing the shackles that he wrapped around me.

Everyone around me was right. I was just a glorified servant with a pussy to fuck. I didn't see it because he made me believe he loved me.

I want to do things like cook and take care of the man I love, to show him he's important to me, but Caleb demanded it. A tyrant who rules and expects me to be blind of all his faults, that he doesn't believe he has.

Be a good girl and do everything he asks. But he never asked. Somehow, he got me used to that, he got me so desperate for any sign of affection, of love, that I would do anything for more of it. Tiny morsels and gestures of affection that were just more manipulations.

In just five minutes with Pike, I experienced more caring and love than in a month with Caleb. Just imagine what an actual month with Pike would be like. How happy I could be again.

There's a lot to do, so many changes, but with Pike beside me I'm not scared of what the future holds. Because I know he'll be right there, always.

After almost an hour, I can't take it any longer and slip from the bed. The house is empty, quiet, and strange, but there is a nightlight in the hall and a pull in my chest that guides me. Caleb's influence has slipped and revealed the emotions I tried to deny. The emotions I tried to force away.

The door to the master bedroom is open, and I don't pause my steps until I'm standing at the side of the bed. Uncertainty slams into me, and I question what I'm doing. Though the fog is lifting, confusion still clouds some of my emotions.

I haven't seen Pike like this in years, splayed out in a bed, his arm thrown above his head. Some things time can never change, and that includes sleeping positions. My perusal is halted when I catch his eyes. Even in the dark, the intensity of his gaze makes my knees weak.

I'm caught, ensnared as that warmth spreads through me again. I'm not really sure what I'm doing, but I do know I can't stand to be alone right now, and the safest place I know of is with him.

"What's wrong?" he whispers.

My fingers tangle together in front of me and I pull my bottom lip between my teeth, then let go. "Can I sleep with you?"

He says nothing, staring at me for a few beats too many before flinging the comforter back. The sheet still rests on the bed, covering him, and I waste no time pulling down the sheet and climbing in. Even less time to settle down in the crook of his arm, my head on his chest.

I let out a sigh as my whole body goes lax. This connection soothes me down to my soul. His touch, his skin beneath my fingers, is perfection.

"That works, too," he says.

"What?" I angle my head back to look at him.

"I was trying to keep it platonic with you on top of the sheet."

My face floods with heat, and my chin draws down toward my chest. I feel like an idiot. "Oh."

His arm drapes around me, pulling me tightly against him. "But I like this a hell of a lot more."

"I'm sorry I just…"

His fingers dance across my skin. "Nothing to be sorry about. Ever."

"I needed..."

"I understand. Trust me, I needed too."

I burrow in deeper and draw in a deep breath. Every sense is assaulted by familiarity and peace. It's changed, aged, but time does that. What time hasn't done is change the absolute feeling of tranquility of his arms around me.

"What do I do now?" I ask. It's more to myself. Do I give in, or is it too soon? Will my decision be a product of emotional turmoil, or hormones and memories of the past?

"Leave him. If he's hit you once, it will happen again."

"I know. And I am. But I'm talking about right here, right now."

There's a low hum in his chest as he blows out a breath. "You sleep, and in the morning, we'll figure it out."

We're so close, but as we lie there, I need to be closer. I need to feel his skin on mine. Need to soak in the heat from his body.

I trail my hand down his chest to his waist, my fingers slip under the hem of his shirt and a sigh leaves me at the softness and warmth of his bare skin. When my palm is flat against him, I draw in a sharp breath. It's small, almost innocent, but filled with more excitement and anticipation than I ever had with Caleb.

Memories of us together just like this flood my mind. The feel of his skin, so soft and warm beneath my touch, covering taut muscles. He's tense, waiting, wondering what I'm doing. I can tell. He won't push me, but he will let me explore, and I do.

Each inch I move up his torso is slow as I soak him in. How many years have I been dreaming about a moment just like this? Not with the pain or how we got here, but in his arms, tempting and teasing before making love.

Soft and sweet minutes absorbing each other.

Still he doesn't move, my hand pushing his shirt up as I go.

I want it gone. I want nothing between us. I need to feel him, feel his love. Need it to soothe me, to wash away everything that happened tonight. To prove to me all the things he's been saying since he got back.

"Aubrey," he groans as he takes slow, heavy breaths.

"Yes?" I ask as I lean down and press my lips against his stomach.

"What are you doing?" he asks.

Another kiss, this time with parted lips, teeth, and tongue. "Tasting you."

My sexuality that had been stunted by men who felt sex was only for their gratification, and used me as nothing more than something to get off in, comes alive. It reminds me that once I was a sexual being who wanted to devour my man. One who couldn't get enough of the man I love.

I desired to touch him, to take him in my mouth. Pleasing him wasn't an obligation or a chore, but something I genuinely wanted to do.

It's something I'm dying to do now. All that bottled-up tension has an outlet and I'm seconds from tearing his clothes off, pushing my thong aside, and riding him.

For our mutual pleasure.

Much quicker than my hand moved up, it slides down and slips right under his waistband. He jumps when my fingers brush against the hot tip of his cock. He's hard. He's needing. Just like me.

My heart hammers in my chest, ready to feel him, my body begging for it. For the comfort, pleasure, I've only known from him.

But I'm denied when he pulls my hand away before I can wrap my fingers around him. There's no time to ask or even react before he has me pinned to the bed underneath him. His hips settle between my thighs, and the bulge of his cock presses against my clit, sending a jolt through my body.

The dim light of the nightlight in the hall doesn't reveal much, but I can see just how heavy his eyelids are. My whole body is a live wire. More turned on then I've been in years, and I know it's all because of the man above me. I raise my hips to press him harder against me.

A groan leaves him that hits me almost as hard as the rubbing. I can feel how wet I am, the physical response of how much I need him.

"No," he says through clenched teeth.

His words are a bucket of cold water, and I freeze as confusions overtakes me.

"Not like this."

Tears prick at my eyes as rejection floods me. "Yes, like this. Don't you want me?"

His groan this time isn't sexual as his forehead drops to mine. "Of course I do, Bree. I know you can feel how much I want you, but after everything that has happened to you tonight, I can't..." He releases my arms and cups my face. "You're hurt, and not just physically."

"That's why I need you."

"Why do you need me? Why me?"

I tilt my head and press my lips lightly to his. "Because you are the only one who can make everything better. Nobody makes me feel this way but you."

His lips crash to mine, lips parting. Each swipe of his tongue against mine is a hit, sending another pulse between my legs. I rub against him in desperate need of that friction.

"I'll help you sleep," he says against my lips.

"It's not sleep I need. It's you."

His thumb caresses my cheek as he smiles down at me. "And you're going to get me, just not that way. Not tonight."

He pulls back and straightens up onto his knees, leaving me to grind against the air, before reaching back and pulling his shirt off.

I wish the lights were on so I could see with better clarity the taut planes of his chest, the desire in his eyes, and the hardness of his cock. I reach out for his waistband, my fingers inches away when he swats my hand.

"Not tonight," he says with a chiding tone and a chuckle.

"But you're so hard." I *want* to touch him, to make him feel good, make him come. And it's not to gain his approval or please him in that way or because he told me to, but because *I* desire it.

He places his hands on my knees and runs them inward, down to where I need him, but his thumbs only swipe just outside my thong before retreating back.

"You have no idea how much I've missed this."

"Missed what?"

"The heady scent of you. This vision of you so needy beneath me." His hands slide inward again, pressing my legs down to the bed, opening me up to him. "Remembering how wet you got for me. The way you would come undone." His thumbs slip under the edge of my thong and run up the length of my slit, swiping across my clit, before retreating back. I nearly jump from the bed, his touch electric. "The way you would writhe when you came, and how you would squeeze down on me."

A groan leaves him and his hips flex forward, nestling his still-covered cock against me.

"Fuck." He cranes his neck, stretching it as his fingers dig into my hips as he rocks against me. "Take off your shirt," he growls, sending a shiver down my spine.

There's such a stark difference between his tone and Caleb's, that I have a hard time believing they're the same words. I take hold of the edge and slowly slide it up, teasing him, testing his resolve. When the bottom curve of my breast comes into view, another groan leaves him as he thrusts his hips against me again.

"Do you have any idea how sexy you are?" he asks. I shiver at the low, gravelly tone of his voice.

My nipples pop out and immediately his mouth is latched onto one, his fingers pinching the other.

"Fuck!" I cry out as my back arches against the bed. Each swipe of his tongue against the pebbled flesh sends an electric zap directly to my clit. With his mouth he begins a trail of nips and kisses down my torso, giving me the opportunity to finally get my shirt off.

Another whimper leaves me when the pressure against my desperate pussy disappears.

"Patience," he whispers against my skin before nipping at my hip bone.

My need for him is becoming urgent and I slide a hand down, but before I can reach my clit, his teeth nip at my fingertips.

"Back," he growls. His tongue traces the edge of my thong, and just when I think he's going to do something, his mouth moves away and down toward my knee.

His teeth nip and scrape at the inside of my thigh, his stubble the perfect amount of roughness, then back inward. With each inch closer my heartbeat increases. I can feel the warmth of his breath, but before he gets to where I need him most, he moves to the other thigh and does the same.

My hips rise, impatient and desperate for his touch.

"Dear heavenly thighs, may your grip be mighty around my head, tight around my hips, and plush beneath my grip."

I blink as I register his words. "D-did you just pray to my thighs?"

He nips again, so close it makes me whimper, then looks up at me. "I told you I would. These thighs are divine." He draws a line toward my knee with his tongue. "All of you is perfect."

My heart thumps in my chest. For the first time in years, I feel worthy. Of love, of praise, of all the things I was told over and over that I wasn't good enough for.

Pike's hands move back toward my hips, his thumbs hooking into the straps of my thong and pulling until it's off before throwing it somewhere on the floor with the rest of our clothes.

A moan leaves him and he reaches out to run his thumb up my slit, this time without any barrier. It's then I realize how wet I've become. The truth is I've never had this strong of a reaction to any man other than Pike.

He grabs hold of one of my legs and props it on his shoulder as he lowers himself, his eyes never leaving mine. He nuzzles my clit, tongue peeking out to swipe against it, my pussy begging for more.

With one last rock of my hips, his mouth opens up and begins devouring my pussy. My mind goes white with pleasure, lips parted as my back arches and my fingers claw at his hair.

I can hardly breathe, my muscles spasm from the overload sending an odd combination of pain from my injuries and pleasure from his touch. It's overwhelming. The build-up from his teasing already had me on edge.

I try to call out his name, but I'm unable to do anything but stunted movements and mewling cries. Over and over his tongue, teeth, and lips are unrelenting as he rockets me to the most intense orgasm I've ever had.

A growl against my clit is all it takes for me to fist his hair, every muscle tensing, and then a cry of pleasure erupts from me. My eyes roll back as my body rocks in a jerking motion as waves of pleasure consume me.

It takes a moment for me to hear my own screams or notice how I have him trapped between my legs until the strength starts to fade. None of that seems to bother or matter to him as he moans with each gentle lap of his tongue.

Aftershocks pulse through me as I come down, panting as I try to regain my breath. All the strength leaves me, and the leg he doesn't have hold of falls down to the bed. On the other he places light kisses as he lays it down.

"Wow," I say. My eyelids are suddenly very heavy, and all the tension has left me.

"I'd say that was a ten out of ten experience."

A giggle leaves me. "Twenty out of ten." He rolls out of bed, and instantly I miss his touch. "Where are you going?"

"Just to clean up. I'll be right back," he says as he pulls something from the dresser.

He steps into the adjoining bathroom and closes the door before flipping on the light. My eyes begin to close. In that half-awake, half-asleep state I feel the bed dip before warmth covers me. An arm slips under my neck and I roll into his side, my head on his chest.

"Goodnight," he whispers before placing a kiss to the crown of my head.

I try to mutter a response, but don't know if I do before sleep takes over.

chapter 20

Pike

THERE'S A SCRATCH AT THE SURFACE OF MY MIND. An ache of pleasure that has my hips moving and my muscles tensing. A warm hand moving up and down my cock, teasing me.

A low groan leaves me as my eyes fight to open.

"Fuck," I hiss as a wave of heat zips through me. It's not a dream.

A small amount of light filters through the curtains, and I look down to find Aubrey's hand down my pants, slowly stroking my dick. I'm hard, so fucking hard, and craving more, my hips arching up, begging.

"Aubrey," I groan. Her eyes are closed, naked body moving against me.

Fuck, letting her fall asleep against me naked was probably not the best idea.

"Aubrey," I say louder, trying to rouse her.

How long as she been jacking me off? Her touch feels so good I'm almost ready to pop. Last night I had to get off before bed because I knew there was no way I was going to be able to sleep. Tasting her, feeling her come, listening to her sounds was all too much. I only lasted seconds before exploding all over the sink.

"Bree, baby, you need to stop or I'm going to come all over your hand."

"Hmm?" she says and moves against me. It takes a few pumps before her hand stops and she freezes. A few seconds pass and I arch my hips up, pushing my cock through her fingers. She relaxes and continues.

"I was dreaming," she murmurs.

"About what?"

"About doing this. Feeling you in my hand, feeling you inside me." Her breath picks up, and she grinds into my side in time with her hand. "I want to feel you inside me." She nips at my skin.

"Fuck," I hiss. I managed to not slip my dick into her last night, but I can only take so much before giving in. She's making it extremely difficult to think of anything other than sinking into her, watching her stretch around me.

I'm trying to be good, to be rational, and to think about what she needs emotionally, but that all goes away when her hand slips down and cups my balls.

"Please," she begs in a breathy moan.

We both need this. I'm no longer wondering if we should. "Damnit." I turn her onto her back and before I can do anything, I'm frozen in place. My blood begins to boil and I have to force myself to look past the bruising that blossomed overnight, otherwise it will whip me into a murderous rage. The beating he gave her shows now that it has soaked in, and it's so much worse than I imagined.

She notices my pause, and before she can say anything, I rub my fingers across her clit. Sliding down, I feel just how wet and ready she is. With my other hand I work my pants down, kicking them off as I settle between her thighs.

Her eyes are heavy as she arches up to meet me. We are both desperate for this reconnection. My eyes never leave hers as I rub the tip against her opening before pressing in. Wet heat surrounds me, and a groan crawls out from deep in my chest.

Her eyes roll back as she draws in a breath, her hands frantically crawl up my arms to cup my face as my hips come to rest against hers

I pull back and start in with long, slow, and steady strokes. All I want to do is get lost in feeling her.

Each thrust in she makes a new sound, and each one speeds my movements up, driven by the desire to hear more, to feel more. My muscles are wound tight, and what feels like sparks walk up and down my spine.

Pleasure in its purest form. I'm lost to the haze, driven by pure need. Each stroke pushes me further and further.

"Come in me," she begs.

My cock twitches, and I groan. Those words alone are enough persuasion. Her heels dig into my ass, holding me in place. She doesn't need to, because there's no question how this is going to end, and I thrust harder.

One last slam buries me as deep as I can go and my cock pulses, firing off, filling her. Our eyes are locked, and I know this is how we were meant to be.

I'm breathing hard but don't want to move. I want to stay in her forever. But my muscles are drained, and I'm forced to slide out with a groan and roll onto my back beside her.

"Wow," it's my turn to say.

She rolls back into the crook of my arm, her head on my chest, right where she belongs. "I forgot how good sex can be."

"So did I."

It takes a few minutes to calm down, and I begin to lazily trace shapes up and down her back.

"You should stay with me," I say.

"I need to go home. I need to…get my stuff from…I need to get a shower, go to work."

"You need to stay with me," I press. I've got meetings scheduled this morning, but I can see if Dave can cover them or reschedule them. Aubrey and her safety are the most important things to me right now. "And you really shouldn't work. Take a few days off to recover."

"Pike." She lets out a sigh. "I have to see Caleb, at least. I need to get my stuff and throw that ring at his head."

"You're not going anywhere near him without me."

"You can't be there," she argues.

I hook her chin with my finger to get her to look at me. "I will be there, Aubrey. He is never going to lay a hand on you again."

"Fine." She relents, but I know that actually being in front of him would be too much, and she knows it too.

She throws the blankets back and slides out, stretching as she stands, a few groans of pain escaping. I'm lost in the trail of my come sliding down her thigh when I notice the discoloration of her skin. I draw in a sharp breath, and as she turns to me, I see the hand-like imprint covering her neck.

"What?" she blinks.

Anger washes through me. I will kill the fucker. I will wrap my hands around his neck like he did to her and watch the last breath drain from him.

A deep pink spreads across her cheeks, and she swallows hard.

Purple and black, yellow and red cover her skin. Markings that hadn't been visible last night are in full bloom. The split lip was just one of multiple blows to the face. This wasn't some small outburst. He was out for her blood.

Tears fill her eyes, and she turns from me to leave. I scramble out of bed and wrap my arms around her waist, pulling her back to me with a hard bounce.

"If he ever touches you again, I will kill him," I hiss into her ear. A shudder leaves her, and I will my muscles to relax by breathing in her sweet scent. I trail my nose up her neck, soaking her in. "You are far too beautiful to have all these bruises."

I press light kisses against her shoulder as my hands move across her skin and I try to cocoon her in my arms. She sags into me, her hand reaching back to run her fingers through my hair.

She is my everything, and I will keep her safe. I will protect her from that bastard until my dying breath, and I will be whatever she needs me to be until she is ready.

"I need to get my clothes," she says.

I don't want to let her go. "You could just stay naked. I won't mind."

A giggle leaves her. "I'm sure you wouldn't, but things need to be done."

"I suppose you're right," I say as I reluctantly step back, creating space between our bodies.

Instantly I miss it, but we can't stand in the middle of the bedroom all day.

chapter 21

A LOUD INTAKE OF AIR HISSES THROUGH MY TEETH AS I stare at my reflection, finally understanding the depth of his words.

The bruises didn't just blossom at my cheek where he hit me. If only. No, I finally see what Pike saw, what made him so angry.

Dark splotches cover my arms from wrists to shoulders, a deep line from the counter, and a black eye from when he bashed my head into it. I can't remember Caleb grabbing me more than a few times, but my body says differently. A tear falls when I see my neck and just how hard he was grabbing it.

What would have happened to me if I didn't fight back?

It's a shock and further strengthens my resolve. I know I told Pike last night I didn't want to go to the police, but I'm not sure I can ignore this.

Those deep-seated reactions and emotions that tell me not to do anything that will hurt Caleb's company, his livelihood, stop me from doing it. I'm not sure I can shake them, but I decide to wait and see what happens today.

After cleaning up a bit, I rifle through my purse for my phone, but when I pull it out the battery is dead.

Carefully, I put my clothes back on, which is proving more difficult than I imagined. Everything aches, and the urge to curl up on my couch grows. Each movement comes with a price.

Gingerly I make my way down the stairs where Pike is waiting for me.

"Do you have a USB-C cord?" I ask. "My phone is dead."

"Yeah, right here." He takes my phone over to the entry table and attaches the cable. "I'll go grab you a bagel. Toasted with butter, right?"

I nod and lean against the wall, then slide down to the floor. I look across the hall and notice the table he'd been working on is gone, the room empty, which makes me wonder if he ever finished the kitchen.

It takes only a minute to gain enough battery to power my phone up. The normal music and swooshing lights go off. Then the pings.

Over and over the phone chimes in my hand. The calm and peace of Pike's presence, of being safe in his home, immediately flies away at the nineteen text messages and six voicemails.

I'm frozen. Dread settles in the pit of my stomach.

I ignore the voicemails. They may not all be from him, but I'm not taking the chance of hearing his voice. Besides, the best judge of their contents is the text messages, which I can see are all from him.

YOU FUCKING BITCH I WILL FUCKING END YOU FOR THAT

Get the fuck back here

I'm not done talking to you

Pick up the phone

Aubrey, pick up the phone

PICK UP THE FUCKING PHONE

Where are you?

Do you really want to piss off the only man that loves you?

If you are with that fucker I swear to God I will make you sorry

You know where I'll be when you're ready to apologize

"What's wrong?"

I stop reading and tilt my head back to find Pike standing over me with a plate and a glass. He crouches down, setting them on the floor beside him. Silently he pulls the phone from my lax hands. I watch as anger rolls through him.

"We need to get this over with as soon as possible." He screenshots the texts and sends them to himself.

"I want this over," I say. "I want all of my stuff out of there today, and I want to forget I ever heard of Caleb Manning."

It takes less than two minutes to drive over to Caleb's from Pike's house. There are no cars in the driveway, but Caleb always parks in the garage, so there is no real indicator of him being home.

I swallow hard as I enter, listening hard for any sounds. There is no evidence of our fight, though I can still feel every hard surface I hit. The ghosts of what happened are still here.

I can't even tell if he's home, but with Pike behind me, we head up to the master bedroom.

The bed is a mess, indicating he had been in it, but the room is silent and empty. Quickly I pull a duffle bag and a rolling suit-case from the closet and direct Pike to empty the drawers of the dresser while I pull my things from the closet.

I fill the suitcase with shoes and dresses, along with a few other articles of clothing that are hanging. Luckily there is a pair of tennis shoes in the closet and I slip them on, since my other shoe is still MIA and I'm walking on the wrappings.

The black dress Caleb bought is all that is left, and I stare at it for a moment before backing out of the closet and shutting off the light.

After that I button up my jewelry case, leaving the necklace he gave me on the dresser before moving to the bathroom and collecting toiletries and makeup.

With each item I pack, the rope around my chest loosens. I feel lighter. This is the right path for me.

The laundry basket catches my eye and I pull things out item by item, searching for anything that is mine, and I stop at a pair of red lace panties.

"I've got the dresser emptied," Pike says from the doorway. "Everything okay?"

I shake my head. "Those aren't mine." I point to the panties, my mind reeling as things click into place. "You've got to be fucking kidding me."

Warmth covers my back, and I know Pike is behind me.

"He's cheating on you?" Pike asks in surprise. "With all his jealousy issues?"

I'm completely dumbfounded, but it all adds up and makes so much sense. All the sudden issues he had to go take care of. They were always there, something was always going wrong, so I never thought twice about it.

He'd conditioned me to his absences.

Anger rolls through me, and I begin to shake. All that I did for him, all that I changed for him, to please him so he wouldn't leave me, but he was never truly with me in the first place.

"Asshole!" I cry out, grabbing his collection of cologne

from the counter and smashing them into the floor. Glass shards fly everywhere, mixing with liquid and splashing.

"Aubrey!" Pike wraps his arms around me and tugs me back.

The last bottle knocks hard against the mirror, sending spider cracks through the glass, fracturing the reflection.

"Why didn't I see it?" I ask.

Pike turns me in his arms and brushes the hair from my face as he looks me over. "Because he manipulated you into never questioning him."

I shake my head. The disappointment in myself is through the roof. How was I with him for so long and never really knew the kind of man he is? He's just a nice façade over an ugly interior.

"If you ever cheat on me," I say through clenched teeth, my fingers fisted in his shirt. "I will tear your heart out with my bare hands."

His eyes widen, and he pulls me closer. "Never going to happen."

It's amazing the calming effect he has one me as I lay my head against his chest. "I'm not ready right now."

"I know."

I reach up and cup his face, basking in the way he looks at me and the feel of him. "But I will be."

His lips press against my forehead. "I'll be waiting. However long you need, I'll be here."

There is so much peace in his arms. So much comfort I didn't understand I was missing.

"As much as I want you to stay right where you are, we should get moving."

I nod and pull back. "You're right." Stepping over and

around glass shards, I make my way back to the hamper and turn it over, dumping the contents out. There are a few things at the bottom, and I gather them up.

Back in the bedroom, one of my work totes sits next to the bedside table and I open it, dumping the contents of the table inside.

"Is this it, or is there more downstairs?"

I wrack my brain and come up with some kitchen items I want back and remind myself to check the laundry room.

"A couple of items, but everything else is his." That in itself is a startling revelation. This was supposed to be my home as well, but after over five months of engagement, the only things I have are related to my appearance or cooking. None of the decor is mine, nor the furniture. I hadn't even gotten around to packing anything in my condo up, which is proving to be a good thing.

Pike nods, and we head back down.

"I'm going to go throw these in the car," he says as he heads for the door.

While he is gone, I check the laundry room and find a few more clothes, then move to the kitchen.

So much time I spent here cooking for him. Hours I toiled to make him the perfect meal, all a waste. There are only a few things I need, and one of the only things he gave me that I'm taking is the pressure cooker, because it really was great. Then again, I can just go buy myself a new one.

I stare at the stainless-steel finish for a moment, then step away. Yep, going to buy myself the one *I* want.

As I pull items from the drawers and cabinets, I realize just how much of my kitchen has made its way over. No wonder I can't seem to cook at home anymore. There is the empty box from the pressure cooker still in the recycle pile in the laundry room and I grab it, placing everything in it and handing it off to Pike.

"Anything else?" he asks as he comes back in.

The longer I'm here, the more a nervous vibration takes hold. I don't want to forget anything, because I never want to step foot in here again or have to ask Caleb for anything.

"Coat," I say as I step toward the coat closet in the front hall.

Just as I pull out my favorite winter coat and my house sweater, the door from the garage to the house opens and Caleb steps in.

My heart slams in my chest, threatening to break through. I didn't even hear the garage door open, but by the sack in Caleb's hand, he just got back.

His eyes meet mine, and he quickly steps forward while I step back. "Aubrey."

Pike steps into view, his arms crossed in front of him, looking more intimidating than I've ever seen him before.

The switch flips on Caleb's expression when he notices Pike. "What is he doing here?" Caleb asks.

"Bodyguard," Pike responds without missing a beat.

"Why the fuck do you need a bodyguard?" He's staring at me, and I know he can see the damage he dealt.

"To make sure you keep your hands to your fucking self," Pike says, not even letting me get a word in as he maneuvers himself to a position between us.

"Aubrey, can we talk? Alone?" His tone is light, sweet almost. "Last night was a mistake, and I'm so very sorry. Please, baby, just give me five minutes."

Before last night I would have given him the five minutes, but not now. The fog is lifted. Finally, I see the truth of him, of me, and of this relationship that never should have gotten as far as it did.

"No."

Caleb's brow furrows, and that feeling comes over me again. That knowledge that he's getting upset, but I don't want to calm him this time. "No? What the fuck do you mean *no*? We're getting married, and you're going to let this guy get between us?"

I shake my head. "We're not getting married."

"Yes, we are. Don't listen to this asshole. He's been trying to get between us since I met him."

I pull the ring from my pocket and toss it to him. He catches it and looks down, his eyes moving into slits.

"I'm done with you. You aren't the man I thought you were, and I deserve more than the scraps you give me. I deserve a better man, and that will never be you."

"You're not leaving me. Especially not for him."

"Yes, I am. You have no power over me anymore." I can feel the strength return within me. "I tried to be perfect for you in every way. Look perfect, act perfect, be perfect so that you would want me, but it's exhausting, Caleb. It's so exhausting."

"Because you're fat and lazy."

Pike's hands ball into fists, but I take hold of his arm.

"Just because you say it doesn't make it truth. We're through. If something happens with me and Pike, that's between us."

"I won't let you leave me. I will fucking ruin you."

Pike steps forward. "You'll what?"

I can tell Pike is looking for the slightest excuse to lay Caleb out. I can also see that Caleb senses this as well, and isn't so sure about his odds for once thanks to the vibes coming from Pike.

"You aren't even all that," Caleb spits. "I've had so many women falling to their knees for my cock."

"Oh, I know you have women falling at your feet. But I'll never, *ever*, be one of them again. I'm done with you and your manipulations."

Caleb's anger fades when he sees he's not getting to me, that I'm not falling all over him to please him.

"This isn't over."

I pull on Pike's arm and back up. "Yes, it is."

Another weight lifts from me as we walk out, knowing I will never be back.

chapter 22

S TAY WITH ME," P IKE SAYS TEN MINUTES LATER WHEN we pull up to my condo.

"What?"

"I'm not comfortable with you being here, especially not alone," he says as he grinds his teeth.

"I'll be fine," I assure him, though I'm not sure I believe myself.

We exit the car and Pike pulls my bags down, along with the box of kitchen supplies. "At least let me change the locks."

I stare at him for a moment before sighing. It's really not a bad idea. I didn't get my key back from Caleb. "Okay, but can we do it later? I just…I just want to crawl into bed and not move for a while."

We walk around to the front door, Pike carrying everything except the coats, which somehow were all I ended up with.

"I can stay."

I hold the door open for him and direct him to set everything down. "I really need to be alone right now. So much has happened in the last…it's only been fourteen hours."

"I understand."

"I'm sorry, Pike."

He takes my hands in his and lifts them to his lips, placing light kisses on each one. "You have nothing to be sorry for."

"Thank you for everything."

"Will you please text me every few hours? I just need to know you're okay."

A nod and a smile. "Yes."

He gives me a strained smile and presses his lips to my forehead. "I'll see you later today."

"Later," I say as I close the door behind him and flip the lock.

I lean against the door and stare at my condo, my sanctuary, for a moment before pushing off and walking back to my bedroom. My clothes and shoes are on the ground in seconds despite the pain, and I slip on a tank top before slipping under the covers.

Only seconds later the torrent of tears bursts from my eyes. From the moment Pike returned, I fought the feelings I still had for him, and for what?

All the time wasted. All the unnecessary heartache and pain.

I want him in my life, beside me, but for now I let everything out. All the anguish releases, sobs rocking my body.

I thought I had the perfect guy to have the perfect life with, but everything about my relationship with Caleb was painted on. Scratch the surface, and there was nothing of substance holding us together but the strings attached to me that he was pulling. Strings he sewed into my mind without me even noticing.

A puppet for him to play with and manipulate into what he wanted.

A knock on my door rouses me from a sleep I didn't know I'd fallen into. In my haze, I bounce down the hall until I reach the door. I freeze for a second, fear that it could be Caleb zipping through me. A quick peek through the peep hole and warmth spreads through me as I pull it open.

"Are you okay?" Pike asks.

I rub my eyes. They feel like sandpaper and twice their normal size. "I'm fine. Why?"

"You never texted me. I got worried."

"I'm sorry. I fell asleep. The whole ordeal wore me out and…" I glance over to the clock hung above the fireplace. Six hours had passed since he dropped me off. "Wow, where did the day go?" I must have really been worn out from everything.

"Are you going to invite me in?" he asks, a lopsided grin on his face.

I blink at him and step back. "I'm sorry. I haven't quite woken up yet."

He places a kiss to my forehead as he passes. "Fucking adorable."

"You have an awful lot of bags with you," I say as count the five bags he's carrying with him.

"New door locks, tools to install, dinner, and some ice cream to drown in."

I light up at the mention of ice cream. "Moose tracks?" I ask as I follow him into the kitchen.

He grins and pulls the container out.

I look from it to him, and my bottom lip trembles. "You remembered."

"We went to four different grocery stores to find it one time."

I poke my head into the bag carrying takeout. "Mmm, smells good."

"Chicken Pad Thai, spring rolls, and a ginger salad." He swallows hard as his gaze moves up and down my body. "You might want to put some pants on."

Pants? I glance down and realize I'm only in my tank top and thong. My mouth drops open and I walk backwards out of the kitchen. "I'll be right back."

Pike changes all the locks on my house as I eat, occasionally stealing a bite from my fork, and even puts a two-by-four in the track of my sliding glass door. It seems like overkill, but I admit that it'll make me feel safer when he's not there.

Which is something I am already not looking forward to. Maybe he is onto something, but can I really just move in with him?

Afterwards we sit on the couch, which quickly becomes him lying on the couch and me pretty much lying on top of him. I finally get to watch more *Lucifer* and find out that Pike likes the show as well.

I think I'll keep him.

"Do you remember when we watched *Runaway Bride* and you swore up and down you would never be with a man that made you change yourself?" he says as his fingers make circles on my arm. "You couldn't ever be that. I never want you to change. Aubrey, I've always loved you just the way you are, and I would give anything for another chance."

"Another chance?"

"I want to start over. I want you to be mine."

"Start over? I don't want to start over," I say, and I can feel him still beneath me. "I want to continue. I want to pick up where we left off."

He blows out a breath and relaxes. "Did you have to scare me like that?"

"But, I'm not ready to jump into anything right now."

"I know. And like I said, I'll be right here, waiting for you when you're ready," he says as he kisses the top of my head. "Do you remember when we would sneak out and go on midnight walks?"

"That seems like such a dangerous thing now."

"It does. We probably made a hell of a lot more noise than we thought."

A small laugh leaves me. "Because everything was silent."

"Walk to the nearest gas station."

My mouth salivates at the treats we used to get. "And load up on Sprees and Reese's Peanut Butter Cups."

"Still my favorite candy."

"Can you even find Sprees anymore?" I ask. When was the last time I saw them? The reds were my favorite, while orange were Pike's. "I've seen chewy ones, but they aren't Shockers."

"Really?" he asks. "I feel betrayed. What happened to Shockers?"

"I think those are SweeTarts Chewy Sours now. I think it says on the wrapper."

"Huh."

I nod against him. "Interesting, right?"

"Yeah. Well, I don't want to be your rebound," he says. "I don't want to be your SweeTarts Chewy Sours."

"I don't want to be yours."

"Impossible."

"How so?" I ask.

"Because they were all rebounds from you. Even at eighteen, I knew you were special. All of my love was meant only for you."

I nuzzle his chest, wishing so badly it didn't hurt.

"I really wish you'd come stay with me," Pike says against my temple. "I have that great guest bedroom. Kate would be so happy to hear you're in there."

"It's so close to him."

"He doesn't know where I live."

I tilt my head back. "But he can find out."

"Maybe, but I haven't lived here that long. And as far as I know, he doesn't know we used to meet up on our morning runs."

I shake my head. "No. Still, I really just want to stay here."

"Okay, we'll stay here tonight."

I arch an eyebrow at him. "We?"

"I'll sleep on the couch," he says without hesitation. "I just don't feel comfortable leaving you alone."

It warms me to know he's so intent on watching over me. "Okay."

"And in the morning, I want to take you to the police station."

"Pike…" I trail off.

"Just to have the incident recorded. Your bruises really blossomed," he says as his fingers lightly trail up and down my arm. "There at least needs to be a record, just in case."

"Just in case what?"

"In case he tries to come at you again. In case he does it to someone else. In case he's more fucked up in the head than either of us can even believe."

He raises really good points, and I find it hard to fight the conditioning that still lingers. But if something did happen, if he attacked another woman, I want there to be evidence to show he's done it before.

And the more I let it sink in, the more I need him to know there are consequences for what he did to me.

chapter 23

IN THE MORNING, PIKE TOOK ME TO THE POLICE station where I gave a statement of events and more photos were taken in addition to the photos Pike took that night and recordings of the voicemails and text messages that we provided.

Turns out I may not have a say on whether or not they press charges, but there is a nice long statute of limitations if I wish to pursue them.

When we stepped out, it felt like another weight was lifted. I thought the ring was the biggest weight of all, but it turns out there are so many little things that on their own don't seem like much but are when piled together.

"Your chariot, m'lady," Pike says as we pull up to the gas station my car has been parked at since I ran into him.

It's hard to believe, to even comprehend that was only forty hours prior. Pike grabs the gas can from the back and pours some into the car's tank, then swings it around to the pump to top it off.

"Thank you, Pike. For everything," I say as I throw my purse in the front seat.

"I would do anything for you, Bree."

"I'm really beginning to believe that now." I lean forward and press my lips lightly to his.

"Are you sure—"

"I'll be fine. I'm going to go to the grocery, sit in my car and order everything from the app so I don't have to go in, have them bring it out to me, and go home and become a hermit. Besides, you can't miss another day of work."

He grimaces like he wants to argue with me. "Did you cancel your meetings for today?"

I nod. "I told everyone in an email that I was sick and unavailable for the week. If they want to reschedule, we can do it via email or wait until next week."

"Hopefully the colors will have faded." His thumb traces under my eye. "Though I bet you could come up with a great explanation for this shiner."

"Attacked by rabid squirrels?"

"Ran into a street sign?"

We both laugh, and I wrap my arms around him for a hug. "Have a good day."

"I'll come over later, okay?" Reluctantly he pulls away, and my body begs for the warmth again.

I nod. "See you soon."

My chest clenches as he drives off, and I miss him already.

A few minutes later I park in the back of the grocery store parking lot and start going through the app, putting stuff into my virtual cart. Right now, I just want to drown in junk food, and so far that's what my list is comprised of. I'll need the week to indulge, to eat my emotions away.

I contemplate calling my parents, but I'm not ready to talk about it yet. I'm not ready to talk to Nora either. I'm still processing it all.

My phone starts buzzing in my hand, Briar's name written across the screen. I contemplate not answering it, but I also know Briar doesn't usually call unless there is an issue.

"Hey, Briar, what's up?"

"Aubrey, we have a problem. I need you to come out to Hummingbird."

I glance at my reflection and sigh. "Briar, I can't. Not today." It kills me to say it, but going there won't be good.

"This can't wait," he says in possibly the most serious Briar voice I've ever heard.

"Shit," I curse under my breath. "What is it?"

"Someone broke in. They made a fucking mess."

"Fuck." I glance down at my clothes. They're passable, and my hoodie covers my arms and all the bruising except around my face and neck. I let out another curse as I stop ordering and throw the car into reverse.

"I'll be there in ten minutes."

When I pull up to the house, there are multiple vehicles sitting in the driveway and in front, which is where I park as well. A glance in the mirror proves I can't go in with my hair up, so I pull the hair tie out and shift my hair to cover what I can. Covering it all would make me look like that girl from *The Ring* with all of my hair in my face. There's nothing I can do to hide the split in my lip or black eye, but I hope the shadows lessen the other bruises.

I walk up to where Briar is standing and watch as his eyes widen.

"Damn, Hart. What the fuck happened to you?" Briar asks.

Fuck. I shake my head. It's not something I can talk about right now. "What's going on?"

His brow furrows, his gaze bouncing between my eyes

before he goes into the damage list. "Broken glass, cement in the toilets, fucked-up drywall, and all the new flooring we installed has been beat to hell."

"Can the floors be salvaged?"

He shakes his head. "No. It looks like someone took a sledgehammer to the tiles, and the laminate is riddled with potholes."

"Shit." That list is tens of thousands of dollars long, not to mention adding at least two weeks to the flip time.

"I left a message for Caleb, but he hasn't called back."

I freeze. "You called Caleb?"

His lips form a thin line. "Unfortunately."

"Briar, we've got more," one of his guys says.

"Fuck," he curses. "I'll be right back."

From the front door, the damage seen is in the thousands, and I can't even imagine how high the final cost will be. I know it can happen with empty homes. It's a risk and why Caleb has insurance, but I haven't experienced it yet. And insurance doesn't cover the cost interest for the extra time before list.

Caleb will be furious, and I want to get out of here before he decides to show up. My heart starts hammering in my chest at just the thought.

"Looks like someone broke in," Caleb says from behind me.

I whirl around, cursing that I didn't make it out in time, and take in the smug look on his face. He's not angry, not blowing up. He's oddly calm. "Did you do this?" I hiss.

"Do what?" he asks.

"You fucking asshole."

"Watch what you say. It's my money funding this project."

"And your fucking money that will have to fix it, you stupid fuck."

His jaw twitches and he grabs my arm, pulling me into the dining room.

"Someone changed their locks. I had to get your attention somehow."

The blood freezes in my veins as I register his words. My stomach drops, and my whole body feels like it's trying to crumple in on itself.

He went to my house. He tried to get in. When? In the middle of the night? I'm even more thankful Pike stayed over.

He releases my arm and steps forward, his brow furrowed.

"Aubrey, we were happy. We were in love. How could you open your heart to another man? And so close to our wedding?" His voice is so forlorn and it almost makes my heart hurt.

"We had such a good relationship, we were making great strides in our goal for your weight." As he continues, that initial feeling quickly fades and I see this for what it is. Another try at manipulating me, of getting me back in line. "Our future was bright. You would give up your job to stay fit and take care of me and our children."

As I listen, I'm amazed at how warped he is. Did this work on me before? Did he really have such control over me that this would somehow sway me?

More importantly, what benefit does he get? Since it's all about Caleb, what is he after?

I take a step back and narrow my eyes. "Give up my job? You mean hand over my company to you? Is that what this is all about? What being with me can give you?"

"That's not it. I just want you to take care of your family."

"Oh, I'll take care of my family with a man by my side who knows what family and love really is. Someone to share my hopes and dreams and heart with, not someone who controls them. Not someone who *beats* women and tries to *rape* them."

I suck in a hard breath when his hands grip my waist, fingers digging in. All smiles and pleading looks are gone, replaced with a sneering, angry man. "That wasn't nice, Aubrey. I'm being fucking nice to you. Have some compassion."

Suddenly I can't move, completely immobilized by his mere presence. "W-why bother coming over besides this charade of the good guy? There's nothing of yours there."

"Oh, but there is. I told you—I fucking own you," he growls.

"You don't," I say, but I can hear the weakness in my voice. What is wrong? Why can't I tell him off? Why do I feel like I'm folding in on myself?

"Nobody disrespects me the way you have," he spits, and I can do nothing but recoil.

A cry leaves me as his grip tightens. "Let go," I whimper.

"If you aren't with me, and you aren't at home, then you must have been with *him*."

"I said let go!" I cry out.

"With that fucking sap you gave your virginity to. Did you cry with him like you cry with me?"

"She said let go," Briar's voice booms out. It's so loud it startles Caleb, and I'm able to turn with enough force to slip from his grip and step closer to Briar.

"You fucking sadist! I can't believe I fell for the bullshit that comes out of that mouth. You are a callous bastard who cares about nothing and no one but himself!"

"I told you to watch your fucking mouth. If you don't stop, I won't take you back."

"Why would I want to go back to you? You're a master manipulator and a cheater, and those are your better qualities."

"Fucking bitch!" Caleb growls as he lunges at me.

"Back off!" Briar yells as he steps in front of me. "You fucking touch her, and I will put you through that wall."

Caleb stops and glares at Briar as he sizes him up, much like he did with Pike.

Briar has a good six inches of height and fifty pounds of muscle on Caleb. It all makes me think that despite all his bravado, he's not confident in an actual fight with someone who can obviously fight back and possibly win.

Caleb's glare finds me. "If you leave me, I will ruin you."

I don't back down and instead lean forward matching his glare, my teeth bared. "Fucking try it."

The anger flares in him again, but with Briar in the way there's nothing he can do. It's Briar's crew, and they will all back him.

"This isn't over," Caleb says as he walks to the door.

"Yes, it is!" I'm fuming, but I don't know who I'm angrier at—Caleb or myself. I crumbled to him, unable to do anything, barely able to lash him with rhetoric.

Briar follows after Caleb to make sure he leaves before coming back over. "Did he fucking do that to you?"

I swallow hard and nod. "Yes."

He brushes my hair back to get a good look, his jaw locking down when he sees my neck. "What else?"

I slip my hoodie off to show him more.

Briar purses his lips and nods, then looks around. "Okay, pack it up!" he yells, and the chatter of the crew dies down. "We're off this project as of right this fucking minute. I want everything packed up, including all materials. If you have left anything at any Home Works site, I suggest you go get it today, because we no longer have contracts with Home Works Flipping effective immediately."

"Briar, you can't," I protest.

He turns back to me. "I can, and I will. Fuck any fines."

"Boss, what's going on?" Tom, his second in command, asks.

Briar glances to me, and Tom's eyes widen. "I don't work for assholes who cut corners, and I sure as fuck am not going to work for anyone who attacks my friends."

I wrap my arms around Briar's waist. "Thank you," I whisper.

He runs his hands up and down my back. "Are you going to tell me now?"

I nod and give him an overview. I can't dive deep into what happened. It's still way too fresh.

"Motherfucker," he hisses, then changes his voice over to a *Godfather* impersonation. "I have this cousin…"

I shake my head. "You don't have a cousin."

"But if I did, I would totally have him taken care of. In all seriousness, I'm so thankful you fought back and stunned his ass. I'm blacklisting him. My reach is hella bigger than his on this side of town."

"Word spreads."

"Rumors spread faster."

"What does that mean?" I ask.

"I think people are going to be talking about this beautiful and strong woman who escaped an abusive relationship."

Tears spring to my eyes, and I bite down on my lower lip. "I hope that one gains traction."

"I think it will. I don't know how deep your businesses are tied, but I'd get away from Home Works and Caleb as fast as you can. Designs With Hart is a great brand, and you don't need him." He pulls his wallet from his back pocket and digs out a small stack of cards and holds them out. "I know he's got some good guys on his payroll. If they want to leave, send them my way."

"Will do. Thanks, Briar." I have one person in mind, and there will probably be more.

The crew races around, pulling materials and tools, emptying everything they brought as I leave.

I race home, forgetting about the grocery store, forgetting about everything. Something Caleb said isn't sitting right in the pit of my stomach, and I know—fuck, I just know he did something. From the driveway everything looks fine, but my end-unit entrance is on the side.

Every fear is confirmed when I walk around the building and see my front door. The frame is busted out and the door is ajar, broken shards sticking out. My heart hammers in my chest as I slowly enter. There's no need to flip on the light due to all the windows, and I quickly scan for anybody who might still be here.

My vision stops on the far wall. Scrawled across the family room wall in bright orange spray paint is a single word—whore. The couch is destroyed, deep cuts with fluff and stuffing exploding everywhere.

There is broken glass everywhere, and it looks like he took a sledgehammer or a bat to anything and everything.

It's a scene of horror movies, and my heart spikes. I don't feel safe in my own home, and I can't stay here.

My hands shake as I pull out my phone and find Pike's number, and I almost sob when I hear his voice.

"P-Pike." My teeth are chattering.

"Aubrey, what's wrong?" he asks, and it almost sounds like panic in his tone.

"I need you," I whimper.

"Where are you?"

"Home."

"I'm on my way."

I don't want to go any further inside, so I back out and wait in the driveway, my whole body shaking. When will this nightmare end?

The Jeep is barely in park when Pike jumps out and runs to me. Immediately he wraps me in his arms. "I'm here."

A sigh of relief washes through me and I lean into him, strength leaving me.

We walk around the side, and Pike pushes the door open. "Fuck," he hisses, then pulls out his phone.

I don't ask who he's calling as I step further in. Everything is a mess, and I don't even know where to begin processing it both mentally and physically. I'm in shock that he would do something like this to me.

With Pike near, I feel safe enough to venture further in. All the shelves are knocked out of the bookcases, the remnants of what they held scattered about the floor. There's a deep scratch trailing along the wall leading to the bedrooms. My office is the first room, and it looks almost normal, just a few things out of place, then I notice my logo on the wall. Whatever he used on the couch and wall is sticking out of my last name.

A shuddered breath leaves me, and I back up. Dread settles in my stomach, and a scream leaves me when arms grab hold of me. I turn to get loose, to get away. That's when I see blue eyes set below a furrowed brow, and I fall forward against his chest.

"Thank God," I say as I clench onto his shirt. "I'm sorry—"

"Stop. There's nothing to apologize for. At all. You're safe.

I've got you." His hands run soothing trails down my back, and my heartbeat begins to regulate. "Son of a bitch."

Pike stiffens, and I know he sees it too.

I tilt my head back. "I can't stay here."

He shakes his head. "No, you can't."

"What do I do?" I ask. I feel completely lost and exposed. What he did to me was bad enough, but this is a violation of my sanctuary, which somehow hurts more. Is it because I now see he'll stop at nothing and that nowhere is safe?

"The police are on the way. We know who it was, but I don't know if we can prove it. Maybe they can. Is anything missing?"

I shake my head. "I don't think so. Just a bunch of broken stuff from what I can tell."

"Are those bags we took from Caleb's still packed?"

We continue down the hall to the bedroom. Nothing looks out of place, not a single crumb. "Maybe he ran out of time?" That's the only reason I can think of as to why he stopped.

The police arrive, and we go through everything all over again. I make sure to mention the Hummingbird property and the destruction there, which was done on the same day.

"You're moving in with me," Pike says as the officers go through the house. It's more of a statement of fact.

"What? I can't."

"Do you really want to move back in with your parents?" he asks.

A groan leaves me. No, I don't. And there's no way I'm staying here anymore.

"Look," He links our pinkies, and it's a shot to the heart. "I have extra bedrooms. You can stay there."

"In your spare bedroom? After we just had sex in the master yesterday morning?"

His lip draws up into a lopsided grin. "Or my bed. I just…" His expression falls. "Aubrey, I don't want to rush you into anything. I can wait until you're ready, but I need you to know I will be right here, beside you. We will take it as fast or as slow as you want. But I need you to feel safe."

"I do feel safe with you. I've always felt safe with you."

"That I'll protect you. Take care of you."

I reach up and cup his face. "You always have." I stretch up and press my lips to his, and there's another electric shot to my heart.

There's no need to give me space. I'm awake for the first time in years, and even with everything that's happened, I refuse to let Pike go again. Even if the space between us is just down the hall.

chapter 24

WE LOADED UP MY CAR AND PIKE'S JEEP WITH AS much as we could and were allowed to. Some areas I was forced to leave alone for now.

It's only a ten-minute drive but with each minute that passes, my excitement grows.

I'm moving in with Pike.

And it's not just words. There's no pretense or expectation, but I know I can't sleep anywhere else but beside him. His home feels like my home. Something about the space resonates inside me, and all the bullshit with Caleb seems to fade away. All that is there is me and Pike and love.

The love I feel for him blows me away. I'm open to it now, to him, and to a future together.

When we reach his house, anxiety crawls up my spine simply due to how close Caleb's house is, but I push it down.

"Don't do anything."

"I'm not an invalid," I say when he swats my hand away from the boxes and bags in my trunk.

"But you're hurt, and I already told you I can't stand for anything to hurt you. So stay. I'm going to run this inside."

I smile and shake my head. "Okay."

The second he's out of my sight, the anxiety spikes and I find myself clutching my keys as my heart rate speeds up.

"Are you moving in?" a child's voice asks from behind me.

I turn to find Mason standing at the end of the driveway, his head cocked and a basketball under his arm.

"Yes."

"What happened to your face?" The concern in his voice is mimicked by his actions. The ball drops from his grip as he runs over, his brow knitted as he looks me over, small fingers running over my arms.

"Someone hurt me," I say in the basest way I can.

"Why?" he asks.

How do you explain jealousy and anger and alcohol to a ten-year-old? "Because I didn't love him."

"Do you love Pike?"

I nod and smile at him. "I do."

I can see tears welling in his eyes. "Mom has bruises like this sometimes."

The words are a knife to the heart. "How does she get them?"

He shakes his head. "I don't know. She won't say. Do you think it's because she doesn't love my dad?"

"Maybe."

"Did Pike protect you?" I can tell by the way he lights up that he looks up to Pike, that Pike has become a mentor and friend to him—a hero.

"He does. He doesn't hurt me, he only makes me feel safe."

He nods and sniffs. "I wanna be like Pike. I wanna protect my mom."

"I know you can. And sometimes the best way to do that is to call 9-1-1 if you hear or see someone hurting her."

He nods vigorously. "I can do that. I know I can do that."

"What's going on out here?" Pike asks as he steps up.

I ruffle Mason's hair. "Just chatting."

"Are you trying to steal my girl?"

Mason chuckles. "No."

"Well, good, because you can't have her." Pike pulls me close, a grin covering his face.

Mason rolls his eyes. "Duh, she's your girlfriend."

"I've got to unload all this stuff. Want to help? Trade your brute strength for a game of H.O.R.S.E."

Mason purses his lips and looks to the sky before smiling. "Deal."

What Mason lacks in brute strength he makes up for in child speed and stamina, making the unloading process so much quicker. There wasn't a ton, but lots of trips' worth.

I watch as Pike and Mason engage in their game, and chuckle at the times Pike purposely misses his shot. It's a short game, and Mason wins.

"Good game," Pike says as he shakes hands with Mason.

"Good game," Mason replies, then suddenly wraps his arms around Pike's waist.

It hits me then. If I hadn't miscarried, our child would be around Mason's age. Seeing how he is with Mason? It's an ovary-exploding scene, and I know one day Pike will be a great father. One day we'll make another baby.

Pike waves as Mason heads home, then that blinding smile is aimed at me.

"I want to show you something," Pike says as he takes my hand and leads me inside.

"What?" I ask. We move through the entry and down the hall.

He flips the light on in the kitchen, and I gasp. When I stayed after the attack, I never went into the kitchen. It's very different from the half-updated state I last saw it in.

The cabinets are painted in the color I picked out, and the backsplash leaves me speechless. It isn't the subway tile I suggested, but the Arabesque lantern style I love. He's taken it and covered every inch of the wall the cabinets sit on, including wrapping them up and around the sliding glass door. It's a spectacular and beautiful sight.

"You finished."

He nods. "Looks good, doesn't it."

"It's beautiful." I look around and notice the new storage cabinets he's added next to the refrigerator, and the table he'd been working on is now in the eat-in area.

My fingers flit across the counters as I take it all in. I stop when I notice the crystal pendant lights hanging over the peninsula.

"Crystal ones?" I ask.

"You always loved sparkles and chandeliers."

"I do love them, they look great, but why because I like them?"

He swallows hard and blows out a breath. "Because I didn't buy this house for me. I bought it for you...for us."

It's our dream house. The one we talked about years ago. The one we sculpted with teenage minds and teenage hearts is still perfectly us.

"What?"

"We used to talk about the future, about what our home would be like. I remember the excitement you would have when talking about what you wanted in our home, and I found a home with those elements that I could make ours."

"Is this a little fast?" I ask, even though I know the answer in my heart.

"It's not to pressure you, just to show you that I meant every promise. With the relationship you just came off of, we will take it at whatever pace you want, but no matter what, I'm going to be standing right beside you. I made the mistake of not coming home years ago, but I'm not going to take the chance of losing you again."

There is no need to think, just a gut reaction. I jump up and wrap my arms around his shoulders and crash my lips to his.

There is no waiting or easing back in. Pike is it. He always has been.

All thoughts of taking things slow are burned away by his touch. I can't get enough, and I draw him closer, tugging at his shirt, desperate to get it off. He gives me no help, his hands flat against my back.

I pull back in confusion. His eyes are heavy, clouded, and it sends a zing right to my clit before echoing through my veins. It's the look of a man who truly desires me, who wants me, just as I am. Whose need for me is so great, but his control to not push me is greater.

He is the man who wants to walk through this life hand in hand with me, as my partner. Someone who will always put my needs above his own.

I spent almost the last two months believing I was in love with two men, but I was so wrong. With Caleb, I was in love with the idea of the endgame we all strive for.

I believed that my chances of being truly happy ended the day Pike walked through airport security. Because of that, I spent almost two years with a man who never cared for me as a person. Not really.

I may not be healed, but my heart is full. I know above everything that I love Pike, and he loves me. He shows it in everything he does. He needs me as much as I need him, like air.

And I want him to let loose, to manifest that need in a physical way.

"Take it off," I whisper against his lips before swiping my tongue across them.

A groan leaves him, but he wastes no more time and sheds the shirt. I reach out and run my hands across his skin. He's vibrating, shuddering under my touch as I map his new physique. I trail down to the waistband of his jeans and pull at the belt, my eyes locked with his so he knows this is what I want.

Hands grip my waist, and my feet leave the floor. The counter pushes into the back of my legs as he settles me onto the edge and steps between my thighs.

He's the perfect height. His hard length presses against my core, teasing me.

"Fuck," he growls. The sound sends a shiver down my spine, and I wrap my legs around his waist to draw him closer.

One hand grips the waistband of my jeans, tugging the seam against my clit and making me cry out.

"These are in the way," he says.

His mouth attacks my neck in hot, open-mouthed kisses. I draw in a breath as pleasure zings straight to my clit when his teeth lightly press in at my shoulder. His movements are frantic and filled with all his desire.

Desire for me.

A shudder rolls through me, and I rock against his length. All I want is him inside me, that base level connection.

"Please," I whimper.

His hips rock harder into me. "Please what?"

My breaths are ragged, desperation rocking me. "Fuck me."

A long, low groan rumbles in his chest, his hands digging into my ass. He wastes no more time and undoes my jeans before ripping them and my thong down my legs. The action only excites me further, and even more so as he opens his jeans and frees his cock.

I lick my lips as I stare at it. From the length to girth, slight curve and hardness, it's like it was made for me.

There's no pause before he lines up and slams in. My eyes go wide as I draw in a ragged breath, my nails digging into his shoulders as wastes no time setting up a rhythm.

He hooks one of my legs over his arm, the angle changing, driving him deeper. My other leg I wrap around his waist, pulling him back in with each thrust. I need him deeper. Harder.

Our eyes are locked, and it feels like my chest is bursting open. All the love I have is exploding, all for him.

"I love you," I whisper against his lips.

His movements falter, and he cups my face. "I love you. So much."

A tear rolls down my cheek, but it's not out of sadness. I'm deliriously happy.

Our breath mingles as our bodies move together, climbing higher and higher. His hand slides down my body, teasing my nipples, pinching and drawing out more mewling sounds that only spur him on.

My eyes widen, and I draw in a breath when his fingers slip against my clit.

"Come for me, baby." His voice sends a shiver through me, right to where his fingers are swiping against my clit.

My breath hitches, muscles draw high as I cry out. Everything snaps, and I'm convulsing in his arms.

His hips pick up in pace before suddenly slamming against mine with a roar. Fingers dig into my flesh, and I can feel him twitching, coming inside me. Filling me.

My muscles continue to spasm as I come down, and a low groan leaves him with each one.

I fall back against the cool quartz counter as I try to catch my breath. Pike follows me down, his head resting on my chest. His arms stretch out until he finds my hand and links his fingers with mine.

"Well, we christened the kitchen," he says after a minute.

A giggle leaves me, and I crane my neck to look down at him. He's smiling that beautiful, serene smile, a sparkle in his eyes. For the first time since he got back, he looks exactly like the boy who left ten years ago.

I brush my fingers through his hair, and he leans into the touch.

We've both been starved, left hungry for the only thing that can sate us. So long living without the only heart that feels like home.

"Which room do you want to do next?" I ask.

"Hmm, how about the master bathroom?"

I quirk a brow at him. "Now?"

"I'll be ready again by the time we get up there."

"And tonight we can move all my stuff into the master."

He raises his head, his eyes locking onto mine. "Are you sure?"

I smile at him and pull him closer, my lips ghosting his. "I'm positive. I'm not sleeping anywhere else but with you."

chapter 25

THE WALKERS REFUSED TO RESCHEDULE THEIR appointment and were adamant I keep to our Thursday at noon.

After the whole ordeal, I took the rest of the week off and I hope the bruising will be down by Monday, but that is still days from now. Restaurants or coffee shops are my usual meeting places, and I find a table in the corner of the bar and grill.

I try to ignore the stares, but it's impossible. I've been a hermit at Pike's house for days now as I get settled and adjusted to my new home.

What amazes me the most is the ease in which it's happened. There's no awkwardness, no special way Pike wants or needs something done. He just goes with the flow.

Oddly, my parents still don't know. It isn't that I haven't talked to them, it's that the conversations are short, and Mom never lets me get a word in edgewise before suddenly having to go. We have dinner planned for Tuesday, and I'm bringing Pike.

Matt and Dana arrive, deep scowls carved into their faces. Neither really looks at me or notices anything is wrong as they sit across from me.

"I'm going to cut to the chase," Dana says, her chin high, lips in a thin line.

The air is charged, and I have no idea the reasoning. "Okay."

"After what you did to Caleb, we can't work with you."

I blink at her in confusion. What *I* did to *him*? "Excuse me?"

"How could you cheat on him?" Matt says. "After all he has done for you."

I don't even get a chance to address the first thing because the second one is a bigger slap to the face. "Done for me?"

"We're not going to work with someone who has no morals." Dana stands up, and Matt follows.

"Then why are you working with *him*?" I ask. This turn of events has me completely blindsided.

"Because he is a far better person than you, you slut," Dana shouts before throwing my water at me.

I gasp as the cold water hits, and I jump up as it soaks my top. "What the hell?"

They stomp off, giving me no avenue to defend myself. Instead, I'm left dabbing water from my clothes and running everything back in my head to make sure I heard them right.

"Are you okay?" the waitress asks as she comes by with more towels.

I nod as I pull my hair back into a quick bun. It isn't until she gasps that I realize what I inadvertently did. There are no more shadows to hide the bruises. They've faded, but they're still there.

There are no words. I don't know what to say. Even away from him, the repercussions of his actions still mar my skin.

"I don't mean to pry, but did he do that? The guy they were talking about?" she asks.

I nod.

She swallows hard. "Did you get away?"

"I thought so."

I thank her and leave a tip for her help before heading to my car.

He's doing it. He's convinced them, manipulated them just like he did me to make himself the victim.

Suddenly I want *everyone* to know the truth, to see my bruises. This ends now. I'm through with him.

I still have access to his calendar—he's at the Zionsville house today.

A sense of unease pools in my stomach, and I call Pike for reassurance.

"Hello?" Pike answers. I can hear voices in the background, and I know I've probably interrupted a meeting.

"He did it," I say, vibrating in anger.

"Who did what?"

"Caleb. He made good on his word that he was going to ruin me."

"What happened?" he asks, all attention on me.

I'm fuming and grinding my teeth again. "He turned the Walkers against me. Who knows who else he's talked to? The asshole made himself out to be the victim."

"Fucking motherfucker," he hisses low.

"I'm going to go confront the bastard."

"Bree, wait. I'll be there in twenty to go with you."

"It's okay, he's at a site. He won't touch me there, and I'll have witnesses." I want to tell him to meet me there, but I also know this is something I need to do on my own. With the crew there I know I'll be safe, and that gives me the strength I need.

"It's only going to egg him on," he argues.

"I'm going to threaten pressing charges. The statute of limitations is years long. That will keep him in line."

"I don't think they're going to wait for you to press charges for that to happen."

"What does that mean?"

"I got a call from the officer who saw us, and they don't take lightly to domestic abuse. They're pressing felony charges against him. He'll probably be in custody by the end of the day."

There is a sense of relief that washes over me. It isn't going to be an empty threat, and knowing it is a loaded one, I'm excited to confront him.

"Even better."

"Just…please be careful and call me as soon as you leave."

"I will."

"I love you," he says.

My heart bursts to hear him say that. For the first time in years, my response is not out of habit or obligation. It's pure and unfiltered and every truth I know. "I love you, too."

It takes me fifteen minutes to arrive and the second I do, I strip off my jacket and shirt, leaving only my cami on. They're all going to see.

Eyes are on me almost immediately, a few mumbled words as I stomp up to the house.

"What happened?" Miguel asks, his mouth open and brow knitted in concern as he looks me over.

"Give me a minute. I need to speak to Caleb."

He nods. "In the kitchen."

I head into the house and make my way to the jackass talking into his phone.

I've had enough of Caleb Manning. He's going to know once and for all he no longer has any power. I'm the one with the power now, and I will destroy him.

"You son of a bitch," I seethe.

He turns toward me, his lips twitching up into a wicked smile. "Pete, I have to go. A little butterfly just flew in." He hangs up the phone and smirks at me. "I told you I would ruin you."

My jaw juts forward, an anger-filled smile on my lips. Revenge is going to be sweet. "Oh yeah? Well, I would think about stopping."

He steps closer and looks down his nose at me. "And why would I do that when this is so much more enjoyable." He leans in and whispers. "I like to watch you squirm."

"Stop slandering me. If you don't stop, I will press charges against you. Don't think for a second I didn't report and submit pictures of what you did to me to the police. You so much as say my name in a demeaning manner, and your ass will be in hand-cuffs faster than you can blink."

He's silent as he regards me. It's a calculating look, plotting his next move, wondering if I'm telling the truth or trying to scare him.

"That's all talk."

"Really? All talk? Want me to give you the name and badge number of the officer who took my statement?" I ask. For a moment he actually looks concerned, but then that smug smile is back. "Don't fucking mess with me because I will press charges. This will go to court, and I will make sure that those photos are blasted everywhere so everyone can see what you really are."

"Don't you fucking threaten me," he spits out between clenched teeth.

His anger is rising, but so is the number of people in the room. The number of witnesses.

"No, don't *you* fucking threaten me. I'm the one with the power here, not you."

"You are fucking weak. You don't have any power."

"I am *so* fucking glad we never got to merge companies, because now all I have to deal with is our current contracts and once those are up, I never have to look at or talk to you ever again. And when it's done, all my clients are coming with me because they can't *stand* working with you."

"You fucking cunt! All I have to do is tell them what a whore you are, and they'll side with me."

A laugh leaves me, harsh and bitter. "Do it. I fucking dare you. And when shit blows up, maybe then you'll learn not to mess with me. I know more of your dirty secrets than you think I do."

"You don't know shit."

I smile and laugh, loving the startled look on his face. It unnerves him.

"You are lowlife scum." I turn to the gathered crowd of workers, at least a dozen men, and hold my arms out. "This is what lowlife scum does to women who don't obey him. I was choked, punched, my head was slammed into a granite countertop, and I was beaten. Then he tried to rape me."

Whispers spread, eyes wide as they stare at the damage to my skin.

"It's not rape when you're my fiancée," he grinds out.

"I'm not your fiancée anymore, and it *is* rape. Relationship status has no bearing on rape. Just because I was with you did *not* give you a pass to do that to me. You were forcing yourself on me after you disoriented me with a blow to the head. The only thing that stopped you was *me*."

His lip curls up, and I know he's remembering the voltage I delivered straight into his chest.

"You stand there thinking you are better than me, but you're not. You want to hit me, attack me again, but you're holding it back because this time there's an audience." Caleb is breathing heavy as he glares at me. I meet his eyes and speak in slow, deliberate words. "This time there are witnesses. They heard. They all know. Your perfect image is tarnished."

Caleb steps toward me, and Miguel steps in front of him. "Go home."

"Excuse me?" Caleb snaps.

My eyes go wide as I stare at Miguel's back. Over the last few days, Caleb has been smart and not taken on Pike or Briar, but they're both larger than him. Miguel is smaller, and I'm afraid Caleb sees him as an opportunity.

"Go home, Caleb," I say in an effort to pull his attention away from Miguel.

"Shut your fucking mouth," he growls, glaring at me from over Miguel's shoulder. His attention moves back, his face inches from Miguel's. "Back to work, Miguel. This doesn't concern you."

"It does," Miguel says, not faltering from his stance. "How could you do that to her? Hurt her like that?"

"Because like you, she doesn't know her fucking place. Get back to work."

I've angered him, and since he doesn't want to test my threat, he's aiming it at another target. There are angry murmurs from the workers, but Miguel holds them off.

"Go home, Caleb, before you make things much worse," Miguel presses.

Caleb's eyes flare, his anger reaching manic heights. "Get back to work before I fire you."

Miguel drops the clipboard in his hand to the ground. "No worries. I quit."

There's a cacophony of things hitting the floor as all of

Miguel's crew drops their tools. One man says "I quit," and others follow.

He's outnumbered, and there's nothing he can do. "Fuck you all!" he yells, and stomps away.

Nobody moves, and a few seconds later the sound of squealing tires filter through the house.

My heart is hammering in my chest, beating like a war drum. I was so amped up I didn't notice, but now that the confrontation is over, I'm feeling the effects.

Miguel turns to me, a sad smile on his face. "Can I have the officer's information?"

"Sure, but why?"

"I would like to be a character witness on your behalf. He runs his mouth on the phone thinking nobody is listening, so I also know more of his dirty secrets than he thinks. You've been so good to me and my family, done so much. I can never return your kindness, but I can help you with this."

I pull out my phone and text him the information, then pull Briar's card from my back pocket and hold it out. Miguel looks at it, then to me. "Call Briar. You'll have a ringing endorsement from me. He's a good man and runs a good company." Standing up for me cost him his job, and I'll be damned if he spends one day unemployed because of it.

He nods. "Thank you."

Confronting Caleb was liberating.

Knowing that he is probably going to spend the night in jail unlocked the last chain holding me down.

I know he will get parole, and I know the anxiety and the

worry will return until he gives up or goes to jail, but for one night I'm going to enjoy my life. Even if that night is filled with packing up the remnants of my home, because the love of my life will be beside me.

"How did it go?" Pike asks from the doorway, a stack of plastic tubs in his arms.

"I think he got the message. If not, I think it'll be a surprise when they put his ass in handcuffs."

"Did you tell him that he's about to be arrested?"

I grin at him. "No." He presses his lips to mine, and I sigh. "Can everything just magically appear in your house?"

"Our house, and I wish it worked that way."

Our house. It really and truly is our house. Our *home*.

"But, I may have bumped into some people who can help."

"Helpers?" I don't get to ask more because Nora walks in.

"I come bringing reinforcements!" Nora says as she pops the cork on a bottle of champagne.

From behind her my parents walk in, their eyes wide in shock from the door that is still a wreck. That and the mangled couch that sits outside the door.

"Mom. Dad. What are you doing here?" I ask as my parents step through my makeshift threshold.

Mom's eyes go wide as she looks at me. "Mercy me. Baby, what happened?"

I'm suddenly very aware of the marks still covering my skin. "I didn't want you to worry."

"When you said you weren't with Caleb anymore, I never…" Dad trails off.

"He did that?" Mom asks.

I nod. "I wanted to wait until the bruises were gone to tell you. He attacked me, I got away, and everything is okay now."

"Fuck him. I hope he gets raped in jail," Nora says as she wipes a drop of champagne from her bottom lip.

"Nora!" Mom cries, but then begins to laugh. "Now that would be justice."

"See, that's what I'm saying. A pretty boy like him, the guys will be all over him." Nora hands me a glass and wraps her arms around me. "Sheesh, girl, you've seen better days."

"Thanks," I laugh and roll my eyes.

"Seriously, what are you all doing here?"

"I called them," Pike says with a grin.

"You called them?"

He shrugs. "I figured they'd want to help you move into your new house."

I stretch up for a quick kiss. "Sneaky sneaky."

"It's a moving and break-up celebration!" Nora yells as she pours five glasses and passes them out.

Nora holds up her glass. "A toast! To karma, may your arrow be true. To Pike, for bringing our girl back to us and being the man. To Aubrey, for being perfectly you."

"Here, here!" I cheer, and tip back my glass. I set it down and wrap my arms around Pike's waist. "Thank you for being perfectly you. I love you. So, so much."

He reaches up and caresses my cheek. "Ditto."

I quirk a brow at him. "Did you just ditto me?"

A chuckle leaves him, and he crashes his lips to mine. "You always have been and forever will be my only love."

"Okay, okay, stop it with the bedroom eyes. We've got work to do!" Nora calls out, bursting our little bubble.

For the first time in a long time, my life feels like it's on the right track.

A WEEK LATER, LIFE IS FINALLY SETTLING DOWN. CALEB was arrested, and a restraining order was granted since he's out on bail. Anxiety plagues me that he might try for revenge, but he hasn't attempted to contact me.

Briar has kept me up-to-date and word is Caleb is moving his business back to the Southside of the city. Briar also sent me a screen shot of Caleb's house up for sale on a real estate app.

It helps to calm me, but I know it will take more time until I feel completely safe when Pike isn't around. I still keep my stun gun charged and with me at all times.

Business is picking up, and I've even had a few clients call to apologize for believing his lies. The Walkers were not one of them, and after our last encounter, that is fine by me.

My bruises have healed for the most part, but there are still some yellowish patches.

I draw in a breath and smile. For the first time in a long time, I am happy. I am deliriously happy.

It didn't take long to move my condo in, especially since some stuff didn't survive Caleb's destruction. My free time has been spent unpacking and merging my things with Pike's.

That and sex.

And more sex.

After a week of pretty much non-stop sex, I thought maybe we'd slow down, but we can't keep our hands off each other. It's like our bodies are making up for lost time. Not that I mind. At all.

In the ten years he was gone, sex always felt like a chore or a duty, but with Pike, it's a desperate desire.

Nights are spent wrapped in the arms of the man I love. He makes my heart so full.

We're opening the pool this weekend, and I can't wait to spend the summer enjoying it.

"I have something I want you to see."

"Did you remodel another room while I was gone? It was just a couple of hours."

He chuckles. "No. It's something I've been wanting to show you for a long time, but never could."

He pulls down a book from the shelf and hands it to me. Once in my hand, I realize it's not a book at all—it's a box.

"What is this?" I ask as I stare down at the faux book box. I remember it. He used to hide things in it, including condoms. But it's different from the last time I saw it. The edges are worn, and the spine is no longer simply a faux, older-looking leather spine. On one end are the initials PW, and the other end holds AH. They are separated by a singular word—Forever.

There are a few scratches through the letters, telling of their age.

"My box of hopes and dreams."

"It used to be your box of condoms."

His lips twitch. "Yeah, well, it got reassigned to a greater purpose."

I lift the lid and stare down at a stack of letters in

different-sized envelopes and colors. There is a red string tied around them, binding them together. My hand shakes as I brush aside the bow to read the letters scrawled across the top piece.

It's my name and address, and it's dated six months ago.

"Not all the dreams are good, and my hopes were often fears, but I wrote you, even if I couldn't bring myself to send them."

"I don't understand."

"Every year on your birthday, I wrote to you. After the first few years of chickening out and not sending them, I began to write them for myself, knowing I wasn't going to send them. It was cathartic, in a way." He holds out another envelope. "Happy birthday, Aubrey."

I stare at the envelope, at my name, noticing that it doesn't have my address on it. "It's a couple weeks early." I glance up at him before gingerly taking it and pulling the paper from within.

"I'll be in the garage," he says, leaving me to his words.

Aubrey,

Happy 27th birthday!

It's hard to believe how my life has changed since the last letter I wrote you. The biggest change happened the day I found out you were engaged to be married.

I was gutted that day. In twenty-four hours, I had a job lined up in Indiana and was working on leaving a decade in New York behind me.

Social media became my stalking outlet, and I could see in the photos how un-you you'd become.

I didn't want that for you. Not for you.

I'm sorry it took me so long to realize that I have no life without you. I was insecure and scared, but not anymore. I want nothing more than to love you and take care of you for the rest of our lives, and I can only hope you'll give me that opportunity.

You're my forever.

All my love,
Pike

Goose bumps spread down my arms and legs. I read the words over and over. I want to jump into his arms, scream out how I want all of that too, but the need for more is greater. Taking hold of the stack, I pull the top letter from the red thread holding it in place.

The date is from the day we bumped into each other at Starbucks.

Aubrey,

I saw you. I held you in my arms and for a moment, I was whole again. After weeks of questioning my decision, I knew I definitively made the right move. In those seconds, every ounce of love for you flooded my heart.

It took everything in me not to kiss you right there, not to beg you like some stalker to see me again.

From this moment, all that I do is for you. Every step, every move, is to show you that I'm the man for you.

I'll prove it.

Prove that I'm the one who will treat you with kindness, protect you with my life, support your dreams, and love you until my dying breath.

Forever and always,
Pike

I waste no time pulling the next letter in the stack. The date at the top is January, and the handwriting isn't nearly as clear as the others. The lines are almost scratches, matching the fury of the words.

Aubrey,

No.

No!

I won't fucking let this stand. I can't.

You're not marrying that fucker. I've seen the photos, I've talked to people, and I know he's not the one for you.

I see now how staying away so long has fucked everything up. I should have come home sooner.

But I'm coming now. Because he can't love you like I can, and I'm going to make you mine again.

Ten years, and I never stopped loving you.

It's only ever been you.

After all the years and the heartache and the distance, I'm coming home. I need you.

Forever,

Pike

I reach up and cover my mouth with my hand. The desperation is palpable.

I pull from the bottom next. It's the first birthday after he left.

Aubrey,

Has it really been a year since I left? It feels like a decade since I've seen you, since I've kissed you. The year has been long and hard. I've missed you. God, how I've missed you.

Resisting the urge to contact you has been agony, but I've managed it. Don't for one second think that it means I don't love you anymore or don't think about you every minute of every day, because it won't happen.

I love you. I promised forever, and I meant it. No matter what and after everything.

Forever,
Pike

My chest clenches as I pull from the center of the stack. All the feelings I never knew, never felt, are laid out in scribbles on a page, but they are the most honest I've ever encountered. Not even during our fights when we were hashing it out did I feel this intensity of emotions.

The next one is from my twenty-first birthday.

Aubrey,

It's only May, but I needed to get this down. I'm not coming home. I want to tell you it's because I got this offer I couldn't refuse, and while that is true, I would have turned it down to be closer to you.

But I've watched, and I've seen—you're happy with Jack. All I want is your happiness, even above my own. You've got another year ahead of you, and him by your side, so I'll stay away.

I want to think I'm being noble, but really I'm guarding myself. No woman can ever replace you or mean anywhere near as much as you mean to me, and I don't think I can take you rejecting me. It wouldn't be fair to even ask something like that.

Forever is still forever, even after everything. Life is life, and we've lived it and will continue to.

But I'm still holding you in my heart.

All my love,
Pike

I set it down and reach for the next. It's dated the year after.

Aubrey,

Why aren't you with Jack anymore? What happened?

Fuck, this complicates things. I want to pack up and come home more than anything now.

But I'm learning so much at my job. I'm excelling, and if I stay I'll be able to get good enough to provide a life for us.

If you'll even still have me.

I'm going crazy over here without you. I don't know what to do. There are so many changes in your life right now, would I even be welcome?

I hate this. I hate the space and the time and the despair. All I want is to wrap my arms around you, to hold you close and kiss the top of your head. If even for a moment.

But I can't have that, and I don't have that, and it's all I crave.

I need you to end this blackness, but I can't ask that right now. You have a fresh start at life. So, I'll give you that. I'll stay here for now. But only because the timing isn't right. Because we both need a little more time.

Good luck. As always and forever, I love you.

Love,
Pike

Tears stream down my cheeks, the writing blurring. The words are so raw, full of vulnerability. They make me ache to hug him, to kiss him, but he's not here.

I set the rest down, deciding to save them for later and weave through the house to the garage. He's been working on a table for his mom for Christmas, wanting to get it done early as he's attempting a few new techniques.

The door swings open and I run, closing the space between us, and jump into his arms. My assault catches him by surprise, and I almost knock him over. Tears stream down my face. I'm unable to process this much love, this much emotion, and so I cry.

I cry for his pain, I cry for his love, and I cry for our time lost. But most of all, I cry because I'm happy.

I'm whole again. I have my soul mate, and nothing will ever separate us again.

"I love you. From now until forever, I love you."

His eyes shine, and he drops his forehead down against mine. "My love has no conditions. There are no strings. I love you unconditionally."

And I know every single word is true.

I am very much loved.

Christmas

OW, THAT WAS…" I TRAIL OFF AS WE STEP INTO the house.

"It was…" Pike trails off.

"At least your mom loved the table."

"She did."

"What did we even end up with?" I ask as I slough my coat off and hang it up.

"A basket of vodka and fruit, and the virtual reality glasses."

A laugh leaves me, and I shake my head. Gotta love white elephant gift exchanges. "What are we going to do with those?"

"Well." Pike's arms wrap around my waist, and I lean back against him. "The vodka is good for drinking. You drink all those little bottles, and I'll have a sultry little elf on my hands."

"You'd like that, wouldn't you?"

In six months I have somehow fallen even deeper in love with Pike. Every dream I had of him, of us, came true, and I've never been happier.

Together, we finished the renovation on the house, making it ours in every way.

In all the months, I've never heard from Caleb. His business has completely disappeared from the Northside of the city, and the latest update is that he'll serve some time, though I have no idea how much. I genuinely hope what happened changes his perspective, that he understands what he did and strives to change himself for the better.

"Very much." Pike's lips press against my neck. "You get so saucy and do a strip tease for me before ripping my clothes off."

My mouth drops open and I turn in his arms, my hand smacking lightly against his chest. "I do not do that."

A chuckle leaves him and he leans down, his lips ghosting mine. "Oh, yes, you do. Especially when you get a little too much wine in you." He nips at my bottom lip.

I narrow my eyes at him. "Is that why you're always pouring me one more glass?"

He nods, a devilish grin on his lips. "That definitely is why. To be seduced by the woman I love who is sexy as fuck? Yes and yes."

I take my turn to nip his bottom lip and lean back. "Maybe I'll abstain for a few days."

His fingers dig into my ass, and a growl leaves him. "And why would you do that?"

"Because I love how handsy you get when you are desperate for me."

He leans in, a groan leaving him. "I'm always desperate for you."

"Well, you're extra desperate after two days."

"You know, there is one room we haven't done it in yet," he says with a waggle of his eyebrows.

"Another room? How did we miss one?"

"Because it's one we never go into."

"You're not talking about that unfinished room above the garage, are you?"

"Mm hmm." He pulls on my hips back out the direction we came.

"Why are we going this way?" There's a staircase in the garage that goes up to it, but there is also access from inside the house.

"Because we never go this way."

There's something different about the staircase, but I can't quite put my finger on it. He opens the door and pulls me in, wrapping his arms around my waist as he walks me in and flips on the lights.

I blink in confusion, wondering if we somehow walked into someone else's space.

"Merry Christmas, baby," Pike whispers in my ear.

My mouth drops open as I step out of his arms to look around, still confused as to what is going on. It was an empty, framed room the last time I saw it months ago, but now it's a thing of beauty. It's a large in-home office. Tears fill my eyes as my gaze lands on my logo covering one wall.

It's *my* office.

Cabinets line one wall, and a beautiful desk with a grey wash sits by the window with matching credenza.

"Did you make those?" I ask.

"With help. Do you like?"

I shake my head. "Love. Love, love, love them." I turn toward him. "When did you do all this?"

"I had some help with it."

"Who?"

"Briar. We're both part of the Aubrey Hart fan club."

I quirk a brow at him. "Oh really? I didn't know that was a thing."

"It's a huge thing. Massive. I think we have at least six members," he says with a grin.

A laugh leaves me and I look around, my gaze hitting on something new with each pass. There's a sitting area at the opposite window from the desk. Every detail is perfect. The furniture is perfect, the window treatments, everything.

The couch looks really familiar, and that's when it hits me—everything is from my online wish list.

"How—" I turn to speak but freeze.

Pike is no longer standing behind me, but kneeling. "I've got one more present for you." He reaches into his pocket and pulls out a small box.

My heart hammers in my chest as I stare down at him in disbelief. He flips back the lid, and I gasp. Nestled inside is a delicate diamond ring.

"I've only ever been sure about one thing in my life, and that is you. I love you, so very much. There has never been a day since I met you that I haven't loved you." He takes hold of my hand and presses his lips to my ring finger. "I wasted so much time, but I don't want to waste any more. Aubrey Danielle Hart, will you marry me? Will you be my partner in life, my wife, forever the love of my life?"

Tears fill my eyes so much it's hard to see, and my other hand covers my mouth. I'm overloaded, completely shocked and surprised and filled with so much happiness.

"Yes," I whisper as a tear falls down my cheek.

His smile is blinding and he pulls the ring from the box, his hand shaking as he slips it onto my finger. I barely look at it, because it doesn't matter what it looks like. What matters is him.

I cup his face and pull him down, my lips pressing to his in small, repeated kisses.

"I love you," I say as I pull slightly back. "Forever."

The only thing in my life I've ever been certain of is Pike, and we were finally going to have our forever

The End

after all the words and the things . . .

Thanks to Netflix, I've had an indulgence of late for teenage romances. One being The Kissing Booth. After watching it my mind started whirling. I wanted more. I wanted to know what happened next. There was no plans for a sequel at the time, and some of the things Elle said at the end really struck me.

What would happen if he didn't come back? And what would happen if she was getting married?

Now, the original idea he crashes her actual wedding, but as the idea ruminated and grew, the characters greatly changed as did the original story.

I wanted to explore how the loss of a first love can affect a person years later. How insecurities can grow and warp a person's internal view of themselves. And how there are people who will take advantage of those that have been beaten down, whether by their own doing or an outside factor.

People like Caleb, and many much worse, do exist in real life. If you are in a bad situation, fight to get out. If you know someone in a bad situation, fight to get them out.

You are worth it.

acknowledgements

Danielle, Pike is still yours. Thank you so much for all of your help. I can't thank you enough for putting up with me and my erratic brain, and helping me make this book the best it can be.

So very many thanks to Massy for helping to straighten me out when I was lost and the doc was a jumbled mess. You're my boo.

Many thanks to Crystal for her last minute beta'ing.

Thanks to Kelley for always keeping it real.

To all women…
You are beautiful. You are worthy of love.

soundtrack

2002 by Anne Marie
Remind Me to Forget by Kygo & Miguel
Back to You by Selena Gomez
Reminding Me by Shawn Hook
Speechless by Dan + Shay
Like I Would by Zayn
Treat You Better by Shawn Mendes
Perfect by Ed Sheeran
Side Effects by The Chainsmokers feat. Emily Warren
All These Years by Camila Cabello
Never Be the Same by Camila Cabello
Sound Of Your Heart by Shawn Hook
Eyes Closed by Halsey
Wish That You Were Here by Florence + The Machine
Better Love by Hozier
Love Me Now by John Legend
Treat You Better by Shawn Mendes
Cool by Jonas Brothers
Hunger by Florence + The Machine
Say You Won't Let Go by James Arthur
Never Really Over by Katy Perry
Electricity by Silk City & Dua Lipa
Almost by Hozier
Nothing Breaks Like a Heart by Mark Ronson feat. Miley Cyrus
You are the Reason by Calum Scott
Just the Way You Are by Bruno Mars

about the author

K.I. Lynn is the *USA Today* Bestselling Author from The Bend Anthology and the Amazon Bestsellers, *Breach* and *Becoming Mrs Lockwood*. She spent her life in the arts, everything from music to painting and ceramics, then to writing. Characters have always run around in her head, acting out their stories, but it wasn't until later in life she would put them to pen. It would turn out to be the one thing she was really passionate about.

Since she began posting stories online, she's garnered acclaim for her diverse stories and hard hitting writing style. Two stories and characters are never the same, her brain moving through different ideas faster than she can write them down as it also plots its quest for world domination...or cheese. Whichever is easier to obtain... Usually it's cheese.

Website—www.kilynnauthor.com

Facebook—www.facebook.com/kilynn.breach

Twitter—twitter.com/KI_Lynn_

Instagram—www.instagram.com/k.i.lynn

Get my Newsletter—http://bit.ly/1U9NSoC

Becoming Mrs. Lockwood

Every girl has dreams of meeting Prince Charming, or at least I know I did.

A fairy tale-like meeting of love at first site.

Real life and fairy tales are very different.

I'm just a small town Indiana girl that had a chance encounter with one of Hollywood's golden boys. You may think you know where this story goes—not even close.

Life is different. Marriage is hard. It's even worse when you're strangers.

Find out more here
books2read.com/BecomingMrsLockwood

Six

I had a one-night stand. It wasn't my first, but it would be my last.

A gun to the head.

A trained killer.

A deadly conspiracy.

Kidnapped and on the run, my life and death is in the hands of a sadist captor who happens to be my one-night stand. Armed with countless weapons, money, and new identities, the man I call Six drags me around the world.

The manhunt is on and Six is the next target. Can we find out who is killing off the Cleaners before they find us?

Two down, seven to go.

When it's all over he'll finish the job that dropped him into my life, and end it.

Stockholm Syndrome meets bucket list, and the question of what would you do to live before you died. The questions aren't always answered in black and white. Gray becomes the norm as my morals are tested.

Death is a tragedy, and I'll do anything to stay alive.

Are you ready for the last ride of your life? Six has a gun to your head—what would you do?

This isn't a love story.

It's a death story.

Find out more here
books2read.com/Six-KILynn
Check out the Trailer: youtu.be/fzpON3PadIA

Breach Book 1

His body was sin, his cock was sin, and I was a sinner.

To keep myself safe I hide in the world and let life move around me.

My new partner, Nathan, isn't safe. Far from it.

The darkness coils around him, hidden by a shield created by a blinding smile. But those who live in shadows see past the façade we create.

Even in darkness, there is light. A spark that ignites, then explodes.

Every filthy word from his mouth, every possessive touch—I crave them, need them. Violent and passionate and everything I need to fill the void inside me, but one thing is missing.

He can never love me.

More than my heart is on the line, and I don't know if I'll survive our breach.

Find out more here
books2read.com/Breach

The Executive

Business is king, and I have an empire to topple.

Ivy is my new assistant and a threat to me. She's my undoing. If ever I was to believe in a cosmic connection, it was the moment I met her.

For years I've had one goal--revenge. As CEO, I have crafted a strategic plan for business, but never a life beyond.

With one touch from her, the veil is lifted. Things are different, and every moment I'm near her, my world begins to change.

A wall of propriety keeps me from her. I need her as my pawn in this war, beside me in battle. Sharing the secrets of my enemies, and her desires in my bed. Her body to claim as mine.

Getting what I want has consequences.

Collateral damage is real.

In the game of crushing kings of men, I never planned on my heart being a sacrifice.

Find out more here
books2read.com/TheExecutive

Cocksure

A life altering lie, ten years, and one wild night later, the game has changed.

Niko

My life is great. I love my job, have awesome friends, and a great family.

Women love me, even if they know it's just for a night.

I always thought love at first sight was bullshit. Then she came storming into my life. She tore through my every rule, rocked my world, and knocked me on my ass.

There's only one problem...she lied.+

Turns out my best friend's little sister isn't so little anymore.

Everly

I stole a night with my fantasy. Lied to him.

After ten years of not seeing each other, Niko doesn't even recognize me.

So I take what I want from him, what I need from him. Without worry. Without consequence.

What I didn't count on was the lingering need for him.

Once the truth is out, the game changes. There are consequences.

I should have known nothing in my life is ever simple.

My brother is going to kill his best friend and I have nine months to figure out what I want.

Find out more here
books2read.com/Cocksure-Lynn-Kelley

Need Book 1

I was Kira's from the first moment I saw her. Maybe it was love at first sight, but I was only ten.

She became my best friend.

My crush.

The girl I can't live without.

But I have to.

She was almost mine, but my father took away my chance.

Now she lives across the hall from me. Instead of the title of girlfriend, she's now my stepsister.

But that doesn't stop how I feel, how I want her. Thankfully, I'm off to college two hundred miles away, but even that doesn't help.

She's under my skin, all around me, and I watch her morph from a sexy teenager to an irresistible woman.

I can't take it anymore, I need her.

Is it possible to ever be happy without the one person you *need*?

"I'm Brayden, baby. The man you've been dreaming about your whole life. And I'm about to fucking show you why."

Part 1 of a 3 part series.

Find out more here
books2read.com/NeedSeries